he
Rooms

The
Rooms

Declan Lynch

HOT
PRESS
BOOKS

What They Said About Declan Lynch

"An exciting name to watch in Irish fiction, and one of the surprisingly few novelists to have attempted anything at all about the strange new country we're living in now. Fantastically gifted."
– *Sunday Independent*

"One of the funniest and sharpest writers in Ireland." – *Who Magazine*

"He's funny, yes, but he writes about serious themes." – *Hot Press*

What They Said About Do Nothing Till You Hear From Me

"The chartacters that populate the pages are big and juicy and full of life, and Lynch's venemous wit and sassy writing style make every page entertaining. Black, tragic and hilariously funny..."
– Paul Howard, *Sunday Tribune*

"This novel breaks into uncharted waters, in depicting the awesome weight of everyday responsibilities, as they fall on the shoulders of one who thought he would never grow up. Do Nothing Till You Hear From Me is superb." – John Waters, *The Irish Times*

"An incredibly well-observed novel." – Kim Porcelli, *Hot Press*

What They Said About All The People All The Time

"A hilarious black comedy, giving us a glimpse of the glitterati with their feet of clay. An obligatory read." – **Valerie Cox**, *Evening Herald*

"Subtly, shrerwdly, truthfully funny and suffused with intelligence. An accomplished and impressively witty piece of work." – **Joseph O'Connor**, *author of Star Of The Sea.*

What They're Saying About The Rooms

"The best writing on alcoholism since Bill Wilson wrote the Big Book." – **John Waters**, *The Irish Times*

"Porter dark but champagne bright, it will dazzle you and break your heart. A truly great Irish novel." – **Liam Fay**, *The Sunday Times*

"Declan Lynch has long been one of Ireland's most mordantly funny writers and, in The Rooms, his laser-like insight illuminates our unhappy love affair with the demon drink. A tough-minded, richly enjoyable and unflinchingly truthful book." – **Fintan O'Toole**, *The Irish Times*

First published in 2005 by Hot Press Books, 13 Trinity Street, Dublin 2.

This second edition published November 2005

British Library Cataloguing in Publication Data is available for this book

ISBN NO: 0-9545516-7-2
Edited by Niall Stokes
Editorial co-ordination by Lisa Coen
Design by Fiachra McCarthy, Andrew Duffy, Graham Keogh

Printed by Colour Books, Dublin

About The Author

From Athlone, Co Westmeath, in Ireland, Declan Lynch began his writing career at the age of 17, with Hot Press magazine. His first novel *All The People All The Time* was published in 2002, followed by *Do Nothing Till You Hear From Me*, in 2003. Lynch is also the author of a play, *Massive Damages*, produced by the Passion Machine for the Dublin Theatre Festival in 1997, and of two books of non-fiction, *They Are Of Ireland* and *Ireland On Three Million Pounds A Day*. He writes for the *Sunday Independent*. Already hailed as "the best writing about alcoholism since Bill Wilson wrote the Big Book", *The Rooms* is his third novel. Declan lives in Wicklow.

"So we'll go no more a-roving
So late into the night,
Though the heart be still as loving,
And the moon be still as bright..."

– Lord Byron

One

If I go in here and have this drink, I will die. Maybe not today, but soon, and it will be a very ugly scene.

That's what they tell me, in the rooms.

But I'm going in anyway, a guy going into a bar like any other guy going into a bar. I'm going into this harbour bar to have my first drink in more than seven years and once I've got that inside me, I'll be ready, ready for the journey across to the island, where the real drinking can commence. And since the boat leaves in two hours, I will actually have time for more than one drink here, on the mainland, for a few drinks in fact, provided I can keep the first one down, which is by no means certain. After so long without it, maybe the first one will just kill me stone dead.

But I've come a long way. And today, I'm not really afraid of dying.

I can see the boat that will take me over to the island, the same ferry that took me across eight years ago, when I still had a few months drinking in me. From the bar I can smell the beer. It has never really left me, the waft of a bottle of beer on a summer's evening, 15 years old and Bob Seger's 'Night Moves' playing on the cassette machine, a bunch of boys in the sand dunes watching the girls swimming in the sea. Twenty years later I am still visited by these blasts of euphoric recall, as if the first tang of adulthood had been tasted a matter of months ago.

It may take me another twenty years to stop this time, but today is not about stopping. It's about starting again in this harbour bar.

For a moment I am frozen. I am frozen in that moment I saw her, knowing I could have Jamaica if I wanted her, knowing straight away how high the stakes would be but unable to stop myself, knowing that I was gambling with whatever passed for my soul at that time. But I kept going anyway, I took the risk. And it didn't feel like I was being strong, or decisive, it felt like just like this, just like now, like I was being led by something inside me that I didn't understand, something that left me powerless.

Something that drove me to drink in the first place, knowing that the drink would make me even more powerless, knowing I still wanted it.

I still wanted it.

I run the scene in my head many times, the moment on that day last August when my life changed again. I come out of an AA meeting in a room in Molesworth Street with Lotte. One of the country girls, as I am later to know them, she is new to the rooms. As we shuffle along the pavement, she's talking about my old band, which bores me. I was never really a star. Back in another lifetime we nearly cracked America, but didn't.

We go for coffee to Café En Seine, a bit fashionable for a guy just out of a small room packed with about thirty recovering alcoholics, but not too fashionable for Lotte. Jamaica is there, waiting for Lotte to chauffeur her home to Wicklow.

I have this vision of them driving back to the estate in a 1930s open-topped Rolls Royce, the leaves swirling behind them as they whoosh through the country lanes.

Jamaica is younger than Lotte, but she comes across like the boss. Unlike Lotte she's all there, with thick black hair that seems both wild and carefully arranged, and cheekbones that tell of a thousand years of effortless cool. And yet her beauty is not the totally intimidating kind. I can see her staying up late at night reading a good book, and that makes me think I have a chance. Or maybe it's the freckles. When you see them first they look like an all-too-human flaw, but when you take them in properly you realise that they illuminate this gorgeous brown skin-colour of hers. They are actually the decisive splash of genius, and so I am mesmerised by the natural colours of her face the way that men would usually be rocked by a great pair of legs. Though I have high hopes too, in that regard.

"I know you," Jamaica says, exuding what I take to be genuine interest and even sincerity.

"Still famous," I say.

We connect straight away. I've seen this happen before, but it never happened to me. It used to happen to Phil, our tour manager. He has this ability to connect with a woman straight away and to get a connection back; they just exchange a certain look before they even say anything, and they know, and everyone in the room knows, it's a deal.

We connect, Jamaica and me. What is this connection? It's a sense that everything else in your life has been hard up to now, but this is going to be easy. It's a sense that this idealised image you have formed of this person will never be darkened by reality; it is burned into you. It is done. I know at last how Phil feels when he does that thing.

As I get the coffees at the bar I reckon I'll say I never met a woman called Jamaica before, but I figure it would come across a bit eager, a bit corny. And anyway her people probably called her that because of a fortune they made in the Caribbean, or some great spliff they had at the time, or both.

I don't want to get into her roots right away, in case I have to say that my father was a primary teacher, and she has to pretend she's deeply interested in that, to feign a look of fascination in those big dark eyes, she who probably went to some primary school where they attended classes naked in fine weather, and the core subjects were yoga, ceramics, and Japanese theatre.

Anyway I know something of Jamaica from a newspaper article about her and what she calls the country girls, who are as talented as they are mysteriously beautiful. They are not constrained by bourgeois inhibitions and they don't wax. I know she's about thirty and she's happening. She does costumes, she does clothes. She'd probably walk down the catwalk herself for the right charity, and carry it off too.

We even look alike, more Spanish than Irish or whatever the hell Jamaica is. Jamaica with that dope-addled English father she talked about in the newspaper article, and her mother whose family lived in some

Wicklow mansion for three centuries with enough bohemian chutzpah to have members of the Rolling Stones sleeping over. I recall this quote in which she laughed off the legend that Jagger had it off with her mother in the gate lodge while her father was outside pruning the roses, tripping, cool about it.

I don't want to push it, but I also know right then, as I bring three black coffees back to the table, that I will probably spend some time with this woman and that I will probably drink again. Probably in that order.

Probably.

As I pick up the coffees, I am thinking: I had no idea until this morning how this would take place exactly, I just knew there was another drink in me somewhere. I am thinking: I can pull out of it. I can down my espresso and leave the table and go but I won't, because this is too strong, this connection. Anyway I am more than six years sober and I think I am maybe ready for it, that I am maybe fixed, even though they warn you in the rooms about getting involved too soon after getting sober.

Six years sober. It sounds like a lot to a normal person but it's not so long in AA time, a point of view which I understand now better than I did that day in Café En Seine. It isn't long at all.

Taking the coffees to the table I run a quick check on myself in the mirror. I look pretty acceptable. Maybe it's just the excitement. I see a dude who knows how to hold a guitar, who has a musician's soul and a troubadour's sense of style. Then I see nothing except Jamaica.

"I loved your band," she says, as Lotte drifts away from us into her own two-weeks-sober thoughts.

"We had our moment," I say.

"I have a picture of you on my wall. Forever." She says it like she means it completely.

And yes, I hear some soft Caribbean music in the way she says "forever." This Jamaica has a Jamaican accent, and I remember that article again, I recall it said she spent part of her childhood in Jamaica. I guess this explains both her name and her accent, strangely like the Cork accent at times, just about ten degrees hotter.

"I'm writing a musical now," I say, taking my chances, expecting her to simply change the subject like most people do.

"Fantastic, yeah," she says, like she's been waiting all day to hear this bit of good news.

"What would you say to a... a boxing musical?"

"I know Andrew," she cuts in.

"Andrew Lloyd Webber mon," she laughs with a note of mischief. "Well, family friend. Not a big fan, y'know?" She laughs again, in the way she probably did when she told Andrew himself she wasn't a big fan, and he took no offence.

"When I say a boxing musical, people maybe can't get their heads around it. Then I say a boxing musical with Matt Dillon and the penny drops," I explain.

"That's it," she says triumphantly. "I can see it now in front of me."

"It's the only way to go," I say. " Broadway." It's my turn to laugh.

"I love to hear positive energy comin' through, a positive contribution," she says. "I got a big t'ing about musical theatre, always."

"Sondheim?" I say.

She closes her eyes in a sort of Sondheim-induced ecstasy and nods vigorously. To meet someone who seems to genuinely understand what I'm talking about when I raise the hoary subject of the musical, is immensely moving in itself. Most people, with pretty good reason, regard it as the ultimate insanity.

"I actually don't call it a musical any more, I call it a tuner, like they do in Variety magazine," I say, something I don't divulge to anyone unless we're on intimate terms. "It's a tuner called Jack Rooney, kind-of an Irish-American thing, except it's good."

For a moment, it feels like I have finally found a companion on a long, long, lonesome trail. Then she touches me for the first time. Nothing tentative, instead a firm grip on my hand like she really wants this.

"Brother, you must let me do the costumes," she says. She says Braddah, really, not brother. Braddah.

I am soon to learn that Jamaica looks with rapt fascination at almost everyone she encounters, and that her interest is sincere, and that she might even offer to work with them if she thinks they're hugely talented.

But she doesn't call everyone "braddah." She doesn't give everyone those sweet sounds of Jamaica, which give words a new life, and the longer the word the better, so that "contribution" gets the full "con-tree-bew-shon," and musical is no longer pronounced "musicle," but "mew-zee-cal," which sounds more, well, musical.

Later I will discover that she can switch the sounds of Jamaica off completely if she doesn't like you.

But sitting in Café En Seine right now, this is the way my mind is working: as a rock'n'roll creature I figure I'm going to be liked and I think I know why. I suspect, anyway, that rock'n'roll triggers something in these aristos because it's one of the last places on earth where the top people are still fenced off from the punters and nobody passes any remarks on it, in fact it couldn't be cooler.

Maybe Jagger was the first to suss this, what a sweet deal it was, with the rockers getting the pick of the high-born ladies and the aristos still looking down on the teeming masses but with all that rock'n'roll cred to soothe their bohemian souls.

This is how it works. I have a handle on this Anglo-Irish rock'n'roll gentry thing, I know these people and the way they work, I appreciate their subtleties. I am well past the stage where I would just lump them together with all the other posh people because, as I sussed a long time ago, these people are not posh. They are far too cool to be posh. They are passionate about the good things in life, about music and art and the life of the mind and money too, but it is a cool passion. And cool passion may sound like a contradiction in terms, but these folks have it.

So I know them and they know me, and I feel we are right for each other. And as the conversation with Jamaica rambles on, it turns out that we have a lot of mutual acquaintances, from way back, a whole generation almost, all of them seemingly doing well for themselves in the various industries of human happiness, except me. Reeling off all those illustrious names of people we have known, makes our coming together feel inevitable. And so, over a few espressos we make a sort of first date, me and Jamaica, though we're too cool to call it that. We agree to meet at the Shelbourne on the morning of an anti-globalisation march in O'Connell Street, have a few drinks or not as the case may be, and then march against the capitalist pigs. I have never been to a demo before, having an aversion to crowds and shouting in equal measure. But I agree to go, like it is the most natural thing in the world for me.

When she and Lotte get up to go, Jamaica shakes hands with me. I don't know how to take it. I decide it means nothing bad. Because as she stands up and takes a few coins out of the pocket of her battered denim skirt to tip the guy clearing the table, I can confirm that she has in fact got great legs, and that's not just the idealised version, the blood still rushing, because I check them out again, I watch her walking tall down the street and those legs are great. I suppose I never doubted it.

And that's without heels, just a pair of runners as battered as the skirt, maybe a little on the drab side for a fashionista. But am I doubting her? Is the ideal starting to crumble already? No, on reflection I don't expect her to be dressed in some spectacular creation just because she designs that stuff, no more than I would carry my guitar around so I could whip it out whenever anyone needed a song. No, from one professional to another, I feel respect for her. The way she is.

On the walk home to my flat in Sandymount, I'm buzzing. I start to have this fantasy. I imagine something less formal when we get together. I work it all out. We meet at the Shelbourne before noon and she starts the day with a tequila, salt and lemon on the side. I want that drink so bad, but I have a mineral water instead and she's impressed. "Soul Braddah Numbah One," she says.

And I imagine that as she throws the tequila into her I'm going mad for it because I've never chased a woman before without a lot of drink involved. And I have one of those little panic attacks we all get when we contemplate the prospect of hanging out with someone for years with them drinking and us on the fizzy water, with no hope of release.

But I'm guessing that 99 per cent of the reason Jamaica is paying me extra special attention is because I'm on the programme. So in my vision I don't want to let her down on the first date, much though I want to lose myself to the sweet madness of drunk love.

And I can see it working out fine that day, because, of course, Jamaica has no intention of actually marching on the actual street with all the punters. She finishes her tequila, just the one, and then she takes me by the arm of my suede jacket and we walk down the street like Dylan and Suze Rotolo on the cover of Freewheelin'.

I can see us reaching this penthouse apartment on O'Connell Street owned by her uncle, who mostly lives in India. And there we support the marchers, or at least we look down on them in a supportive manner. And I don't make any smart remarks about this because it wouldn't be cool, and anyway we're soon making love on a big leather couch while the marchers put the world to rights on our behalf down below.

This is my vision anyhow, as I walk home to Sandymount, and as any alcoholic will tell you, even thinking about sex is probably progress. Thinking about Jamaica's lovely skin glowing post-orgasmically as I pass some rancid tumbledown drink-shop in Ringsend can only be a good thing. And it is.

Relationships are different, you're never really ready for any of them, but to have the simple desire to see a woman with her clothes off, and to be able to conjure it up like this with no drinking involved, is as near as a lot of us get to the healthy mind in the healthy body.

So there we are in the penthouse, becoming lovers. I can see myself at the balcony looking at her taking her clothes off as casually as if we'd been married for twenty years. Which I don't like. I still prefer a little shame with my sex, a little embarrassment at least.

Passing another of my favourite dirty old pubs in Ringsend I play the scene again, except this time it's a bit more complicated. Reality is starting to intrude, because this time Jamaica kicks it off by taking a condom out of her purse and throwing it in my direction like a skimming stone. I'm so glad, at that moment, that I'm sober: it's not just that I wait until she makes the first move, but that I catch the condom when she throws it, rather than spilling it like a donkey.

When you're sober you can give it the time it needs instead of belting away. I guess you have more time for everything. You don't charge in with that old drunk passion, you are struck by odd thoughts, even misgivings, like why is Jamaica using condoms when she was surely brought up to believe that nothing made in a rubber factory should interfere with the natural order?

And in my mind's eye we're screwing, as I'm walking up the street towards Sandymount Green. It's great and we do it a few times on the sofa in that penthouse suite. But I lose it there, because as I walk though Sandymount Green I see Ryan's pub and that gets me thinking that a penthouse suite belonging to a member of the bohemian aristocracy is bound to have a drinks cabinet. And I love a drinks cabinet.

Great sex all day in a beautiful apartment is a fine thing, but my heart is not in it any more when there's a hundred bottles of booze in the room and I'm not able to drink them.

I put away this daydream because now I'm just suffering.

Six years off it, and the drink still brings me down. The lack of it. The craving.

And here I am thinking that I actually have a chance, with Jamaica, to start drinking again. Drinking and smoking again, because with a voice like that it seems odds-on that she will light up a spliff at some stage of the proceedings, and that stuff totally destroys my resistance to all other forms of temptation. I am anybody's after partaking of the 'erb.

But this badness won't leave me, it keeps whispering to me that she's only known me for about two hours, maybe she doesn't know enough about addiction to make a stand against it when we get to the penthouse and I charmingly suggest that the odd glass of wine is probably feasible for a man of my experience in the rooms.

I'm getting a bag of chips on Sandymount Green, seriously thinking that this might be my chance for another shot at drunk love. I'm figuring that all those Wicklow types are basically free spirits and degenerates anyway, so why should Jamaica be any exception? Why? Ah, but I can't convince myself of this. I know for sure that something has passed between us, this feeling I have that she knows everything, with those ancient eyes she knows me, and she understands me, and she'd never buy a line like that. Would she?

So outside of this daydream, it's foolish to suppose that she'd meet this guy just out of an AA meeting, and he'd tell her it was alright for him to have a glass of wine or two, and that would be cool.

I can go on daydreaming, but that's not really a good idea either.

I can go to the rooms again, where I belong, the second meeting of the day, which seems like a lot, but then I was a long time out there drinking. Fifteen years.

I eat my chips on the street outside the chipper and catch a meeting in Sandymount, in the front room of a little old house with a coal fire. There's only seven of us in the meeting, so I can't really avoid sharing. "I'm Neil and I'm an alcoholic," I start as usual. "I met a woman today." And the guys laugh. I love these guys, they've kept me together for six years. Not these guys exactly, but guys like them. Guys trying to do the twelve steps, or just trying to pass another hour sober.

"I met a woman today, and I'm not saying anything but..." I say, and it sounds like I'm cheating on them, especially the hardcore who are wedded to the twelve steps and the twelve principles of AA, and who have genuinely handed it all over to a Higher Power, which I happen to know doesn't exist.

Anyway, I want to share this. "I think I'm ready for this, after six years in the rooms," I say. "I met her coming out of a meeting. I owe it all to my sobriety." And they laugh again, not a mean-spirited note to be heard, but genuine goodwill, such a strange thing to feel in the company of drunks.

Why would I want to go back to the world, when I have these people? They have saved my life, of that there is no doubt. But even as I sit in that warm old room sharing my good news, I'm figuring that I don't want to be saved any more. I want this woman, whatever it takes. And if that means staying sober, I think I can just about do that. And if it means something else, I'm ready for that too, I fear.

I get home to my apartment block. I turn the corner into the long narrow hall that leads to my flat. Jamaica is sitting at the door, waiting for me.

Two

She couldn't wait until Saturday, she had to lay it on me now, so she got my address from Lotte, who came here last week, after a meeting, for coffee and a load of smokes and who's probably back in Wicklow now thinking she's done me a big favour. Which is my first impression too, until Jamaica starts talking, even as I'm making the mugs of instant coffee.

She talks to me in that downhome Jamaican way like she's known me forever. In fact she's generally acting like she's known me for years instead of a few hours; there's none of the usual extra effort you make with someone new, nothing too polite; it's like we're old friends just catching up.

That's how it is sometimes with fans of the band, but Jamaica seems to have too much going for her to be coming from that place. In fact I think she was lying when she said she loved the band. I think most people are lying if they say that.

She sits on the arm of one of the blue couches that came with the apartment, getting settled before telling her story. Sharing, as we'd say in the rooms.

I guess this old-buddy act is nothing to do with me, she just feels comfortable in any company. And I start to suspect that some of the accent may be an affectation, that she sprinkles the patois over her speech as a matter of personal seasoning. But so what if it's optional? It works sublimely well for me. And anyway, I enjoy her lapses into plain English, when to me, she sounds just like Chris Blackwell, the founder of Island Records, who himself was raised as a white kid in Jamaica and who used the family business acumen to more or less single-handedly bring the reggae music he loved from the Third World to the First. I had dinner with Chris once, and Jamaica at these odd moments sounds like him, not posh of course, just casually elegant.

The subject of her story turns out to be drink. When I drank, there was nothing in my world except drink. And now that I don't drink, there's nothing in my world except not drinking. Like the man said, I dabbled in it and it became my life.

"I've got issues around alcohol," she says, opening up, a line of plain English that conveys a hint of anxiety.

I raise my coffee-mug in a join-the-club sort of way.

"I t'ink I may be goin' bananas," she drawls, downhome Jamaica again on the 'ba-na-nas'. And then she seems to get lost, like the topic is so big she doesn't know where to start.

"Just talk about it," I say.

"OK, OK, listen, everyone I know is in Alcoholics Anonymous and they all drink less than this lady," she says, pointing to herself accusingly. I think I could listen to her saying Al-co-hol-ics An-on-ee-muss all day.

"OK, fine," I say, like I'm a GP taking notes.

"Naturally I'm curious. I t'ink, maybe, just maybe Lotte is not an alcoholic and the rest of dem are not alcoholics they're just... what-you-call it? depressed? deluded? Or am I talkin' about myself?"

She's making me feel like a world authority on the subject and I'm pretty comfortable in that role by now.

"Talk away," I say, with a little nod of the head, like the judge telling the witness to proceed.

"Are you OK about dis?" she says, but she sounds like she's just being mannerly, not seriously concerned that a man of my wisdom and experience might be prone to doubt. "I'm bringing dis to you because... because you're one of dem... but you're not really one of dem, are you braddah?" We both laugh.

I'm getting a flashback to my penthouse dream of drunk love. I try to be responsible. I remind myself that the most important thing at this moment, and indeed at all times of the day and night, is my recovery. But at this precise millisecond, when there's a woman called Jamaica giving me serious respect and maybe the promise of something more than respect, my recovery doesn't seem quite so important.

"Go on," I say, drinking deeply of the Kenco Caribbean Gold, a poignant choice, all things considered.

"I mean, we are all drinkers in my family goin' back a long, long way. I get drunk maybe once a week. I've always got a glass o' wine... I hear Lotte talkin' about alcoholic behaviour and I figure, that is me, you know? But still, I just don't feel like I am an alcoholic... whatever that is supposed to feel like... I guess I'm confused."

I lean back on my couch. I don't like where she's taking me with this, but I keep up my GP mask.

"Forget about other people," I say. "Does your drinking bother you?"

"Somewhat," she says.

"Can you have two or three drinks and then leave the pub?"

"If I want to..."

"But..."

I pause for effect...

"Do you want to?"

"Depends," she says.

"Could you give it up?" I say, working well.

She wraps her hands around the mug. She's got dirt under her fingernails. I drift away for a moment, pondering the meaning of this. Dirt. I decide I like it.

"Could I give it up, mon?" she repeats.

She thinks about it. She swirls her coffee like it's got brandy in it. She spills a drop on her battered skirt; it's probably designed by herself, like the plain black sweatshirt. Part of her student collection. She puts the mug down. She keeps thinking. I'd say she is the devil to be sitting there looking like that and planting bad thoughts in my head, but there's this seriousness about her which reassures me, a look of 1930s Cambridge idealism in her eyes.

"I mean, could you give it up, like, totally? Like, forever?" I ask.

"Maybe," she says, not really to me, to herself.

"OK..." I say.

"The t'ing is, why should I even t'ink about giving it up if I don't drink too much of it in the first place? I think that is my issue."

This is dangerous turf for me. Talking like that, she might as well be standing there pouring me a large whiskey. I'm also convinced that, at any moment, she's going to start skinning up, at which point I think I will join her.

"Do you... smoke?... as in... drugs?"

I blurt it out, like a teenager.

"As in ganja?" she says with a huge Jamaican smile. "On very, very special occasions. I need to control myself, because if I start on the ganja I can't stop, and I never get my work done, none at all. Just smoke, smoke, smoke..."

She laughs.

I make a decision right there. I choose the rooms over Jamaica. I know in my soul I can only do drunk love, and stoned love. I just can't let myself go with a woman until the drink loosens me up. It's been like that right from the start. It's not a sex thing, I can have sex with anyone in any condition, but for the full works, the full Jamaica, I would need wine, I would need blissfully drunk days in country pubs, I would need Christmasses drenched in brandy and champagne, I would need twenty beers in a marquee at a big wedding, I would need plastic cups of Guinness backstage with The Pogues, I would need to be collected from JFK in a record company limo, with a fully-stocked bar from which we select a couple of fine whiskies as we toast the Manhattan skyline, me and Jamaica, Jamaica and me.

So I decide it's a straight choice between staying sober and taking it further with this woman. And my dread of the booze wins the day. I choose the rooms over Jamaica, and I feel like the Dalai Lama, though it strikes me that, wherever the Dalai goes he is hailed as a spiritual giant, which must help when it comes to getting on with doing the right thing. No one will hail me for this.

There's another drink in me, for sure, but I think that if I can somehow avoid getting deeply stuck into this woman today, then maybe I won't drink that drink, today. Maybe I won't tomorrow either. Because there is no tomorrow, as I have learned in the rooms.

"You're OK," I say abruptly. "Just watch it."

I can still feel the electricity. I'm still outwardly bursting with positive vibes in her presence. And maybe later she'll understand that it's me I'm really worried about at this moment, not her. Maybe she'll understand.

"Seen," she says, and I have to think back, far back, to my rock'n'roll days to recall this patois. I remember that Sly and Robbie and all the top reggae guys were always saying 'seen', meaning, I understand... I'm stoned out of my gourd, but still I understand. And what's more, I agree wholeheartedly with you. Seen.

"Seen, and thank you very much, and now let us have some music and enough of dis psychobabble," she says, psy-cho-babb-le never sounding more seductive, and then a nod to the synthesiser which seems to fill half the flat, a big Korg which can reproduce fifty instruments, and on which I've been able to create something very like the sound of a Broadway orchestra. I really think I'm getting pretty good at that stuff. It's actually easier to write the full score of an original book-musical than to handle this mess that Jamaica is stirring so sweetly, so sincerely, in me.

I get up from the couch. I'm pulling back from this intimacy she is offering me, and she knows it.

But in case I'm coming across like some insensitive asshole who just doesn't want to talk about her troubles any more, I figure we can share the music. And as for the bile inside me, I'll sit with it.

As soon as the first song comes out of the Korg and through the speakers, a stately eleven o'clock number called 'Suddenly', she's offering to do the costumes again. Though 'Suddenly' probably isn't the ideal choice of soundtrack, bringing up the goosepimples with lyrics like "suddenly she turns out to be, who I've waited for." Suddenly.

That's where the line is drawn and that's the way it remains for the next few weeks. We skip the anti-globalisation march because it's all about the tuner now. She comes back to the flat every other day to hear all the songs and to read whatever I've got by way of a script, more an outline really than a script, but strong stuff nonetheless.

She especially likes the song 'Manhattan Moon', reckons it would make a killer opening number. She's sketching all sorts of costume ideas and backdrops and I sense she really understands what I'm trying to do here, she really gets it.

One afternoon she arrives with a bunch of superb 'Jack Rooney' logos for promotional purposes. Way ahead of me, she's already thought it all the way through to the official merchandising. I'm impressed.

And then she makes what seems like a pretty sensible suggestion in the circumstances.

"Braddah, I have this gate lodge you know?" she says. "This gate lodge down the road from my stupid old house? It's not that I mind coming here, in fact... I just feel the way we're goin' with this t'ing, it would work better if we were more... available."

I'm still far from free of those thoughts of drunk love, or stoned love, so to be on the safe side, I should leave things the way they are. Stick with the programme. But I also have a strong desire to be available. Av-ail-a-ble.

"Available for work," I say, nervously mimicking an official from the Department of Social Welfare, of which Jamaica presumably knows nothing.

"It's down at de bottom of de lane," she says casually, while showing me a drawing of Jack Rooney singing into an Elvis-type microphone. "Not much bigger than dis place but it's got somethin', you kno'? An atmosphere you kno'? And it's Wicklow..."

"You in the big house and me in the gate lodge?" I say.

"You get the better of that deal. The house is an absolute shambles," she laughs.

Yes, she lapsed for a moment there into plain English. I've heard members of the aristocracy talking like that on TV documentaries in which they insist that they have no money – "ebsolutely no manee" – while sitting in a forty-roomed palace on a thousand acres. But I'm inclined to believe this one, because I want to believe her. And if I can't make drunk love with her, I want to be near her at least, mainly I think because of the colour of her skin. Her voice is enchanting, and it's not that any other part of her has gone down in my estimation, but you can get accustomed to a perfect body until in some strange way you don't see it any more. But I gaze at the colour and texture of her skin every time I see her. I can't help myself, it's an astonishingly attractive shade of brown, enriched if anything by that dash of Irish freckles. I keep having to remind myself that she is basically a white woman, maybe just one-quarter Spanish. Though of course being one of those bohemian types, she would probably claim that her soul is black. Which indeed it may be.

As for mine, it's adrift here, because I'm also thinking that I could do without paying rent for a while, now that I'm a full-time writer of tuners and none of my old rock'n'roll buddies would insult me by offering me session work.

"You mean, I just move up there?" I say.

"Straight away if you like," she says.

"I guess Sandymount's a long way for you to come... from Wicklow," I say.

"It's not for me, braddah... well, let's say it's for Jack Rooney," she says

"I might give up this place so," I say.

Did I hear myself say that?

"Move on up," she says, perhaps a bit casually for my liking. But then I take it as a signal that I'm to feel secure in my new premises. I keep taking the optimistic view because, basically, I can't help myself. I am intoxicated by her. And now I remember the agony I felt as a teenager, eye-ing some astonishingly beautiful girl at a gig, feeling so desolate because I knew I could never approach her, because she was just made differently, like Jamaica is made differently. From me.

Then the band took off, and suddenly women like her started approaching me, and I was still the same guy, except it had all turned around for me. Still the same guy who didn't really feel entitled to all that attention, who needed a good few beers to feel normal at any social gathering. Still the same guy, with the ego of a pop star but the self-esteem of a slug.

Whatever is wrong with me, this alcoholism thing, I sense that some of it is just the old story of a guy who's a failure with women, who doesn't have the strength of character to get through the realities of a relationship, and who, at an age when he might have had the chance to mature a bit, was transformed instead into a rock'n'roll guitar hero.

And while I am full of regret for my degenerate years, I am also about ninety-five per cent sure that I would do it all over again tomorrow, for all the obvious reasons, but also, perversely, because it has brought me to this place, to Jamaica. And after all, it has not turned me into a complete fool, has it? Because I am in recovery, and I am left with this crucial five per cent of hard-won wisdom which is stopping me from taking Jamaica gently by the hand and fucking her right here, on the floor.

There is another thing too. Somewhere inside me, I also feel I must have accomplished something in my life, if such a fine creature as this is casually organising the gate lodge for me. Such a fine, fine creature. And she's not fooling. It is going to happen. I believe my life is going to change again.

Then I remember Susan. And I remember Stephen. My wife Susan and my ten year-old boy Stephen, the two of them always delighted to see me for an hour down in Captain America's in Dun Laoghaire, where we eat huge banana splits and I never go back with them to our old flat, which is only about a hundred yards away. For fear of I don't know what.

I haven't a clue how to function in that world either I never did. I remember the day I realised that, realised it for certain – when Stephen was a baby and I nearly burned the place down by falling asleep with a cigarette going. I remember the big hole scorched into the back of the sofa, which somehow burned itself out beside me while I sat sleeping. I remember the fear now, like it's a living thing.

"I need to visit Dun Laoghaire now and then... to visit my... eh... wife and child. A ten year old boy," I say.

She looks up from some sketch she is doing.

"Wife as in ex-wife... it's amicable," I say.

"Lotte told me all about it," she says, implying that no more needs to be said.

I try to discern if this has lowered me in her estimation. But she seems cool about it, detached even. I reckon it genuinely doesn't occur to her that any other relationship I might ever have had matters a damn, now that she's here.

She has me out of the flat and up to the gate lodge 48 hours later, really buzzing with this notion that we're soul-mates of the best kind, the mystical kind, artists working on a special project, partners who can bond in a pure union, the kind where you can screw anyone you like apart from each other. And she will keep on drinking, and worrying about it sometimes. And I will keep on not drinking, and worrying too.

In those first few days up in Wicklow I don't get settled into my new place because she keeps me outdoors most of the time. She takes me walking through the fields and woodlands, just to get me acclimatised to all this fresh air, and to talk about the tuner. Actually I suspect she is talking too much about the tuner, overdoing it just to emphasise that this is a serious project, and we are serious people who wouldn't be using some half-formed boxing musical to get us to the next stage, the part where the clothes come off.

And of course if we're outdoors, then we can't be indoors, doing what men and woman do in that situation.

As if to mock us, the leaves are falling at the start of autumn, creating a scene of chocolate box romance wherever she takes me. But we say nothing about that.

We are being so cool, so cool about everything.

I discover that she has even less interest in food than I have. She drives me down to the local Supervalu store, where I buy about a hundred-weight of pasta and Dolmio sauces, on which I mainly survive, along with some fruit and loads of Kenco Caribbean Gold coffee and Ena Baxter's finest tinned soups. Every woman I've ever known would judge me harshly for living like this, on such a basic diet, especially when I explain to them that this is a major improvement on the years when I had no diet at all. But Jamaica is genuinely different, in her indifference. Up at the lodge that evening, she introduces me to the small gas cooker with an air of total apathy, as if it's this bizarre gadget left behind by some eccentric who used to live here.

She mutters something about the big fireplace in the main room, something about coal arriving, but her heart isn't in it. Anyway there's central heating, which suits me fine. I guess they installed the radiators when the dirty job of shovelling coal into the fire proved too much for whatever rock'n'roll legends were here before me. But by now I am so impressed by her disdain for the usual comforts of the bourgeois lifestyle, I start babbling. "You know these guys in the AA are always talking about how they could taste food again when they stopped drinking? One guy keeps talking about all these brilliant desserts he eats."

I am babbling. "I don't know about you, but after a few bottles of brandy a day, I'd need more than cream buns to keep me satisfied, know what I mean?"

She just chuckles, not really interested. Food and heating and life's little necessities don't concern her at this moment. Instead she seems to be lost in some reverie, absorbing the vibes of the gate lodge, maybe still wondering if Jagger really did have it off with her mother in here, while her father was outside pruning the roses.

I feel so close to her at this moment, I have a real problem letting her go back to the big house.

"It's got a special atmosphere, dis place," she says, looking like she's reluctant herself to leave. But then she's at the door, setting off the wind-chimes.

"You're in the country now, when it gets dark, it gets really dark," she says.

Then she's gone, a swift but gracious exit. I wonder if she practised it, or if it just came off naturally. Even the way she says a little word like 'dark' has music that lingers when she's gone.

She was right about the dark out here. Night is really night.

There is none of that comforting neon, but a sense of death, the final passing of another day.

I don't miss the city, you can get no peace on those streets. I find it easier to get out of bed in the morning up here, where day is really day. It feels like I'm in the right place, that this is not just an illusory change in which you simply shift all your problems to a new location, doing a geographical, as they call it in the rooms.

But within a week, when we get settled into a pattern of work and idleness, Jamaica starts probing again at the raw stuff like she did that first day in the flat, wondering what it is that scares me so much about the drink. It feels more intimate in the gate lodge than in my flat, we feel more like a couple, we know for sure now that the lack of drink is all that's coming between us, that I just can't risk making that move, and that if I did, we'd probably make it in every room in her daddy's mansion. And she doesn't want all that on her conscience, so she doesn't go for it, she just picks at it. Or that's the way it seems to me.

So after a week, when I'm feeling the benefit of all this clean and sober country living, on a day when the tuner is sounding like gold, I'm able to tell her this story of how I reached my rock bottom and I think it makes things clearer for both of us.

The story goes, I'm in this pub in Camden Town with this mate of mine called Jesse Nestor. It's an old stomping-ground of mine, Camden, full of venerable rock'n'rollers and class acts I met when the band first got a deal and we moved to London and were on a sort of a permanent binge.

I keep going back there in a haze of nostalgia; it is one of the great joys of my drinking life that I can hop on a plane wherever I am and go down to Camden and drink in the Devonshire or the old Mother Redcap with the likes of Jesse Nestor.

I go there on a whim or I go there if I really need it, like this time when I split with some woman I can barely recall now, and it seems like a sensible thing to do, just to go drinking on the back of it, to spend my days in pubs where I can't harm anyone except myself.

So I'm about a month solid on the booze, drinking all over Dublin and sleeping with drunk women and crashing, and I'm in Lillie's Bordello one night when I get the old urge to catch an early flight to London and a cab straight down to Camden.

Arseholes drunk, drunk beyond being drunk, grinning like a maniac on the red-eye, I'm delirious by the time the tube takes me to old Camden Town and I hit the Devonshire straight away and there's Jesse Nestor. My old mate.

Jesse is a star. He has two singles and an EP to his name on an indie label that went bust in 1979, but he is a star all the same. I don't mean that he has the attitude of a star like you need to have if you're in rock'n'roll; I mean that in his own mind, Jesse Nestor is a star just like Lou Reed is a star, a legend of 20th century popular culture.

When he finds himself ransacking his flat looking for fifty pence for the meter, it doesn't strike him that this is an odd thing for a stupendously successful man to be doing. To Jesse it's just a distraction. It's like when a normal man has to scratch his leg, a mere irritation.

The people who groove with Jesse have always been able to negotiate this by simply accepting it. Jesse Nestor is a rock'n'roll star. Don't fight it.

I accept it myself throughout that day when I find him in the Devonshire and we drink pint after pint of Stella Artois like I've just dropped in from next door. Jesse's not really interested in my travels or my career. I'm just a small-time operator who was on Top Of The Pops once or twice while he, with his long grey hair and his sparkling white shirt and his leather trousers and his cowboy boots, is an immortal star.

I've drunk myself sober and I'm getting drunk again, but my rock'n'roll stamina keeps me going as I buy a couple of bottles of Southern Comfort at closing time to take back to Jesse's flat, which is just up the road over a cool record shop, so cool they probably even have a copy of Jesse's EP and his two singles, and they'd find them too if they looked hard enough.

Jesse's not totally drunk, exactly, but I start to notice he's not the man he was. He trips going up the steep stairs to his flat, and it takes him a while to get the key into the door. He goes to the toilet for maybe half-an-hour, leaving me looking at 'The Blues Brothers', which I find totally hysterical after about thirty nights on the tiles.

And I'd love to share it with Jesse, this wild hilarity, but he's quiet on his return, like he's done something in the toilet that he can't quite get his head around. The movie ends and Jesse starts talking about this new album he's working on, as if he's actually made about twenty mega-platinum albums so far.

I'm angry all of a sudden at Jesse's horse-shit, I can't keep the bile down, my own band has probably got about six months to live and it's getting to me now, it's like the drink is turning bad on me and I'm trapped here in a world of irredeemable failure, with nothing to entertain me except Jesse's fantasies. I don't make the usual allowances for Jesse, I just kill the conversation.

I get up and start looking through Jesse's video collection. I turn my back on him as he reveals that Mr. Bob Dylan wants to work with him on this one. Then I turn to him and say, "Dylan? I've got to tell you this Jesse, Dylan was in town last week. And he said you were an asshole. A total fucking asshole."

I say it in a nasty tone of voice, and I can tell Jesse is waiting for some relief, some sign that I'm winding him up about this. But I can't give it to him. I can turn putrid like this when the booze is going down the wrong way.

"Jesse Nestor... the biggest asshole in all the worrrrlllllld," I say in my best Dylan accent.

And Jesse just ignores me, of course. He goes silent for a while, like he's lost his train of thought and then, tossing back his long grey hair, he starts dissing Prince, who according to Jesse has finally been found out.

As Jesse drones on, eventually I don't hear him any more. I lose consciousness. I am woken up by the police maybe a day later, and I learn that Jesse Nestor is dead. Fell down the steep stairs and cracked his head and that was it. A shell.

They let me go after a few hours. Frankly, I don't think they care what happened to Jesse Nestor. His people take him back to Somerset to bury him, while I'm getting tanked up again in the Mother Redcap, just another Irish loser on the batter. I never knew his people were from Somerset, I think through the fug, certainly Jesse never talked about them after he became huge. My mind is beginning to slide. A magnificent career and a golden life and I destroyed it all, as surely as if I threw him down those steps. I am in a bad way, thinking like this. It might as well have been David Bowie who died.

It takes me another few weeks back in Dublin, drinking and guilt-tripping about this, convinced I am the man who killed Jesse Nestor with my harsh words, before I collapse. And when I am eventually taken to St. Pat's drying-out department, after passing out in an early house where, I dimly recall, Dirty Harry was on the telly, they tell me that my liver has just about packed it in and another drink will kill me. And there's an AA meeting tonight, which is highly recommended.

I meet a nice old man I recognise from the newspapers in the canteen, a man who until recently had a title, something like Lord Chief Justice, and who is now dipping a biscuit in his coffee, expressing delight that he has just been let out of his room unaccompanied. So I mooch along to that AA meeting.

That's how it is with the drink. You nearly burn the house down with your wife and child in it, and after a few deep breaths, you carry on like before.

But you try to tell Jesse Nestor the truth, and it all unravels.

Three

I tell all of this to Jamaica and she's pretty convinced now that I'm a genuine grade A alcoholic, that one drink might kill me. So it's a pretty serious scene as she leaves me there on the estate for a few weeks while she goes off to do something successful in New York.

Just before she leaves, she drops a small television in to the cottage. I'm not there when it arrives, so I'm only guessing here, that she did it herself, but my heart sinks a bit when I see it there on the table by the window.

I'm sure I heard her say that she never watches the box, and I distinctly recall telling her that I like 'The Sopranos' but otherwise I hate nearly everything about television – though I look at Sky News occasionally, to find out what time it is. I even refused an invitation from the Late Late Show to talk about my booze hell, because I don't believe in that stuff, and because backers for some reason tend to go cold about trusting you with their money to create a stage musical, when they discover that you're a well-known drunkard.

So my suspicious mind starts up, and I figure she's sending me a message here, lowering the tone of our relationship, throwing a bit of rubbish in my direction, an exercise in studied indifference. I told her I hated television and still she gives me a television. This dumb line keeps repeating itself in my head. I told her I hated television...

And it feels so bad, it gives me a jolt of panic. I suppose at the back of it all I am still leaving my options open, assuming that she would always be a willing partner, that at the smallest signal from me, the party could kick off. The TV tells me no.

Then again, maybe she just dropped a television in because she's great. But that bad feeling gnaws at me. And later that evening, as I fix it up on the floor in the corner, shoving an upturned ashtray under the front of it to get it to tilt just enough to look at, I am becoming dangerously bitter about the choices that a man in my situation must make.

It's not even much of a television, but it plays videos, and I watch videos. Mostly videos of tuners. I root around in a black bin-bag containing the fifty or so I brought up here, a smattering of empty cases and loose cartridges included, that reek of black holes and days of chaos. I select 'On The Town', a brave choice in the circumstances, Frank Sinatra and Gene Kelly on shore leave in their sailor suits, ripping it up in New York to take their minds off the Second World War. Yes, I will confront this bad feeling, I will watch a tuner about people arriving in New York and having a wonderful time, I will have only happy thoughts of Jamaica on her way to this place, and I will be free again. But it doesn't work, it just fills me with longing for the life I used to live, it gives me another shaft of regret to think of Jamaica running into her own Gene Kelly, who will show her a good time for a change, like I can't.

The move to the gate lodge has already told me a few more things I didn't want to know. When you're in your late thirties and you can still get all your stuff, including the Korg, into one car belonging to someone else, you have to wonder if you've been wasting some of your precious time. Even if it is a very big car, a Volvo estate driven expertly by Jamaica through the narrow little tree-sheltered roads up in the Wicklow hills.

But during those first few days in situ, I'm buzzing again about the tuner. I get another blast of hope from her reaction to 'Suddenly' and 'Manhattan Moon' and from her sketches and from studying her skin-tones as she talks up the show. I can see it happening again. It's taken me four years to chop it down from an insane Irish-American epic spanning three generations, featuring the St Patrick's Day Parade on Fifth Avenue, at which world champion Jack Rooney's manager is murdered by his father, with his grandfather there or thereabouts, to one night on stage with Jack, retired prizefighter, who takes his night-club act on the road like any other boxing cliché, but with one small difference: Jack is good.

Played by Matt Dillon he'd be very good, singing his own stuff in this Irish-American musical style I think I've invented, maybe raising the stakes as a theatre piece when Jack apparently loses his drift and drops his guard, as the demons get the better of him on the feverish and fateful night during which the action takes place. His songs, which are my songs, tell the story of his heart's journey, his journey towards manhood, his Irish-American showbiz mother Julia, who worked with the great George M Cohan, and his debauched father Loftus, his dead brother Frankie, his trainer Tosca, and a woman called Nora, with whom he has had a long and tempestuous entanglement; Nora, who was a Jewish reporter when she started out, but who is now just a dark presence, just Nora.

And they wouldn't give me five million dollars to put this on?

I do some good work when I'm alone on the estate, alone except for various workers like Eddie, who rides an old Suzuki, making me nostalgic for my own motorbiking days, short-lived though they were. With the first big cheque I got from the band I bought a motorbike, a Harley of course. Maybe I'll take it up again; I imagine myself roaring down an imaginary freeway, the wind racing around my head fit to make you dizzy. I only ditched it because our manager persecuted me about the stupidity of getting up on the bike, and the danger to life and limb it involved; he thought we were going to make billions, but if the main songwriter ended up splattered across the highway...

Then again, it might have been a good career move.

Anyway, I'll talk motorbikes with Eddie some time; he's always knocking around doing whatever workers do. Probably something that makes more sense and pays a lot better, come to think of it, than trying to finish a big duet between Jack and Nora called 'Last Night I Dream I Am Dancing', sounding on-the-money now, I believe, after a hundred rewrites to allow for the fact that Nora was once a totally different person. And Jack's been through some changes too.

It doesn't take much to get me settled in. I don't have a lot to unpack. I'm not too fussed about my surroundings anyway, but I like the gate lodge, the one main room with a small kitchen attached and a mirrored sliding door that leads to the one bedroom with a bathroom off it. Probably fetch about £450,000 at today's prices, and when you're a retired rock'n'roller living on occasional royalties cheques, that's a fine premises, a fine premises indeed.

At least I assume I'm alone on the estate, once the Volvo pulls out onto the road and drones away, fading into the distance. For all I know, Jamaica has a few of her mad relations up there, but she says she lives alone and she likes it that way. But she also likes to have someone in the gate lodge, just in case.

Which sounds a bit cold and businesslike to me, but then I'm the one setting the boundaries. I'm putting it across that, in my condition, I am available for work, and nothing else. Nothing untoward.

So during those first few tentative weeks she doesn't even offer to show me around the big house and I don't question it. I'm just inside the gates here, covered in trees, farther down the lane from the big house than I imagined, a few thousand yards, not a few hundred. And I've only seen the big house once.

On the first day, she takes me up. It's a grey old place with mullioned windows that looks more like a monastery, brightened up by manicured lawns and flowerbeds, which probably explain the workers. Again she calls it an absolute shambles, muttering something that seems too aggravating for her to talk about properly, something about her mother packing to leave several times, and never getting around to it, but never getting around to unpacking either.

She leaves me sitting in the Volvo while she collects the keys of the gate lodge, making me feel small and undignified, and she doesn't even ask me what I think of the place.

I guess it's no big deal to her, it's just the house where she's always lived. I mean, I never asked her what she thought of my flat, did I? And she didn't offer an opinion.

I share this at the meeting which I sussed out down in the old Protestant village hall, built in 1928, according to the legend above the front door. I decide there's no point keeping any secrets from these guys, a small but elite crew of rural alcoholics, on average ten years older than me. I guess the countrymen can take a few more years of bombardment out there in the wilds, before they put up the white flag.

I say I've just moved into the gate lodge and I'm friendly with this woman up there and I feel deep down that I don't deserve to know people like that at all, but then I felt deep down that I didn't deserve Susan either, who has no money but who is basically a better person than me in every respect. I get a lot of recognition for these morbid reflections. The room is paying attention.

I'm talking about this fragile self-esteem that we all have, and how it makes us unfit for lasting relationships. I leave it at that. I decide to skip the bit about my fear of falling into drunk love, because with these guys it sort of goes without saying.

I like this old room with the bare floorboards and the Super Ser. You don't get more than ten at the meetings here, and they're real, serious drunks, massive abusers of alcohol, who have come a long way to be sitting listening to a prat like me talking about issues of self-esteem.

I like the walk back up to the gate lodge too, the sounds of birds and animals of which I know nothing and the smell of some terrible shit on the fields, which I presume has a higher purpose. And I like that sense of well-being I always have after a meeting, a sense that I've been with a bunch of men who are trying to do the right thing for once in their lives, who are putting down something they loved and loved in vain, and opening themselves up to things of the spirit.

It's a feeling that hit me straight away at that first meeting back in St Pat's, something I know I want, a lightness in myself that goes way back to the beginning, that offers the promise of a fresh start. An end to the madness. And yes, as the big book says, a life beyond your wildest dreams.

It does it for me nearly every time, and it stays with me at least for the mile home, as I try to figure the meaning of that line, a life beyond your wildest dreams. What I'm doing now, spending my Friday nights in a broken down hall, built in 1928, and then walking home alone sober, is definitely a life beyond anything I imagined when I was miming our first hit on Top Of The Pops, sober for some bizarre reason. But I can see that this lifestyle, each long day in the country, is helping me to finish the tuner, which is the kind of wild dream that I can still relate to in my shallow way. So maybe I'm getting there. One day at a time.

But when I get back to the gate lodge I'm looking at it another way. This is how it happens when you're a slave to the drink, cunning, baffling, powerful. I'm sitting there in the soft light on this windy autumn night listening to A Collector's Sondheim on the Walkman and thinking about Jamaica over there in New York, just hitting the bars no doubt, when I notice there's a mobile phone on the table with a scrawled message: "I dropped this in from Jamaica." Signed Eddie.

So the workers can come in any time. But that's OK, in fact it's a real touch of class on Jamaica's part. I feel there's no hidden meaning here, like there might be with the television. She doesn't know I don't use a mobile any more, for my peace of mind I say, though in truth it's probably because I can't afford it. She just notices that I don't have something I probably should have, and she puts it right for me, and I'm crazy about her at this moment. I think she's sensational. I don't encounter an act of kindness like this every day, and of course I'm not entitled to it.

And then I get the phone working and there's a message on it and I've really got the butterflies now as I hear Jamaica's voice saying "Hello from New York City." In fact I stop it there, because I need to settle myself and make a mug of coffee to prolong this, to savour it.

"Hello from New York City," she begins, sounding strangely calm, but then it's only people like me who think you have to shout down the phone, all excitement just because you're in New York. "I felt you'd need this t'ing so I asked Eddie to drop it in. Hope you don't mind the... ah... intrusion, but we all use dem up here just for security. I'm out tonight with someone you know, Jason O'Brien, sound engineer, sends you his love... ahh... told him about the musical, he says it sounds excitin'... . I'll call you..."

It ends there and my mood has swung the other way again. I'm deflated. Sure, I loved listening to her voice afresh, giving words like in-troosh-on and mew-zee-cal the full Jamaican, but the message is somewhat on the dry side from someone who's supposed to be my new soul-mate. More like something you'd say to the lodger, this line about security.

But what's really wrecking my head is the thought of her on the town with Mr. Jason O'Brien. Yes, I know this man. Jason engineered both of our hit singles and the hit album and the minor hit album and the flop album. He's the best there is, a powerful bearded type with enormous energy the way those large guys have sometimes. And we drank like madmen together; in fact Jason appears in many of my fondest memories of days and nights in The Docker and The International, then down to Suesey Street for rivers of wine, before it all went bad on him too, it became a job of work, a fulltime job.

I remember towards the end we got on this riff one night about all the drinking we'd done, how the days on the bottle become months and then years, until one day you add it all up and you discover you've spent more than half your life in the old battle-cruiser, or generally under the influence.

We were uncorking a few at the mixing desk of our old studio at about five in the morning, reminiscing, when I put it to Jason that Jimmy Carter was President of the United States when the two of us started to drink seriously, and so this riff started.

We had been drinking from the time of the Carter administration, through to the end of Bill Clinton's first term. Three Republican administrations had come and gone, two Democratic presidents had served full periods in office, and we were still out there, banging the bottle.

When we started, James Callaghan was still the leader of the Labour Party in Britain, and Tony Blair played in a rock'n'roll band. We drank steadily through the entire Thatcher era and deep into the time of John Major. We were drinking at the time of the Falklands War, the Iran-Iraq war, Reagan's dirty war in Nicaragua and El Salvador, the first Gulf War, the war in the former Yugoslavia, and for a sizeable chunk of the war in Northern Ireland.

Jason did the sound for us at beer-maddened benefit gigs for the release of Nelson Mandela, when the prospect of Mandela ever getting out seemed remote. Indeed, for about the last ten years of Mandela's imprisonment on Robben Island, our drinking became progressively alcoholic.

We saw the Ayatollah Khomeini coming and going in a haze of booze, we were in a pub when we heard of the death of Pope John Paul 1, in fact we still believe the man was murdered in his bed, which he probably was. And we were drunk for much of the Pontificate of his successor Pope John Paul 2.

Comrade Leonid Brezhnev was still king-of-the-world around the time we were moving from Macardle's ale to something a bit stronger. We carried on, oblivious, still broadly sympathetic to the Soviet Union, until eventually we witnessed the collapse of Communism and the fall of the Berlin Wall. Which we celebrated in the only way we knew how. I can still hear the dull clink of our pint glasses, the head spilling carelessly over the top upon impact.

We drank through five World Cups, in Argentina, Spain, Mexico, Italy, and the USA.

We drank through the entire career of Diego Maradona, from his emergence as a teenage prodigy and on through the glory years in Italy with Napoli and on again to immortality against England in Mexico, until they got him in the end, banishing him from the Argentina squad on drugs charges. And, at the end, we figured we were holding it together better than he was.

Five World Cups and five Olympic Games. In fact when we started, Athletics was still an amateur sport, so they said, and the world record for the 100 metres was over 10 seconds. But we watched them whittle it down over the years, raising our glasses to each new landmark in human achievement.

Meanwhile, immersed in alcohol, we went through a seemingly endless world recession and enjoyed the boom that followed. We saw Japan rising to become an economic superpower, and then falling back to where it started, and we took it all in our boozy stride. When we joined the drinking ranks there was virtually no such thing as a video recorder. By the time the old hooch was catching up on us, we were roaring uncontrollably down the information superhighway.

We got through punk rock, new wave, powerpop, the New Romantic movement, Live Aid, World Music, raggle-taggle, grunge, Britpop, hiphop, house, and hard house. We saw Ireland winning the Eurovision Song Contest seven times. And we never stopped drinking, we just gave it a rest from time to time, to get us properly up for it again.

We were going on three-day benders before MTV was invented. By our best estimate, we had not been properly sober for approximately 750 episodes of Top Of The Pops, apart from the one on which I actually appeared. We saw U2's early gigs on Saturday afternoons at the Dandelion Market, drunk.

In fact Elvis Presley was still alive, just about, when alcohol was starting to play a significant part in our lives. And so was John Lennon.

We riffed like this, Jason and I, until the dawn was breaking outside the old studio and the early houses on the quays were opening. It was maybe the last great night we had together.

So I don't think it's presumptuous to say that my man Jason is an alcoholic, and that's exactly how the man describes himself when he appears at his first AA meeting about a month after me. It happens like that; the rooms start slowly filling up with guys you drank with out there, who have finally stopped or been stopped.

So Jason is full of it for six months, maybe a year, reading the Big Book which I only skim, mad to do the steps, fired up with AA lines like Let Go, Let God, keeping it simple, keeping it in the day, keeping away from that first drink. Jason O'Brien is an alcoholic but that's OK.

In fact he soon reckons it's OK for him to start drinking again. He gets so wrapped up in the rooms he's not available for work any more: he seems to be totally devoted to this higher quest. But then he is offered this astonishing gig in New York and he agonises about it in the rooms, but I tell him to take the gig, he'll find plenty of rooms in New York.

On the Concorde he breaks out. A little champagne to celebrate life's mystery, then a lot of champagne, because it's Tuesday. And inevitably, as night follows day, we expect to hear of his life coming apart again, Jason soaking up bourbon in Makem's Bar twentyfour seven. There's no way it won't happen.

It all goes quiet for a while, until I meet Jason as I'm going into Bewley's to see a lunchtime play, written by another guy from the rooms. Jason's with this woman who's like Sharon Stone and Jason himself looks stupendous, like everything has gone spectacularly right for him since the day he takes up that first drink again. And I get a faint aroma of beer from him, but nothing drastic, it's only noon.

We stand there hugging and high-fiving and I don't barge in on the booze front because in the rooms we're super-sensitive about anonymity, about being a friend of Bill and Bob as we say, about not saying the wrong thing at the wrong time. Because, for all this woman knows, Jason may never have had a late night in his life.

But Jason isn't shy.

"This is Tanya," he says. "We met at a meeting."

"Great," I say.

"I'm so grateful to you man, for getting me into that room. You were my shining light," he says.

"Great," I say. "And now, you're... you're out of it?"

"We just figured we could handle it out there. We've got each other now, you know?"

"Jesus, man, I'm very happy for you," I say.

"I still envy guys like you who can take it all the way," he says. "Guys like me, we just take the good stuff and go out there again."

"You want a coffee?"

"We're late for this meeting. Guy up in the Shelbourne says he's got a gig for me. Give me your number..."

"I don't have one right now..."

Off the leash again, Jason storms up Grafton Street with Sharon Stone, clearly bound for more success, to be celebrated with a lot more drink, and yes, a life beyond his wildest dreams.

For sure it's beyond mine. And he has the good grace not to tell me he's about to get a gig with Leonard Cohen.

Four

I get a meeting the night before Jamaica comes back. I need it.

She calls me from New York this morning and it's different this time.

"Braddah you'll never guess what I've just done," she says, the voice full of energy now. I get a mad burst of hope that she's going to tell me she's raised five million dollars for the tuner, but I know better.

"Ehhhh... you slept with Jason," I say.

She lets out a loud laugh.

"He's a lovely person, but no," she says.

"You slept with Tanya," I say.

"Who is Tanya?" she says.

"Interesting," I say.

"Listen, I think I'm just after doin' something big and I'm feelin' pretty good about it. I want you to go with me on dis, y'hear?"

"Ehhhh... sure."

"I've stopped drinkin' alcohol. I don't need it in my life."

"Oh Jesus," I say. I hate this. It seems these amateurs don't understand that we alco's are mostly concerned about our sobriety, not theirs. They're alright at the end of the day, we're just hanging on.

"If you want a drink, have a drink. Really," I say.

"Just don't need it, mon," she says.

"Well I do," I say. "But then..."

"You are different," she says.

"So now we're the same," I say, trying to hold myself together.

"Yeah, but I'm doin' dis for me, for Jamaica," she says.

Somehow I don't like the sound of that either.

"There's nothing wrong with you," I say.

"I want what you have," she says. "And to tell you nothin' but the truth... I just want you... I want you."

It's almost understated, matter-of-fact, the way she says it, which only makes it sound more powerful, like the feeling is obviously so strong, and so sincere, it doesn't need the big production number. For a few moments I am floored by it; then I remember how beautiful she is and the agonies of my youth and how far I have come and I feel sanctified.

"On second thoughts, maybe there is something wrong with you," I quip, with my knee-jerk wit. I have always been able to disguise my true feelings with a one-liner. It's part of my disease.

"I'm over here in New York City missin' you and there's only one t'ing that can put it right. We are of one mind, and now I want us to be of one body," she says, as if she's giving me another chance after that false start. And I decide I'm going to take that chance. She has pushed me over the edge and as I fall I am exhilarated, and hell, if the two of us eventually end up in St. Pat's, in the wet brain ward, there's always the rooms again, where they'll call it a slip, just a slip.

"I've waited a long time for this," I say. I sound emotional this time. My voice conveys what I feel in a way I hadn't intended.

"Oh fuck," she says, a blast of Anglo-Saxon, suddenly sounding like she's elated. Maybe it's just the immense relief of getting the right response. Or maybe her credit is running out. "Look I'm goin', I'm goin'," she says, like she doesn't want to wreck this wonderful thing with any more talk.

"And hey, braddah... .you listenin' to me, braddah?" she says breathlessly.

"Listening," I say.

"And listen to me... .you listenin'?" she says, like she can't quite get it out.

"What is it?" I say

"Gonna have one more drink on the plane... for luck?" she says, as if beseeching my approval.

"Have one for me," I say.

Then she's gone.

Yes, I need that meeting.

So the old manoeuvres start in earnest with me and Jamaica, Jamaica and me. Now, a new fear overtakes me, the fear that she won't come through, that it will all look different to her when she gets back, or that she was just drunk on the phone and that she'll have forgotten all the things she said.

An old girlfriend told me once that I was so full of fear I didn't even realise how full of it I was, and I dismissed it at the time, but I have come to believe that there was something in what she said. So I will try to get through this one day without fear. I figure that if I can't enjoy this sense of anticipation before Jamaica arrives, if I can't get the old butterflies about it, if I can't travel in hope and deal with the arrival when it happens, if I can't get it up for this, I am not a man at all, and I might as well just hang myself from a tree out there in the woods.

And anyway, I didn't just dream it, she really said those things, and she meant them. I don't claim any special knowledge of females, but when a woman like Jamaica starts making "I-want-you" phone-calls from New York, it's safe to say that she is making her move. In a situation like ours, it takes one of the parties to make that move, to show courage. Turns out she has what I lacked.

Within twenty-four hours I will have to respond, with my best shot, but I think I'll be ready for it. I feel ready for it now; in fact if she walked up to me this instant I would say nothing, just rip her clothes off and go at it like a hog. But there's nothing much I can do, this far away from New York, except wait for her to come back.

And get a meeting. I'm doing the chair tonight, a sign that I'm becoming an ace face down at the room in the village hall. I help old Theo G to prepare the room. We set up the chairs and the table with the big book and the cards with the slogans, Think Think Think, Let Go Let God and Keep It Simple. We organise the tea and biscuits, Theo G and me, he a fit old army man in his sixties, the sort of AA elder lemon I am becoming one day at a time.

There's eight of us boys in here tonight, but the usual woman, Kay B, is away.

As chairman I kick off by reading the twelve steps and the twelve traditions of AA and a passage from the big book and then I tell my own story. Or edited highlights of it, because I haven't yet mastered the art of telling one definitive version of my drinking life. And I can never bring myself to put in the routine words of appreciation to my Higher Power, because I don't have one.

But that's OK, the only qualification required by AA is a desire to stop drinking.

And we've all got that, as well as a pretty fierce desire to start drinking too.

That's why I'm in the right place tonight. All day I have been entirely ruled by my dick, which is still that of a normal man and thus increasingly mad for a piece of Jamaica. I am horny. She's due at my door at about six o'clock in the morning, and there is nothing more complicated in my head than about a thousand snaps of us humping and sucking and shafting and scratching and groaning, my bitch and me. But as the night comes down, my head is also swimming with images of Jamaica and Jason on the town in Manhattan, knocking back shots of rye in the late night bars, images which to me are paradise.

I can't work either, not in this state. I've got this woman in my blood now, stirring it up. I feel I'm close to picking up a drink. I don't know if she and Jason even went to a late night bar, but with this disease it's the thought that counts. The thought of all the great times that I am missing because of this programme I'm on, this rage in me, this basic character defect. ·

But I can come across all positive when I start talking from the chair. It's genuine too, while it lasts, just like the positive blast I get when the tuner goes right. I know, then, what Keeping It In The Day means. I'm fully alive in the present tense. I'm not lacerating myself with regrets or dreading the approach of another Christmas.

So in these moments, in this room, I can tell my story and leave it there, knowing that it's all over now. And there is no tomorrow.

"My name is Neil and I'm an alcoholic," I start. A murmur of recognition comes back. I've said it before and I'll say it again, I love these guys. Looking at their faces charred with the effects of whiskey and beer, and spurred on by my own mad sense of well-being, I suddenly feel I can go further with my story tonight. I can try to talk for the first time about something that happened a long time ago, something I couldn't even talk to myself about until now, maybe the last ugly secret that is keeping me sick.

"It's great to be here tonight... I feel I'm in the right place... I suppose I had my first drink when I was 13... bottles of Harp in a field." Another murmur of recognition. "And even before that I would see the cowboys on TV throwing back shots of whiskey and I would copy them using water... and later whiskey."

They all laugh. I'm working well, I think I'll be able to spit it all out tonight. Or maybe not all of it, maybe just what I can remember. Two steps forward, one step back. Maybe some of it wouldn't be safe to tell, if there were criminal aspects to it, for example. Even as I speak, my mind is playing games. And I'm not convinced anyway by this secrets-making-you-sick line, I don't really connect with it, I just go through the motions and hope it hits the spot some day. So on second and then third and then fourth thoughts, I won't spit it out tonight after all.

I am weak, I lose my nerve, I baulk at going all the way. I can't tell them that story, not the way it's reared up now out of the depths. But I'll tell them a story anyway, that isn't a million miles away from the full and final version, and I'll see how it plays in this room. Much the same, I imagine, as it's been playing in all the rooms where I've been telling it for the last six years, in another slightly more watered down form.

"I just loved what drink did to me," I continue. "It loosened me up, it made me comfortable with my body, as they say. I wanted that feeling all the time, and pretty soon I started to need it. My story... well my story involves this party when I was about 15... a rich kid's party... a barbecue... when I played a few songs with a friend of mine... I'll call him Bill...

"I remember how awkward and angry I felt towards all these other kids. I recall some ugly scenes."

I'm not sure where all of this is going, except that it's not going far enough. Or is it going too far?

"I can tell you now about something that happened that night that should have been a warning to me, except it only sank in about twenty years later. Maybe only tonight, if the truth be told. We were kind-of chased out of the place in disgrace that night, but when we got outside the big gates we found we had company... this girl about our own age with... eh... these terrible black spectacles was tagging along with us. She clearly saw something in us that no-one else could see... and maybe she was feeling as... despised as we were, so we had common ground.

"When we couldn't get rid of her, we asked her down to the beach to finish off a few cans of Harp. Nothing wrong with that. But we sort-of went the wrong way and found ourselves in this place called... ehhh... the ferns, which was a popular spot for courting couples."

I'm starting to sweat. I take a drink of water. I have the full attention of the room.

"The ferns," I say, longing now for their protection, to be hidden from everyone, smoking cigarettes and drinking beer. "In my mind I'm back there now. I can clearly see the three of us up in the ferns and, though it was about twenty years ago, I can still see the girl in those terrible glasses, having a few swigs of Harp, probably thinking we were the two coolest guys she'd ever met, and the best musicians. Oh yes, she alone among that wretched tribe liked our playing, but then she'd had a few on board already."

I get a couple of chuckles for this, but mostly I'm getting deep silence.

"So we're talking about this and that and then my friend starts to get a bit... heavy... then he makes a grab for this girl and starts kissing her. But she's not really ready for it, at least she doesn't respond in whatever way he wants her to respond, and he gets angry like it's her fault."

I stop and swallow, but it doesn't go down easy.

"So he's getting angry and getting drunk and she looks to me for a way out but at this stage of the evening I'm getting angry and getting drunk too, and she starts to get scared. I can see it in her face, behind the glasses..."

I take another gulp of water. I look at Theo, whose eyes are closed, he's smiling peacefully as if he's heard worse, a lot worse.

"She mustn't like what she's seeing in those drunk little faces of ours, so she tries to make a dash for it. But between the two of us, we get the better of her. And I get even more angry because in the struggle I spill most of my drink... luckily we still have an armful of cans lifted from the party..."

Theo, if anything, looks more serene; I am encouraged to continue.

"I think she was just too drunk to run away and anyway she didn't want to draw attention to herself, because next thing we two boys come up with the hilarious idea of taking all her clothes off and leaving her there, naked... which is more or less what we did... and here I got cute, because while my friend talked about binding and gagging her like they do in the movies, I saw the big picture. I said it would be better if she took off her own clothes.

"By this stage I guess we were getting a bit scared as well, so we let her take off her own clothes, like the gents we were. And it kept the noise levels down... and just to show there were no hard feelings, while she was doing this, I opened another can of Harp and gave it to her, saying it was a warm evening."

I can feel the tension in the room, the recognition from these guys, most of whom have done one thing above all others that they can't face, but one they must at least approach as best they can. It doesn't have to be a war-crime, a crime against humanity even; it can be anything that has a specially foul meaning for the teller. But among the men it tends, on the whole, to be some crime against women. So they can sense me approaching my own dark place, we can all sense it together, and I'm sure now that I'm going to disappoint them with the manifest triviality, the small-time banality of my evil-doing.

"We could have walked away but we didn't," I continue. "We weren't as drunk as she was, we knew we were taking advantage... So she drank her beer naked and we drank ours with our clothes on, and we all started to see the funny side. In fact it was getting quite pleasant and she may have thought we were all going to be friends and she'd get out of there with dignity. And then the two of us ran off with her clothes, laughing."

There is silence.

"I don't know what happened to her after that. I guess she never blew the whistle on us. Maybe she went back to the party and they despised her even more... and OK, we've all done things as adolescents that we're not very proud of, but there's something about what happened up there in the ferns that has this special meaning for me. It's not my rock bottom, it was more like the rock that started the landslide. It's like I took the wrong turn that night and I've been stuck up there ever since..."

"Or just thinking about it, about going up there on the sly, for a drink and a smoke..."

I hear a few mumbles of recognition, but I feel the tension has lifted now and the rest is going to be routine. I'm sure they're all thinking they've done a lot worse themselves with no drink involved at all, and they probably have. But in the rooms we don't judge each other in that way. It's not a competition to tell the most hideous tale; we are in spiritual kindergarten and we hail the slightest advance as a sign that we are growing, one day at a time.

"Soon I didn't need the ferns," I continue. "The everyday world was meeting all my drinking and smoking needs anyway. I was going to pubs. Maybe it was always in my system. Even these days I feel weak at the knees sometimes, when I remember the first pub my father took me into, and that amazing waft of drink, which took a grip of every cell in my body. But the music was there too, and just when I really needed it, the band started going places. I think I was already addicted and here I was in a rock'n'roll band. How good could it get?"

There is laughter.

"And of course for a while, for a long while even, it was great. You didn't really need to have a fully-formed personality when you were drinking all night at festivals with rock'n'roll characters, and you were with the band. We roughed it once, and slept in a tent at this festival in Denmark, and Phil our tour manager woke me up saying, quick, quick, there's a hippy on fire. And I look out and sure enough there's this long-haired guy jumping up and down and yelping because his trousers got caught in the campfire.

And we're nearly hysterical, still drunk from the night before. It didn't get much better than that, I guess."

The boys respond to my mordant line. Black humour. Do we know any other kind?

"The band only made it so far and it all got progressively uglier and there wasn't much laughing any more. But I still had a few years drinking in me yet. I managed to get married around this time and have a son. A lot of it was just immaturity. No way was I ready to be a husband or a father or anything except what I was, a drinker.

"And I want to put in a word here for the kind of drinker I am, not the three bottles of whiskey a day man, just a guy who drank a few pints, and then a few more pints, and then a few more on top of that, until it became my life. Alcoholism, as we know, is progressive, so it always gets a little worse, but it doesn't necessarily mean you can't function at all."

Some of them already know that.

"So I got married and it wasn't all bad, not by any means. It was only when I nearly set fire to the house one night that I moved out. I fell asleep with a cigarette going... a lot of it is just immaturity. No way was I ready to be a husband or a father or anything except what I was, a drinker."

I am repeating myself, but that's part of the process.

"But I was a free man now and I was drinking more or less constantly, and when I wasn't drinking, I was thinking of drinking."

I pause here again because I should be getting to my rock bottom with Jesse Nestor here, but I figure I've disappointed the boys enough for one day. And I've disappointed myself too.

"When they drained it out of me in St Pat's they said another drink would kill me," I say, which sounds impressive enough in its own quiet way. "Liver damage. And they sent me to my first meeting. And I think I got it immediately. I was ready for it. I wasn't put off by any of the God stuff, even though it wasn't my thing. I suppose I just wanted to save my life, simple as that.

"And so it's great to be here tonight telling my story again, because every time I go back over it I know why I'm here, and I know I'm in the right place. Now I don't want to go on too long because I know that other people want to get in..."

I sit back as Theo shares. I don't really hear him, I suddenly feel weary at the thought that I'll be telling that same story or something like it when I'm as old as Theo. I'm thinking of the effect that first drop of drink had on me, how it changed the way I felt straight away, and even sitting here in the room I crave that feeling again, now that Jamaica is coming home. Especially now that Jamaica is coming home.

I'm not being rigorously honest with these guys either, because Jamaica doesn't have a place in my story yet. I just can't talk about her in this room. And squirming away inside me is the thought I'm still not giving them the full SP about what happened a long time ago...

So what am I doing here?

I ask myself this as big Michael B shares, and I'm not there for him either, because I'm hearing bits of his story for the second time, and while it's scarier than mine, even that's not enough to raise my spirits. He's babbling away about getting down on his knees every night for the last fifteen years, and how that has kept him off the drink. And when the guys start talking like that, I'm always tempted to say, "interestingly, I came into AA to get up off my knees."

For the first time I'm not getting a lift from a meeting; I actually feel I'm in some version of hell, in which we are all doomed to keep telling the same stories until we die, rather than accept the merciful release of drink.

But you don't stay sober for six years without a certain ability to suffer when the night has come, and the land is dark.

I lead the boys through the Our Father and the Serenity Prayer and I hang on in there through the tea and biscuits, and I tidy up with Theo.

"You fucked her didn't you?" he says calmly, folding the top of a packet of Fig Rolls.

Somehow I knew I couldn't give these guys an abridged version, and just get away with it.

"What do you think?" I say.

Theo seems to take this as a "yes." I'm not entirely sure, because he turns away from me for a few moments, tidying up the rest of the tea things. I get this weird feeling that he's blanking me out, re-arranging the cups on the counter so he doesn't have to make eye-contact. I sense that something has come over him and he's trying to hold himself together. But maybe that's just me.

For sure, that's just me. Theo turns and looks at me quite calmly.

"Think Think Think," he says, just like it says on the card.

As we switch off the lights and the heater, Theo spares me the lecture about how we're only as sick as our worst secret, which I take as a mark of respect. I could reciprocate by telling him about this woman I'm friendly with up at the lodge, that we're going to be a lot more than friendly very soon. But I'm all rattled now, my head is racing again. I want to take a pill which will delete everything from my brain except all the horny stuff that was in it today. A pill, maybe washed down with something...

"You want a lift?" he says casually, locking the heavy wooden door.

A simple question, but I don't know what to say. We are creatures of habit, Theo knows I always walk home.

I really don't know what to say.

"You want a drink?" he says.

Just like that.

I look straight into those clear blue eyes. He's not fooling.

"Yes Theo, I want a drink," I say quietly.

We stand on the steps outside the hall for maybe a minute, just looking at the cars going past, most of them to the pub for Friday night.

"Me too," he says at last.

"Pint?" I say.

"Pint of stout and a chaser," he says.

We watch a few more cars going by, couples out for the night.

"You don't miss much, Theo," I say.

"Sixteen years..." he says.

Theo taps me on the elbow and we walk slowly to his car, a beautiful old pale blue Morris Minor.

"Sixteen years," I say.

He talks to me across the roof of the car.

"You've six years under your belt," he says. "You've come a long way and you've learnt a lot. Maybe you can go out there again."

"And get away with it," I say.

"And me, I'm so old now. My wife is dead, my daughter is dead, and my son won't talk to me. In all seriousness, why am I coming down here annoying myself when I could be over in Regan's, skulling pints?"

"Regan's," I say.

"Maybe we'll do it like this," he says. "Are you listening?"

"Yes."

"Maybe we'll have that drink."

"OK"

"But maybe we'll have it... tomorrow," he says.

We get into the car. I think about it.

"Sounds right," I say.

He lights a cigarette.

"Tomorrow then," he says. And he drives me home.

Except I have no home, I say to myself, as I shut the door of the gate-lodge behind me, setting off the wind-chimes. I slump into the couch. Not my couch. For a while I just listen to the wind shaking up the trees, my Friday night entertainment. Night is really night up here, but I don't think I'll be sleeping. It's not just the attack of adolescent nerves at the prospect of seeing Jamaica at six o'clock in the morning, it's this other darkness that has visited me tonight. In my solitude in the gate lodge it creeps back into my mind, like vermin.

Yes, Bill and I made a disgrace of ourselves that night at the rich-kids party. But no, we didn't go up the ferns later on. I just make that bit up, when I'm telling my story in the rooms, because it has the shape of something that really might have happened. Except I haven't been strong enough to describe what did happen in a different time and place; I described it to Phil, of course, but Phil is a creature of rock'n'roll, he has seen terrible things. In the real world where Phil and I have been trying to live in recent years, I haven't been strong enough to admit to another human being the nature of my wrongs. The exact nature.

I want to be liked, I want so badly to be liked. So I leave myself a margin.

I was just a kid, after all, in the story of the ferns. But that night in Camden Town we were men, two drunk men, me and Jesse Nestor. And a woman. Everything happened that night exactly as I described it to Jamaica, up to and including Jesse cracking his skull, and my drinking to the repose of his soul across the road in the Mother Redcap. And my arriving in the rooms soon afterwards, at rock bottom. Except I left out some stuff. Stuff about a woman. A woman who had changed a lot since I last saw her at that party when we were kids, but who recognised me that night in the Devonshire, who started drinking with us, and who wanted to party. She said she was still friendly with the girl who threw that party. They always talked about the old days. And she said she had a recollection, a vague recollection it seems, of my playing some music that night with some other bloke, but even so, said she always knew I'd be a star. So I didn't bother explaining to her what I thought about that.

So we went back to Jesse's place. And shortly after Jesse Nestor made me snap with his Bob Dylan spiel, the three of us found our way into Jesse's rock'n'roll bed. And Jesse turned out to be something of a bondage freak. So he started tying the woman to the bedpost with a belt. She started not to like it, started to panic. She was in a pretty bad way, like she was having some sort of a fit, but Jesse steamed ahead anyway.

Jesse screwed her, then he defiled her, speaking in tongues like some deranged beast. He did his worst, and I stood there watching it, and honestly I would have taken my turn, except I was too far gone.

So I watched. And I stayed watching. From the moment Jesse started slapping her in the face to break her resistance, five or six hard slaps until one of them must have caught her on the nose, because it started to bleed. Just a trickle, but it had the required effect, it quietened her down. Softly now, she pleaded with me to do something, to do the right thing. It would break your heart, to hear someone plead like that, but it didn't. I remember thinking, it's too late now, through a haze of beer and Southern Comfort, it's too late now to change your mind, to decide you just wanted a late-night beer and a few sounds, it's too late now for all of us.

And then she stopped fighting it. I remember her looking at me over

Jesse's shoulder, her face a mask of suffering, her eyes blazing with hate, and I remember saying to her, "It's rock'n'roll." That's what I said to her: It's rock'n'roll. Baby.

Then Jesse does the genius bit. He calls a cab, and when the cab arrives, he releases her, nonchalantly, as if nothing has been going on except some party game. He dabs her nose with a tissue like he's just fixing her make-up. He's not speaking in tongues any more. He asks her where she lives, in a perfectly friendly fashion, and when she says Brixton, he says he has some friends down there on the Railton Road, we must all hook up again some time.

And as the city is waking up, as all the good people are going to work, he leads her downstairs very gently, very sweetly, and puts her into the cab, and pays the fare to Brixton.

I imagine her still in the back seat of the cab, in shock. Disorientated by the new morning, I guess she swore she'd get us locked up, and wept with frustration when she recalled that about forty people in the Devonshire saw us having a marvellous time. And then the next day I imagine her hearing about the death of cult figure Jesse Nestor, feeling that for all its cruelty, there is some divine justice at work in this world.

As for me, I went into the rooms for about six years, though I might more properly have been getting my meetings in prison, most likely in the sex offenders' wing.

So that was my last big night out.

Yes, that put me off the drink for a considerable time.

Night is really night up here, but I don't think I'll be sleeping. I switch on Sky News, to keep an eye on the time. And for company.

Midnight comes and I think, this is tomorrow, Theo, wish you were here. Wish you could explain to me how all these high hopes got tangled up with all the black stuff, how I can be seeing Jamaica in the morning and feeling like Hank Williams, when he heard that lonesome whistle blow.

Because that vermin keeps gnawing at the inside of my head, swarming all through the night.

This woman who's coming from America to get it on with me, someone should tell her it's not a good idea.

Five

She's at my door straight off the plane. The taxi outside must have woken me up. I must have fallen asleep on the couch at about five, but I manage to get to the door before she can open it with her key. The night is fading into an autumn dawn, a good omen perhaps. She's in some soft Lainey Keogh-type bohemian thing, including a very long purple scarf that she takes off and puts around my shoulders.

"From New York City," she says, though her voice is all Caribbean warmth. Ah, it kills me.

We kiss, the first time. Softly to start, then hard. She grabs a hold of the hair on the back of my head, I grind into her, squeezing her arse with both hands. She starts to unbutton her long dress at the front and quickly the two of us are getting our clothes off, all off, and tossing them on the ground; we are of one mind and now we are going to be of one body.

There's a beanbag just behind her, a great oversized beanbag with a leopardskin pattern, a timeless rock'n'roll kinda thing, and she sinks back into it, showing me a great mound of pubic hair, drawing me down on top of her, and then we're lovers; we are lovers, and that is a fact.

It's intense, it gets more intense until it's unbearable, and it's over soon, but we both want it that way, a rush, a rush, a rush, a demented release.

We lie back, recovering. We can see ourselves in the mirrored sliding door. We know we will be remembering this scene for the rest of our days, remembering what we did, and how we felt, the first time.

What I felt... I will know rightly in about ten years time what I felt, because feelings tend to take that long to settle in me. In these moments as they're happening I am driven more by a raw instinct that seems to emanate from a Power than is even Higher than the one we have in the rooms.

The Highest Power.

A Power so great and beautiful I believe it can release me from that thing I did in Camden Town, and kill all the vermin in my head, and redeem me, and make a man of me again.

"Braddah," she says.

"Yeah?" I murmur.

"Again..." she says.

We get it going again. We connect on the beanbag like we connected the first time, with the same rush, the mad intensity. It takes longer this time. There are moments when I slip out of her to stop myself coming and try it another way, taking her from behind and then rolling over as she takes control on top of me, the two of us locked, out of our minds. We finish up on the other side of the room.

Now, as the energy rushes out of me, I remember this, the way you suddenly feel so tired and so empty but incandescently, so empty of all the bad stuff.

"How are we?" she asks, getting her breath back.

"We're great," I say.

We roll back to the beanbag. She wraps the long purple scarf around us. We look at the image of us in the mirror. We've got the same dark hair and dark eyes, but her unwaxed body is much browner than mine. And unwaxed is putting it mildly: her pubic hair is luxuriant, verging on the overgrown. Her breasts, by contrast, look almost artificial, they're so perfectly proportioned. She gives a little moan of exhaustion, yes she too is empty, incandescent. I get a duvet from the bedroom and slide it over us. It would feel wrong to get into the bed and to fall asleep there, it would take away from the significance of the beanbag and the mirrored door. It would feel like we were just falling asleep because the old jet-lag was kicking in. We can do that any time, but not now.

She drifts off to sleep first, her back turned to me. I am thinking about all that pubic hair. Strange thoughts, like, what will happen exactly if we ever go for a swim in a public place? Will she get it waxed, at last, or would that be against her religion? Her underarm hair doesn't spill out the same way, and her legs are smooth. Maybe that's natural too, or do I doubt her? Maybe I'll just leave it in her capable hands, let her manage her own hair.

I drift away too, one arm draped across her belly, my dick throbbing into the softness of her arse, remembering some old Shakespeare line, about the honey-heavy dew of slumber.

I know this professor of English in the rooms, who swears that Shakespeare had a bit of a drink problem because his vivid descriptions of the pains and pleasures of sleep reveal a man who must have suffered terrible hangovers, and hated himself for it. According to the professor, The Bard refers to "the swinish sleep," the most perfect description of the drink-induced semi-coma which boozers call sleep. And the honey-heavy slumber is the best kind, the post-coital kind that I am drifting into now.

With the grace of God and the help of Alcoholics Anonymous. As they say.

When we wake up, we try to guess the time.

"I t'ink it's five fifteen," she says.

"Why five fifteen?" I say.

"Well the light is fadin'..."

"I mean, why not just say, like, five o'clock? Why be so accurate?" I say.

"It's just somet'ing I can do, tell the time pretty spot on. I guess it comes from bein' a country girl."

Her head disappears under the duvet.

"One of my useless little talents," she says, as she starts with the tongue.

With the duvet on top of me, and her down below, I can look at myself in the mirror receiving oral sex from some unseen entity. I think if the boys in the rooms could see me now... well, let's just say they'd want to share.

They'd say, Let Go Let God.

I want to return the compliment but she suddenly decides she's got something she needs to show me. A Jackson Browne album she got in New York.

"You'll love dis, I promise you," she says. "You like Mister Jackson Browne?"

"I love Mister Jackson Browne," I say. "I love nearly anyone from California. It's part of my disease."

"Look at the track listin', mon."

I see what she means: the song 'Jamaica Say You Will' nestles in there among the gems listed.

"Great," I say.

"Jamaica is me," she says. "Sort of."

I feel a tremor of unease. She picks it up straight away.

"No, don't look at me like I'm one of dem lunatic people from Wicklow. I'll tell you 'bout it, all right? It's a family legend. And accordin' to this family legend, my father was hangin' out with some old friends of his on the West Coast, and I had just been born back here, he wasn't around of course, and he told dis friend of his on the West Coast that I was to be called Jamaica, and dis friend happened to know Mister Jackson Browne and happened to mention it to him...

"That is the family legend anyway," she says, a faint note of Cork reaching my ears at the end.

"That's great," I say, genuinely impressed. "That's just great. I love that. I love that song."

"My father was smokin' an awful lot of ganja at the time," she adds.

I pull my jeans on, and a t-shirt. I can feel the mess of sex on my skin sticking to the clothes, but I like it, the strangeness of it after so long. I put the Jackson Browne album into the machine and I stand there listening to Jackson's gorgeous angst-ridden song about Jamaica, the daughter of the ship's captain. I know this song because I used to dream of being Jackson Browne, with his fine cheekbones and his vast talent — and no doubt a vast bedroom in his cool Californian house overlooking the sea, where highly intelligent and socially aware and, yes, beautiful women would have sex with him.

I think back again to the night when I was fifteen at the rich kid's barbecue. I can recall it now, almost without pain, now that I'm in this room with this woman. I can run those twisted scenes in my head and Jamaica will still be here at the end of it.

I'm fifteen again and Bill and I have just formed this band and we find ourselves amongst the rich kids in this summer house overlooking the sea. And most of them don't know us, but we're asked along anyway to sing a few songs, while all the rich kids get on with dressing their hamburgers and pairing off, all comfortable in their own skins, or so it seems to me.

The way it was supposed to be, I would sing a few Eagles numbers and play the piano and Bill would bash away on guitar and the rich kids would gather round and check us out and we would find love that night. But it didn't work, not that night, not that summer, not that year. We felt that they despised us and we spat teenage bile at them and eventually we were asked to leave.

So we left, and no, we didn't go up the ferns afterwards with some unfortunate young woman: we just went home and felt sorry for ourselves, a pair of wetback losers. None of that stuff about the ferns is true, like I said, I just use it in the rooms for... for dramatic effect. We boys were able to disgrace ourselves without going near the ferns. It's like Bill and I were a step below those people on the evolutionary ladder, but they were showing us the way up. It's like we went from the middle ages to the 20th century with nothing in between. Maybe our children would have lives like that, but we'd just have the music and the beer and the bile and the bad clothes. Small wonder the rich kids looked the other way while we played, and small wonder we went to the pub the next night to get more comfortable with our bodies the only way we could. Beer was the answer then and it was the answer for a long time to come. My soul still sighs whenever I hear the soft California rock that got played that night on the stereo, while Bill and I sucked on bottles of Harp and watched all this sex going on around us, guys getting what they wanted, like it was pre-ordained. I'm right back there, nursing the agony of rejection, while Don Henley croons about desperadoes coming to their senses. Tell me about it, Don.

I should hate Don Henley and all the Eagles and curse them as I greet every tequila sunrise without the tequila. But I am weak. Yes, even still, with that rigorous AA honesty of mine, I can't help loving that West Coast sound all the way up to Mr Jackson Browne. Maybe it's got something to do with a lot of those guys being wild drunks. But there I go again, reducing every story to a story of drink. There I go again.

What if that's all baloney too, and your West Coast headbangers like David Crosby and Dennis Wilson only dabbled like anyone else? You read some line in the paper, that Mr. Jackson Browne himself is having some serious woman trouble and you make about fifty connections straight away; you wonder if those guys maybe had some addictive thing going on, and you make a connection with yourself, with your own addiction which maybe attracted you to that sound back then in ways you didn't understand at the time.

But maybe there's no pattern to it. Maybe there's no connection at all between me and California, except the totally random events that led me to liking that music, and a lot of other music I heard, along with a million others, except that I got to be a rock'n'roller. And in that world, and even in the shadow of that world, you can meet women called Jamaica. Yes, maybe it was worth it all just for this day, to know that I am with Jamaica – and the guys who jeered me when I was fifteen are not, and will never be.

Ah, those rich kids. Their houses had a different smell, like the very stone and the wood and the glass and all the inanimate objects had some fragrant promise, for them but not for me.

But I have risen above them all. I am here now with Jamaica, I am listening to Mister Jackson Browne playing that song and it's sublime, it makes me feel like a full person again. And I'm not just saying that to the boys in the rooms to make it through these empty hours, I'm living it.

The song ends.

"That's it," she says, breaking the perfect silence.

"Wow," I say quietly.

"Are you alright?" she says.

"Yes... yes."

"You kno' what I mean?" she says. "Are you... alright?"

Ah, for about five seconds there, I had moved beyond the drink. But she's bringing me back now, back to reality. Apparently life goes on. And on.

"Yes I'm alright," I say.

"I did not have that drink on de plane," she says, like she's looking for my approval.

"I've got something better than drink," I say. I set up the Korg to play the finished backing track of 'Last Night I Dream I Am Dancing'. I don't want her lying there thinking that maybe Mister Jackson Browne is better than me, at least not when I'm on form. Because he's not.

At least I've got to cling to that possibility.

I bang it on and it really sounds like it's happening. I'm discreetly studying Jamaica's reactions and she seems mad for it as she lies there naked on top of the duvet. I get a blanket from the bedroom to cover her back, lest the evening chill prevent her giving the piece her full and undivided attention.

This would be the big duet between Jack and Nora and I've added a trumpet solo during the section where they dance under a starlit sky. You can easily imagine it bringing the house down. Jamaica loves it.

"It is so... so exhilaratin'," she says. "It sounds like..."

"A show," I say, ex-ill-ar-ate-ed too.

"A musical," she says. A mew-zee-cal.

"Just five million dollars and it's yours."

"Writin' a musical. Very, very smart," she says, like it's all still new to her, still fresh.

"They're even getting trendy again, have you noticed? Chicago is everywhere, Baz Luhrman's at it. I've got to say, I thought of this nearly six years ago and people figured I was loco."

She lifts the blanket, inviting me in. She gives me a long hard kiss.

"I love that," she says. "I really love that. I love to listen to you talkin' about your work, about the musical. It makes you so... upful."

"You're the one... you've got the career..."

"I can't tell you what it feels like when you get positive. When you get upful," she says, repeating the word.

"I believe in this tuner."

"Then it will run for ever," she says, the sweetest words, in the sweetest accent.

"I'm positive about it, even though I've had some brutal experiences with it. Six years of them, actually. But you won't want to hear that."

"Maybe I need to know. I'm doin' the costumes, am I not?" she says.

Apparently she means it. Apparently she cares.

"I assure you there's nothing upful about it," I say.

"I can take it, mon," she says.

We'll see.

"I'll give you the short version, will I?"

"Shoot," she says.

I go blank for a moment, overwhelmed by the sheer volume of rejections I have received, not knowing where to start. So I start with the first one that comes to mind, a random selection, and as it happens, it's a bit special.

"OK, I make a demo of the four big numbers," I say. "The really good stuff. And I give it to Chris Rodham. You know Chris, he's a big shot in London and he's mad for it. Wants Harry Connick to play Jack, wants the best of everything."

She cuts in.

"I kno' Chris" she says. "I met Chris at a party. He's a very nice man."

"A lovely man," I agree. "Many phone-calls, bags of enthusiasm. Then one day he's in a meeting and I can't talk to him. Next time he's gone to New York for two weeks. He'll call me when he gets back. That was three years ago. I haven't heard from Chris since."

She finds it hard to accept this.

"Did you try him again ? Maybe some confusion?" she says. Con-few-shon.

"No. I had called him twice or three times in fact. Now it was his turn to call me. Pride you know?"

But I lie. There was no con-few-shon. I called Chris' office many times after that. In fact before Jack Rooney ever existed I used to talk to Chris on the phone every few weeks, shooting the breeze, then I give him Jack Rooney and the man doesn't want to know me any more. I crack on.

There is much to tell.

"No problem, I have the band's London lawyer on the case and he's mad for it. He'll organise some finance. And so I go to a meeting in the lawyer's office with this money-guy and I mention that the character of Loftus has shades of Eugene O'Neill, and he says, I know Eugene, he used to run Ryanair... you want any more?"

She bursts out laughing.

"I am moving in a world where men hear the name Eugene O'Neill and think Ryanair," I say.

She's still laughing, I didn't think it was that funny.

"And so are you," I add.

She steadies herself.

"Did he give you the money?," she says.

"No. But my lawyer gets the message that you need to have a business plan for a big project like this. So he gets an accountant on board, does up this brilliant business plan. I mean, it really is a brilliant plan, everybody says it's nearly a work of art in itself. I must have met with about thirty different rich guys at different times up there in the Westbury Hotel and they've all been hugely impressed with the business plan. They take it away, along with the CD with the songs on it, not to listen to, never to listen to, 'cos that's not what they're interested in. I eventually started giving them empty CD cases because it was costing me a lot to run off these CDs, and nobody ever complained. Then you get back to them and usually they're in a meeting. And then they're in New York for two weeks. Everyone goes to New York for two weeks when they meet me."

"Soon come," she says, meaning, I guess, that success is coming soon.

"Everyone goes to New York, but you're the first one to come back to me," I say, a hint of sentimentality creeping in.

It's only now the notion hits me that if we can somehow deal with the drink, money might become an issue with us. I mean, Jamaica's parents are presumably dead, so she probably owns half of Wicklow. Which means she could finance about forty major Broadway flops if she felt like it. And I know that old line, that you never use your own money, but if, say, she wasn't doing the costumes... ah, it's vile to be thinking these things, especially when you happen to have your hand softly squeezed between the person's hot thighs... it's just that I genuinely don't understand why it's such a no-no to use your own money. I mean, if you have loads of it... why not?

But then I already know rich people. I know anyone who's anyone in rock'n'roll. I had dinner once with eight people, one of whom was Bob Dylan.

And if I could have asked any of them for a load of money, I would've done it long ago. But, somehow, that's not allowed in the high places in which I moved. Money is such a dark subject among my rock'n'roll chums. As free spirits, we're supposed to regard it as something sinister, something best left to all those sick people on the management side. Money is not supposed to be an issue with us, and yet some of us have made incredible amounts of it. So I have friends who still feel that they are brandishing the true flame of rock'n'roll, when in fact they've become little more than property tycoons in leather trousers. In some part of their heads, they still genuinely believe that they're outlaws and vagabonds. And so the issue of giving money to someone like me, a fellow gunslinger, would simply never arise. If it did, I'd just be out of the gang straight away.

And it's not that they don't like me, and it's not that I don't like them. I know them all, and after my band nearly cracked it, I sat in with the best of them on guitar, just jamming after-hours, the odd blast at a studio session. Shit, I've been around. I know all these guys and I like them, and they like me and this sideman vibe of mine that tells them I can play a bit − but also that I know my place in the pecking order.

Maybe that's why Jamaica and her country girls like me too. They can sense I won't get out of line. They can smell it with their highly-trained noses, even as they're getting off on this rock'n'roll guitar-man thing that I've still got going for me, nearly ten years after the band went down, like I'm up there but I'm not the boss man, you know? More like the guy in the cowboy picture that John Wayne thinks is a bit loco at first, the kid throwing shapes, who turns into Wayne's top man. But not the top man. Never the top man.

And I guess they like me too because I'm easy on the eye, like some cute-looking gaucho, Jamaica says. It's always gaucho with Jamaica and not cowboy. And I give the impression I'm easy on the nerves too, always likely to flash you a big grin no matter what you do, no matter what you're looking for. Mostly I look like I have accepted whatever happens to be for the best, coming down from a high place as gently as I can, my cool never completely blown, despite the whiff of failure.

And is any of this worth any money to me?

Not a dime.

"Soon come," she says, opening her thighs just a notch, freeing my hand to venture up into the forest. "Soon come, soon come," she whispers, opening wide, letting me feel how wet she is, how ready to be fucked.

"I'll never mention this subject again," I say.

Then she closes her thighs on my hand again, remembering something else.

"Listen, Jason O'Brien is gettin' to know a lot of important people in New York city. You must send him a CD straight away. He's such a fan of yours. He says you're his shinin' light."

"Where did you go?"

A reflex question.

"Some bar... we talked about you all night."

"You stayed till two in the morning, three?"

"Three-thirty approximately," she says. "

"Gad Almighty, the man can drink." Gad-Al-might-ee is right.

"Makem's?"

"Some place on Seventh Avenue. Mulligan's?"

Ah, the way she says Mull-ee-gans, it sounds too good.

"I know it."

" I had my last drink in Mulligan's of Seventh Avenue with Mister Jason O'Brien," she says wistfully.

She opens her legs for me, and we're about to go again, and I can hear the boys in the rooms urging me to get down on my knees and give thanks to God for what I've got. But in some dark corner of my heart, I still believe I might trade it all for what Jason's got.

Six

We're not living together as man and woman, though this we most certainly are. Man and woman. Jamaica always leaves me in the morning to drive back up to the big house, allowing me to spend my usual few minutes sitting in the lotus position with my eyes closed, trying to get my head straight. It's not meditation exactly, but since I don't precisely know what meditation is supposed to feel like, maybe it is.

These early days are the best I've had since I went into the rooms. The honeymoon period with Jamaica is like the honeymoon period when you first get sober; your spirit soars, you've got an entirely new way of looking at the world. You've still got the cravings, but you're high enough on the new thing to make it through.

There's the frequent sex, dumbing down our relationship at times to the level of the animals; the life of the mind is always there for us when we need it, but we don't, in these happy days almost devoid of meaningful speech.

I know I'm supposed to be doing a 12-step programme, but, even after all this time, I still don't get it, or maybe I just don't want to get it. It must be the old rock'n'roller in me, but on this guide to the good life I go with Eddie Cochran instead of Bill and Bob, Eddie who advocated three steps to heaven, not twelve − though I can still be heard, reading aloud the 12 Steps whenever I'm required to do so at the start of a meeting. I know them off by heart at this stage, and I imagine the constant repetition in itself is doing me some good, the way a mantra might.

1. We admitted to ourselves we were powerless over alcohol − that our lives had become unmanageable.

2. Came to believe that a Power greater than ourselves could restore

us to sanity.

3. Made a decision to turn our will and our lives over to the care of God as we understood him.

4. Made a searching and fearless moral inventory of ourselves.

5. Admitted to God, to ourselves, and to another human being the exact nature of our wrongs.

6. Were entirely ready to have God remove all these defects of character.

7. Humbly asked Him to remove our shortcomings.

8. Made a list of all persons we had harmed, and became willing to make amends to them all.

9. Made direct amends to such people wherever possible, except when to do so would injure them or others.

10. Continued to take personal inventory and when we were wrong, promptly admitted it.

11. Sought through prayer and meditation to improve our conscious contact with God as we understood Him, praying only for knowledge of His will for us and the power to carry that out.

12. Having had a spiritual awakening as the result of these steps, we tried to carry this message to alcoholics and practise these principles in all our affairs.

Fine words, intimidating to some as they attend their first few meetings, although lots of us figure out the loopholes pretty fast. We note that God is mentioned a lot, and we turn away in despair, thinking we have arrived into some weird offshoot of the Knights of Columbanus, which just happens to contain several of our old drinking buddies. But as our minds drift at meetings, and we gaze at the steps printed on a large scroll, contemplating the enormity of what lies ahead, the more we like that part about God "as we understand him." God as I understand him − or her, to be less old-fashioned and sexist about it − can be anything from moonlight in Vermont to the transcendental force that was Mr.Van Morrison circa 'Astral Weeks'.

God-as-I-understand-him tells me that I don't have to go back to the real God, and face His wrath.

It's that fifth step, along with the eighth and the ninth, that trouble me at present. What happens if you admit to wrongs that didn't happen? Or if you twist the wrongs that did happen into something else, something less noxious, something that is not quite unspeakable? I have admitted to Theo the general nature of the wrong I did to that girl, up the ferns, except it was all basically bullshit. Yes I did something bad to a woman once, but it wasn't when I was a kid, and it wasn't up the ferns, it was up in Jesse Nestor's place. It was in the rock'n'roll jungle. How many of the others in there are speaking under false pretences too, are lying through their decaying teeth? I know this: the exact nature of the wrong I did is something I am not ready to admit to another human being. And I don't know if I ever will be.

Like I said, Phil doesn't count as another human being for this purpose. But Theo does, and I know that Theo's door is always open.

Then there's that stuff in Steps 8 and 9 about making amends, real shiver-down-the-spine stuff there, but maybe Step 9 offers a way out, with the consoling suggestion that we must make amends to persons we have harmed, "except when to do so would injure them or others."

Yeah, there's a fair amount of wriggle-room in there for the worms that we are. And I might lose that luxury if I came straight out and asked Theo to be my sponsor – the guy who's been in AA a lot longer than you, who takes you through the steps one by one. I should have a sponsor after six years in the rooms, I know I should, but I don't, partly because it seems to me that what we're looking for ideally comes in three stages, not twelve. At least I think you can get away with three, at a stretch. And I'm now at the third, which is possibly the most dangerous.

The first stage is when you just try to get by without the drink in your life. You try to get your head around the concept of powerlessness, of admitting that you are powerless over alcohol. Which is a lot more complicated than it sounds, and to prove it there are men coming in and out of the rooms for years who think it means that they have no power over themselves at all, that the prospect of drink entirely overwhelms them, that they are virtually automatons programmed to drink, vegetables like

Father Jack Hackett on Craggy Island, or some similar cranked up wino who shouts and roars and belches at you in the street. Which is a different thing.

But most of us grasp it to some extent when we first go into the rooms, delirious on the ninety meetings in ninety days which are highly recommended. We're still deeply addicted at some level, but the honeymoon period gets us through a lot of it. And then there are times when we're just hanging on. It can go either way. And I guess I made it across that first precipice somehow.

The second stage is when we're looking for something deeper to get us through it, some level of serenity. And to me it comes not from some positive engagement with the Higher Power but maybe from what I think of as the absence of madness. The days, that is, stretching into weeks and into months, in which you start to notice that you haven't done anything completely insane for quite a while now, and you're beginning to feel the benefits. Which don't necessarily come with a fanfare; there's just the occasional sign that suggests, in a small way, that you're starting to become a vaguely decent human being.

And the rooms can make the difference here, a guaranteed injection of something like serenity, and expert advice. Maybe the only guarantee we've got is that most of us will be sober for the one hour that we are in that room. If we approach it in the spirit of fellowship.

So here I am at stage three, where we involve ourselves in a relationship again, an adult relationship the like of which we have never had before, because we were almost permanently out-of-it. Risking it all for a higher prize again, in my case for a woman, a move which can either bring me peace of mind or whatever the opposite of that is? Bad craziness I guess.

Love to me is peace of mind and I've got it this morning. Peace of mind and the little extras like waking up with Jamaica explaining that she's usually not that horny first thing, but guess what?

Little things like that.

I wouldn't say we've got anything revolutionary going yet, but there's plenty of that cool passion, and that warm Caribbean passion too.

Generally she likes it the usual ways, me on top, her on top, from the side and from behind, usually when we're naked in bed, like everyone else. But she likes it with clothes on too, her beautiful clothes which I like to think she is designing with these scenes in mind, she standing up and bending over and gripping the table while I get behind her and slip it home into what she calls her punani, a word she swears she was using for years before Ali G, and which sounds immeasurably lovelier coming from her. Funny, I always thought that Ali G just made up that word, but if this is one of her little Jamaican affectations, I figure it's the one she's most entitled to – it turns out anyway that she's right and I'm wrong, he didn't make it up. Not that I was ever going to make an issue of it, but I checked anyway, just for the hell of it.

And this sex-standing-up-with-clothes-on thing is new to me because behind all the rock'n'roll bluster I guess I'm a bit repressed; like I said I've never been all that comfortable with my body. But once she gets me into the position, I don't know how I lived without it. It goes straight into the routine.

She's also completely open to me licking her punani, though I have known some women to have reservations about this, women who will fuck you with abandon but then with a firm hand stop your head from heading south until – what? – until they know you better?

Jamaica loves me working away down there in the forest. I hear a lot of "soon come, soon come," and she reciprocates at the other end. I tell her about this line in The Sopranos when Uncle Junior is talking about some girl tongue-ing his balls, just the right word, tongue-ing. Jamaica likes the sound of that word too, she tries it, and it works. Tongue-ing.

So the way things are going Mr. Eddie Cochran was right, there are three steps to heaven, not twelve.

I put on a cowboy hat, like the gaucho I am, and walk down to the village for a meeting. I think I'll share properly about Jamaica today, about the peace-of-mind side of it rather than the tie-me-to-the bedposts-with-a-set-of-rosary-beads side. The guys aren't ready for that yet.

I'm having a coffee in a little restaurant we use before and after meetings. I'm talking to Theo about our little conversation the other night, just thanking him, and no more about it.

I see Theo at times as the last decent authority in a world in which no-one is any good. He is like that cranky old woman in 'Night Of The Hunter' who protects the runaway children from the forces of the night because no one else will do it. They are all too stupid and vain.

"There's my woman now," I say.

Jamaica walks by with Lotte and another woman whose face is familiar to me.

"Which one?" Theo says.

"The nice one," I say.

Smiling.

Lotte sees me just at the last moment. She steps back and acknowledges me. I'm expecting the three of them to clatter in to join us, and maybe Lotte can come with me to the meeting, though I know she prefers the one inside in Molesworth Street. For the anonymity.

Theo and I are poised there, waiting for the three ladies. By the time Theo has finished his third cigarette we figure it's a no-show and we leave for the meeting.

I share in a general sort of way about Jamaica, but again I'm not focused on it because something is bugging me about what just happened. Not the fact that Jamaica knew I was there and wouldn't stop to say hello, she's a free spirit after all. It's the other woman I can't get out of my head, the one whose face is familiar to me but whose name escapes me in that completely maddening way. Not just her name, but who she is, what she does, and where she's coming from. Otherwise she's well known to me. I think.

In situations like this I always wonder if it's just some woman I slept with, drunk.

There's a scary little thing I do sometimes. I find myself flicking though my address book and looking at the names and telephone numbers of women who clearly played some significant role in my life at the time I entered their details in there. But if I sit around looking at their names and numbers until the end of time, I won't be able to place them.

There's a grotesque void out there containing loads of my drunken nights, gone forever from my memory, which is deeply disturbing in one sense, but also a relief, as if the god of drink, having taken your soul, is repaying you by simply erasing some of the worst atrocities from your mind.

Gone, gone, gone for all time, otherwise you'd be walking down the street and you'd suddenly remember who the woman at 6969696 is, leaving you with no option but to sink to your knees right there in the street in mortification.

What did you say to that woman? What did you do to her? You just don't know.

But she does.

And I'm talking about this to Jamaica later that night. We're sharing a pizza and a couple of Cokes that I collect on Eddie's Suzuki, Eddie the worker.

"Then there's the dead ones," I say, handing her a quarter of the pizza. "You get to the age of 35 and you're browsing through your phonebook and you discover on nearly every page there's the name and number of someone who's dead."

" Other alcoholics?" she says, non-judgementally.

" Perfectly normal people who just got a bad break," I say. "For example… there's two women in my book who ended up committing suicide. Not one, but two… and there didn't seem to be much wrong with them when I knew them."

I get a shudder at the feeling.

"You mean… relationships?" she says. Re-lay-shon-ships?

"Enough for me to have their phone numbers," I say. "One I got off with in Leeson Street, the other I spent a weekend with, a lost weekend…"

I shudder. All the things that happened between me and that woman, all the ways you could describe that weekend are now covered by just one word. Lost.

"And they ended their lives, like, soon afterwards?," she says, implying nothing that I can divine.

"A lot later actually. One took pills in a flat in London, the other hanged herself in Australia..."

"Gad Almighty," she says.

"You think I should cross their names out or leave them there as a mark of respect?"

"Whatever feels right to you," she says.

" I should just throw away that phone-book," I say.

She's apologetic about not coming into the coffee shop. Her friend Grace Bannon was running for a train. I understand. That's OK.

"Grace?" I say. "Grace Bannon?" I don't recognise the name, just the face.

"I wouldn't worry 'bout it," she says.

"I'm going to check my book anyway," I say.

"Silly t'ing," she says.

"She didn't give the slightest hint, nothing at all to suggest she might know me?"

"She's been married ten, twelve years. She leads a quiet life," she says.

"Come on, everyone has a night out."

"She's not de drinkin' type," she says.

"So she'd remember everything," I say darkly.

"I said you were in the band and she sort of knew who you were then, but..."

"Has she children?"

"Two children..."

"Have you... eh... met them?" I say.

"Actually... .one of dem has your first name... I wonder... ?" she says, winding me up.

"Sorry," I say.

"OK, so."

"He doesn't really have my name?"

"No, he does not," she says.

"I suppose, if I did something really bad to her, she'd warn you about me. Right?"

"Right. She's a good person."

"So she can forgive."

"Put it behind you," she says absent-mindedly, just making whatever sound will reassure me.

"I'm telling you I know her. I know that face," I say.

It comes to me three days later. I'm chairing my old meeting in Molesworth Street and I'm telling my story again, for a change leaving out the bit about the rich kids' barbecue and the pain of it, and I see her face now, Grace Carey. Or Grace Bannon, as Jamaica is calling her. She was one of them. Maybe not the worst of the rich kids, just one of that crowd. The one who gave the party. Grace Carey.

The last time I heard her name was in the Devonshire, the night that Jesse and I showed that woman what we were made of. That was the last time for many things.

And luckily I can tell my story in my sleep at this stage, because an awful feeling hits me. A feeling of doom, that there always has to be a catch, that Jamaica disappeared from view the other day because she's not levelling with me over this Grace Bannon – using her married name, I presume, to put me off the scent. Or just a made-up name, who knows?

We drinkers know when we're being gulled. We're the experts. We have a fine instinct for knowing when the honeymoon is over.

Here I am supposedly deep into recovery, chairing an AA meeting, "doing the chair," talking the talk, but now my heart is sickened.

Keep it simple, they say, keep it simple, but this all seems brutally simple to me now, this domino effect which goes like this: if that woman in Camden Town was still friendly with Grace Carey six years ago, and Grace Carey is still friendly with Jamaica, maybe the real reason Jamaica couldn't come into the coffee shop to see me, was that she was too busy hearing about Camden Town, and what an utterly twisted fuck I am.

There is a clear connection, I figure, from way back. That day I connected with Jamaica in Café En Seine, I also connected with my own most disgraceful episode. In my effort to break free, I find myself right back there. Right back there, except now I've got something to lose. In fact, I've got a lot to lose.

This is how it looks to me as I quickly finish doing the chair, on AA automatic, the usual twaddle.

Lotte is at the meeting and, the fear rising, I'm determined to pump her. I take her to Café En Seine again. We find ourselves sitting at the same table, the one we were at when she introduced me to Jamaica. I get the coffees.

"I know Grace Carey, and I'm pretty sure Grace Carey knows me," I start. "Grace Carey, Grace Bannon, whatever she's called now. There was a party... a barbecue... and... it got pretty messy..."

Lotte knows what I'm on about. She's rattled.

She's coming to the end of her AA honeymoon. Looking well on it too, but she's got too much of a mournful look for my taste; she must have done a hell of a lot of crying before she got to the rooms.

"Secrets keep you sick Lotte, that's what we say."

"Are we in the rooms now? Are we talking confidentially?" she says.

"No, we're not. But I'll be wise."

Lotte composes herself. She takes a few deep breaths. She takes her time. She composes herself very well. Then she begins.

"I personally don't think you'll have a problem with this..." she says.

"I won't have a problem?"

"Jamaica thinks you will, I say you won't," she says, with a certain edge of country-girl menace.

"Maybe I won't then," I say.

"Grace Carey and Jamaica are very old friends. Jamaica would meet Grace if anything important happened in her life and you are an important happening, my boy. And as you say, Grace was at that party, you were at that party and, well, she says you were absolutely atrocious that night..."

"She came to say that?" I say.

"Of course not, it just came up... . But she said you were absolutely atrocious in every way, how you looked, how you sounded, how you drank..."

I think she's starting to enjoy this. I fear what's coming, out of my past, out of that grotesque void.

"You were playing some terrible music with your friend from the band, who couldn't sing..."

"Bill..."

"And some of the crowd were giving you a hard time, but most of them just ignored you. Frankly, I'm told you made a disgrace of yourself."

She is enjoying this.

"So, we weren't ready for it..."

"Anyway, next time she sees you, you're on Top Of The Pops," she says.

"Right," I say, still waiting for Lotte to tell me something really bad that I did, something really bad that I know I did, years later, to some girl who was at that party.

"These are the breaks, I guess," she says. "From zero to hero!"

I get a rush of relief at the cliche. The kind you get when you thought the baleful gods were out to screw you, but it turns out they were only passing through.

"She... eh... she just thought it was, like, ironic? Like, how bad we were and how well we did?"

I'm starting to enjoy this too.

"Yes, but Jamaica felt you'd be sensitive about it, as an artist, so she chose not to tell you what Grace told her. She feels it could upset your morale."

"Oh, it would, it would," I say.

"I'd forget it if I were you," she says.

"Still, there's no reason to keep it from me," I say, with a nauseating air of self-righteousness.

"Jamaica's an angel," Lotte says.

"Yes."

"So, while she feels it's wrong to keep this from you, she also feels it's important for you to move on from all of that. You were only a kid.

What does it matter, now?"

"Of course," I say, affecting a little sulk.

"It's not a very, very deep wound, you understand," she says, as if she's experimenting with the language.

I look away from Lotte and out the window at the people walking up Dawson Street, all the normal people. We sit in silence for a few minutes, letting it stew.

Lotte has an appointment with a specialist, who will tell her if her liver is damaged. She gets up to go.

"It's OK if I bring this up with her?" I say.

"Maybe it's the best way... rigorous honesty," she says, quoting from the twelve steps, of which she is hardly even at number one.

"Did Grace mention... at the party... was there anyone that we... insulted?" I say.

"No."

"Thanks, Lotte."

"That's OK," she says.

Seven

I'm due to visit Susan and Stephen, so I take this new piece of information out with me on the DART to Dun Laoghaire. It shortens the journey somewhat.

Passing through Sandymount, I realise I don't miss my old flat, any more than I missed any of the other places I've lived for the last fifteen years or more; always, it has felt like I am just passing through. I recall that one of the guys in the rooms gave me a kitten to raise in the Sandymount flat, suggesting that its playful antics might divert me. And it worked for a while, until the kitten grew up and left me; apparently she too was just passing through.

Still it was an education to watch this creature, just a few weeks old and yet so skilled at negotiating its new world. I became fascinated by the way it used the litter tray so expertly. I would watch it getting into the tray and having a cat-crap, then using its paws to kick up the whitish clay in order to hide the crap under it, always a perfect job of concealment. All covered up but still in there, like these stories we tell; like the story of the ferns and other, darker stories, all our old dirt half-remembered, but still somehow covered up because we're so good at that, it's in our nature.

I get out at Dun Laoghaire station and walk up to Captain America's wondering how I am going to face our usual family feast with so much important work to do, that tuner to write, such a need for everything to be alright with me and Jamaica.

Susan's got a crew-cut now, and Stephen's had one for some time. Almost twins, they're delighted to see me; they both have these huge smiles. In fact I miss those smiles more than I care to admit and once in a while I imagine I'm not an alcoholic and we're still a family. I feel I could nearly deal with that now, eight years after. Eight years too late.

Stephen actually sticks his fist in the air and lets out a whoop, which I feel is laced with irony. I seem no longer to represent a father figure to Stephen, just some headbanger who arrives into Captain America's now and again, claiming to be related to him.

Susan doesn't do much to discourage him in this attitude. She's not the controlling type. She stopped being bitter about our break-up five minutes after I left the house that last time; now she genuinely believes I'm making progress in the rooms, to the extent that I'm slightly more mature than Stephen. But it's a close run thing.

I give Stephen a Liverpool FC picture book. My one undeniable contribution to his development is that I have him supporting Liverpool rather than Manchester United. Thus, already his young life has been speckled with failure.

I never have a problem discussing other women with Susan; in fact it still alarms me that about a month after our break-up I was knocking back the beers, right here in Captain A's, giving out about some chick who was giving me a hard time because she seemed to be under the mistaken impression that I drank too much. No, I don't like to remember that, and as for nearly setting the house on fire, well, I keep that in the rooms.

So when Stephen goes off to mess with the other tables, I'm jabbering to her about Jamaica.

"You've done well," she says.

"So far," I say.

"High maintainance?" she says.

"The usual..."

"The drink?"

"Not the drink exactly... not that the topic doesn't come up... these secrets everyone has, things they might keep from the other person in a relationship, secrets that make you sick we call them in the rooms, some of them that don't matter at all, some of them that matter a lot..."

"Such as?" she says, helping me along.

"Well, she decided not to tell me that this woman saw me playing at a party years ago and thought I was rubbish."

Susan considers this. She knows how morbidly sensitive we alcoholics are; she's always trying to toughen me up.

"I'm sure it doesn't matter," Susan says, deadpan.

" If it doesn't matter, I'll raise it with her. Right?" I say.

"You're the man," she says.

"How will I do that Susan?"

"I think firmly but gently..."

"I'll say secrecy is a bad habit of mine as well."

"That's good," she says.

"On the other hand, what would you say," I ask, "if I told you that after that party, Bill and I took some girl up the ferns, got her more drunk, got her naked, and ran away with her clothes?"

I'm trying on the old reliable, seeing how Susan reads it on the atrocity-meter.

She contemplates this a bit longer.

"I'd say... I'd keep that a secret if I were you..."

"You think?" I say.

"Even if it makes you sick."

"Yeah."

"Even if it makes you as sick as a dog."

"Right."

Susan looks like she wants to laugh, except she senses this is big stuff for me, that I won't be seeing the funny side for a while.

"It's just gnawing at the back of my skull, you know? I tried to share this sort of stuff at meetings but I bottle it," I say.

"Keep bottling it. That's my advice."

"Thanks."

"God, you were a little prick," she says.

"There's just a lot of stuff coming up for me right now," I say. "All the good things that have happened in the last six years, I feel they're all down the toilet if I make one false move. And frankly if I'm still with this woman at the end of it, I won't care what state I'm in... you know?"

"I know."

"So even the smallest thing is bugging me, like why is she keeping anything from me, even stuff that doesn't matter? Especially if it doesn't matter."

"Just don't push this honesty shit," Susan says.

"Otherwise I'm in heaven," I say.

"Listen, she's done something here," Susan says. "She's done something I didn't do. She's met this guy who's liable to go bananas on drink at any moment, she's risen above it and she's done something. She's taken a risk. She's even doing something about your musical. Sometimes you get lucky in your life and someone rises above it and does something when they might just as easily let you fuck off and die."

"Right," I say.

"I let you go," she says.

"But you were right."

"That's what I needed, and that's what you needed," she says.

"So what do I need now?"

"You need to stay cool, and you need to stay sober..." she says.

"Right."

"Then like any normal person, you take your chances. But the thing now is that you do have a chance."

I'm flattered. Susan would not lightly class me as normal. I think I may be able for this after all.

"She's even stopped drinking for me," I say.

We order our usual banana splits. I've got just about the right money, no more.

"I'll get this," Susan says. "I got ten grand from my uncle's will."

Susan calls for a bottle of Heineken. The atmosphere is suddenly merry again. Neither of us will ever have a proper job, but Susan is bizarrely starting to play the stock market with some success – and now this wind-fall. You need a bit of luck too.

"Like to invest in a musical?" I say, about 95 per cent in jest.

"What about Jamaica?"

"Doing the costumes."

"She's stopped drinking, has she?" Susan says.

"She doesn't need it in her life," I say.

Susan takes a swig of Heineken.

"She needs it," she says.

They see me off at the DART, Stephen again raising his fist in triumph. I think I've got a strutting rock god in the making there. There'll be a chance to bond, maybe, when he realises what a rock'n'roller goes through.

Susan is working well today; as we wait for the train she tells me again not to get too wrapped up in head-games, just to do something human for the rest of the day, like meeting Jamaica out at Bray and maybe even buying her a drink.

"Do what?" I say.

"Just get her a can or something, and watch the tide coming in. Women like that stuff."

Yes, it would be a fine declaration of trust; it would even be quite grown-up. And that's what we all want to be some day.

"My guess is, she doesn't really want to give up drink, she just wants to know it's all right with you," Susan says. "So I'd say, give her what she wants."

"But is it all right with me?" I say.

"Well, is it?"

"I've told her it is... obviously within reason... I told her..."

"Just show her... show her you can handle it... and if you can't handle it, she can always give it up again," she says, as the train comes into view.

"I guess you're right," I say. Susan is always right. I even agreed with her wholeheartedly when she threw me out.

"And remember this, what you did when you were fifteen is not totally irrelevant, but there are other reasons why men drink too much, the main one being that they like it," she says, as I get on the train.

"Thank you, Susan," I say.

I call Jamaica, using the mobile she gave me, suggesting we meet half-way, in Bray, for a walk along the pier, or something. I need to express these good thoughts, to free them from my system before they fester.

The journey around the bay makes me feel less tense. I'm able to enjoy the scenery now just for what it is, without a drink in my hand. And a walk along the pier is progress for me, something that was once inconceivable without a pub at the end of it.

These are the small steps you take in recovery, until one day you find you've earned a fifty-fifty chance of a giant leap.

I wonder what's out there for Stephen. Maybe it will all go the other way, and he'll be like my father, a regular guy. I really hope he won't find himself visiting his son whenever he gets the chance, in between trying to raise about five million for a tuner and chasing a woman called Jamaica. Or India. Or Persia. Naturally, I hope he won't be a hooch-monster.

And I now understand completely what they meant in the old days when they said you should have something solid. That's what I want for Stephen, and I stopped saying it with a sneer about six years ago.

I don't know anyone who has anything solid. What we have are fast-fading memories of the golden age of Irish rock'n'roll, of helicopters bringing us to the liggers enclosure at Slane, of waking up in Denmark to look at a hippy on fire, of stinking, booze-ridden nights with Jesse Nestor in Camden Town.

We have talents but we can't make a living. We're all addicted to something. And we're excitable. We talk too much. And we think too much about stuff that doesn't matter, like whether Ronan Keating will crack America.

As Jason O'Brien put it when he was gung-ho, mostly we live on illusion. We build our dreams on the clouds above our heads, we set our caps in that direction and we strike onwards in hope. The failure of this mechanism is the key to what we know as alcoholism.

We scramble desperately to connect, we make a religion out of looking inside ourselves at stuff that happened when we were young. But we're still making it up as we go along, we're still seeing what we want to see. Like, when we stop drinking and look back to figure out where it all went wrong, naturally we're going to be looking out for bad stuff that happened to us, that made us drink too much. We're going to be looking really hard for that stuff, because the only alternative theory is that we drink too much because it's more enjoyable most of the time than anything else we can think of doing. And anyway, who's to say what's too much?

We used to have religion to tell us what was responsible and respectable, now we just have Americans on the radio with a book to sell. We are so weak, we have so little to guide us except these random connections; we're easy meat the way that our fathers were.

Except the priests were more honest than the gurus, they told our fathers to forget about happiness in this life, forget about drink and women, just offer it up. They told of a life beyond your wildest dreams in the next world, if you died sober. They never dared to suggest it was all there for you in this life if you could only figure out what upset you so much in the first place. Maybe they knew they were talking to men, and not boys, boys like me who sit in the rooms telling the same old stories about how they hit rock bottom, stories of pure evil, and sometimes stories that amount to nothing more when you boil them down, than incompatibility, some guy's wife freaking out about their relationship after hearing that American on the radio, who drank a bottle of gin a month and decided he was a hopeless alcoholic. With a little help from his partner who co-wrote the book.

And you wonder if there's some vast Puritan conspiracy afoot, which has ensnared even us wild men of rock.

But hell, it wasn't the Americans who made us do all that drinking. We did it, we had the good times our fathers were denied, and here we are now. We have our struggles, for sure, just trying to make the rent, but somehow they lack nobility. We are entitled to a lot of the credit for seeing off the priests, but it will leave Stephen with another problem, the lack of something out there to rebel against. You gotta laugh at that little twist...

And after all that, we finish up in a room with bare floorboards reciting the Our Father and the Serenity Prayer with a bunch of people who swear by the virtues of prayer and abstinence. Go figure.

So maybe going off the drink is the one struggle that counts, it's our cause, our Spanish Civil War, our fight against an evil force within and without, in which we are prepared to make the ultimate sacrifice. We can't choose our comrades, but we accept that they are on the same side as us, and that is all that matters. We respect what they are doing because we know how much it hurts. And without bragging about it, for this, we too are entitled to respect. Not that we always get what we're entitled to.

The train is pulling out of Shankill, the last stop before Bray.

The other thing my father didn't have to cope with is women. Certainly not women called Jamaica.

We assume a lot about our fathers; we assume we are the first men in history ever to spend the whole weekend in bed with a woman drinking wine and ordering pizza.

But we assume also, and with some justification, that they got away with stuff on a scale we can't imagine. They weren't expected by women to have emotions, or to entertain their children, or even to talk to them if they didn't feel like it. They were men. Just men.

So not long before he died, when I told him I was giving up the drink, my father said it would make a new man of me. But I suspect deep down he felt that this was all part of some dark scheme got up by women to control men, to make them feel bad about themselves and the few pleasures left to them. He would still cling to the view that an alcoholic is someone with a wet brain roaring in the gutter, not some fairly presentable guy who just lets himself go from time to time.

On this journey, en route to Bray, I don't like to let those thoughts into my head, but they come anyway, the comforting sound of the train seeming to invite them.

Jamaica meets me at the station and we head for the seafront. I got my head kicked in, in this very place, one night long ago; I think on that particular occasion I deserved it, but it doesn't make the memory any sweeter. This time I just hope to break even.

It's getting chilly, so she takes a raincoat out of the Volvo estate, opposite the promenade. A self-designed raincoat to go with her self-designed jeans. She seems completely relaxed, which only ratchets it up for me.

It's always the way, when you're about to bring up something new or unpleasant, the other person always looks contented in themselves, yet another reason why they invented drink.

I know I'm going to have to do this quickly. I mumble something about getting chocolate. I leave her on the seafront then, while I trot across the road to the off-licence.

I have lost all sense of grace around drink, all finesse.

I'm back again and we wander down the promenade, hand in hand. I'm still stalling, looking for the right spot as if there is such a thing. Just trying to do something natural involving alcohol.

We sit on the wall, looking at the tide coming in.

"I got something in the off-licence for you," I say.

I take a can of beer out of my coat, and hand it to her.

She looks at it for a while, speechless.

"It's cool..." I say.

She keeps looking at the can, then she smiles.

"I rather like this stuff," she says, the words sounding formally English, the accent all Jamaica.

"I've got six years under my belt," I say. "I reckon you're entitled to the odd can."

"Certain?" she says.

"Sure," I say.

"You're a good person," she says.

"If I can't handle it, you can always give it up again," I growl.

"This is goin' to work," she says. She throws her arms around me with an intensity that actually makes me lose my breath.

"You said you were doing it for you, but you were doing it for me. And I don't want you doing that for me, it's miserable. I want you doing other things for me," I say.

She lets out a salacious chuckle.

"This is goin' to work," she says.

"I just want to say one thing," I start, before she gets into the can. "This party when I was a kid. Lotte tells me I got a bad press from Grace what-ever-her-name-is. You can tell me, I can take it."

"I know, I know," she says, unruffled.

"I pumped Lotte, sorry about that," I say.

"I just felt it was a bit cruel of Grace, disrespecting you like that, you and your music. You'd be sensitive about that sort of t'ing," she says.

I catch myself gazing at her skin again, not imagining for a moment that it was ever blemished by the filth of puberty. No, it was always fine, it was always adorable.

"I'd like you to tell me everything," I say, "but if you don't want to, that's all right too."

"Seen," she says. She kisses me quickly on the lips and then she opens the can.

I look away to the amusements. More images of childhood fill my head; there's no escaping it, I only need a jukebox playing 'Young Girl' by Gary Puckett and the Union Gap and I'm right back there.

She starts to drink the can, a few sips to start. She takes longer, more contemplative draughts, as she looks out to sea, inscrutable.

Crazily, I am reminded of West Indian men I used to know in London, standing outside Ladbrokes all afternoon supping cans of lager. I also think of an old girlfriend, who used to torment me in restaurants by taking an eternity to finish her wine, while I sat there, not long in the rooms, drinking water. I still don't know whether she was doing it on purpose. I couldn't bring it up at the time, and there's definitely no reaching Jamaica now, wherever she is.

She drains the can to the last drop.

Then she gets up and walks across the stones to the incoming tide.

She goes right to the edge of the water. She hurls the can into the sea, where it bobbles uselessly.

"Finished," she says.

Eight

She's finished until we get back to the gate lodge, by which time she's picked up another eight cans in a supermarket on the way, which is still fine by me; it's the smell of a bottle of red wine being opened that tends to break this old heart of mine. Then we talk most of the night, sometimes jokingly, mostly in earnest.

She says she felt that connection with me straight away, that day in Café En Seine, and by the time she's got three or four cans inside her, she's prepared to say that she was sure she'd met me before in some previous existence, probably as far back as the thirteenth century.

So while our relationship, like any other, may go through some changes, she'll no doubt be able to deal with it in the context of the many lives we have led.

And this is not the joking part, this is Jamaica being earnest. People like her don't automatically scoff at the mention of reincarnation. That's why they're different. They believe that anything is possible, and in their world it is. They may talk in an earthy accent that isn't entirely their own, but it's ninety per cent their own and the rest is allowable, because the result is so beautiful, and anyway they feel entitled to talk any damn way they like.

I hear her out with a solemn look on my face, remembering Theo's wise words that cynicism is one of our deadliest enemies, we must beat it away with a big stick. But I can't resist the urge to ask her if I was also an alcoholic in the thirteenth century. We laugh about that, though she doesn't actually answer the question.

And anyway, I can sort-of relate to what she's saying, although on a far more modest scale, as befits the son of a primary teacher. I believe we all find our soul-mate, someone who won't be uncritical, but who will appreciate all the good in us – and bring it out of us in time. We all find this person we can be happy with; it's just that we don't necessarily know it at the time, maybe because we're drunk or just otherwise engaged when it happens. But as we get older, if the ship has indeed passed us in the night, we look back and realise that it got away, that we'll never get back there; like the man says, we'll never have that recipe again.

It seems that Jamaica was my soul-mate all the time, except I never knew she was out there for me, and I could have done with that knowledge when I was too young and too foolish and too angry and too full of Harp because those rich kids wanted to listen to The Eagles instead of me.

But I know it now. And it deepens this thing we've got going up here, deepens it every way.

And by the time she's draining the last can, we're nearly ready to compare notes on our respective childhoods, except we instinctively move off that subject; she says it just causes her too much pain to start rooting through all that rubbish again. Another area in which we connect, I surmise. But she was happy for a while as a child in the Caribbean, and I suppose I was happy too, when I got the waft of a bottle of beer on a summer's night, 15 years old and Bob Seger's 'Night Moves' playing on the cassette machine, a bunch of boys in the sand-dunes watching the girls swimming in the sea.

We decide this is the best time of all, the best life we will ever have, the one we are living now.

Yes, two women I kissed committed suicide. I kissed them and they kissed me and we spent nights in bed together, rock'n'roll nights. One of them hanged herself, the other took pills, and though I hardly knew them at all, I understand, I understand only too well, how things can get so bad, you just can't keep clinging to the wreckage. Maybe there was some darkness within them that attracted me, and vice versa, but at the time they just seemed to me like bright, sexy women who were probably going to have interesting lives with plenty of options, none of which involved suicide by hanging in Australia. Or anywhere else for that matter.

The one who took pills, I can still hear her voice as we were making love, whispering in her London accent, "it feels so good in there." She must have had a lot better sex than that over the years, but she paid me handsome tribute all the same. She was one of those stunning rock chicks, and I doubt she even remembered my name the next day, though for all I know she regretted for the rest of her life that she never got it together properly with me, and eventually it just got too much for her. I mean, if you can form the notion of killing yourself, and follow it through, who knows what sort of craziness can get into your head?

Maybe when the pills kicked in, some hazy vision of that night came back to her, and she heard herself saying "it feels so good in there," and she slipped away easier. But I doubt it, I doubt it very much.

I knew nothing of her inner life then and I know even less now; in fact, I know nothing of her life at all, in any shape or form, since that morning about fifteen years ago when she left my basement flat in Rathmines and we said we'd hook up again, knowing we wouldn't. At least I knew she wouldn't, so I figured there was little point in me running after her and pleading, though in truth at the time I would happily have spent the next forty rock'n'roll years with her, to hear her saying just one more time, "it feels so good in there." Why didn't I go after her? Because I'm lazy, for a start. And because I just knew she wouldn't have me. Or at least I thought I knew. But of course I knew nothing. Nothing at all.

How do we ever pretend that we know what's going on in somebody else's head?

Whatever was going on inside her head, as she was busy ingesting those pills, as she was killing herself, is known to herself alone; she left no note, but it seems that all she wanted in the end was the certainty of death.

And yes, I have indulged in a form of suicide myself, but my way is the best, the slow suicide of the barfly, slow enough to walk away from it, because there's always the slim chance that one night, for a few minutes, you might just find yourself up in the Wicklow hills thinking, this is the best time of all, this is the best life we will ever have...

A few days later we're on a plane to East Midlands airport and Jamaica is drinking again, so she takes wine with her food. Red, red wine.

"Alright?" she says, like she's asking if I mind the air-conditioning.

I gave her the can of Harp after all, and therefore I can't be that bothered about her drinking, can I? And like I say, it's not her drinking that really bugs me, it's mine.

Still it's a wondrous thing for us alcoholics to observe, the casual brutality of the normal person as they choose to drink or not to drink and opt for the former, with one of us sitting there beside them. Minding our own business.

When the waft of Jamaica's red wine hits me I recall a flight from Dublin to London on which I find myself sitting beside George Best, George looking terrific in a white suit, fresh from the Late Late Show the previous night, in which his then wife Angie had insisted that she would leave him if he had one more drink.

I'm hung over, and when I try to milk my coffee I squirt some of it on George's lovely suit.

And George is really cool about it, but I want a drink now to stop the trembling, so the hostess reads out a list of drinks available and I stop her at the brandy.

I unscrew the miniature brandy, releasing the fumes. I pour it and drink it, George, in the seat beside me, apparently oblivious to the ceremony. Deep down, I know now he wanted to kill me, very much.

But I survived, and I guess George has survived too, in his way, not going to Alcoholics Anonymous because, well, how could George Best be anonymous?

Ah, George...

We're collected at East Midlands airport by Phil, the band's old tour manager, who drives us the ten miles to his house in Nottingham, where I still go to restore my musical spirits. And I want to show Jamaica off to him; Phil appreciates fine women.

Meeting him again reminds me that it must be nearly seven years since I started this tuner, because I'm in the rooms seven years or thereabouts and the two things happened within a few weeks; I gave up the drink and

I got into tuners.

Clean and sober for the first time in my life, I hung out for a few days with Phil and got dug into his vast collection of tuners on CD and vinyl and video. I connected with it straight away, I got it, it brought me back to whatever turned me on to music in the first place, the optimism of it all reflecting my hopes for a clean and sober future.

Rock'n'roll had left me with nothing but alcoholic poisoning in the end, and a close encounter with the reaper. No question, you lose all your prejudices about show-tunes and the middle-class theatre when you've taken a beating from rock'n'roll. And we were the smart guys, we didn't get totally ripped off, we didn't actually end up owing the record company a few million. But we were all pretty sick towards the end.

I had long forgotten what music meant to me when I was a kid, hitting that first chord on the electric guitar. I had forgotten that rush. Now I was rediscovering a similar kind of feeling.

Besides, I have an even older memory of being totally blown away by a stage production of Oklahoma! when I was about ten. Maybe that's where this tuner thing comes from. But going back that far sounds like counselling and I don't need counselling. I know what's wrong with me, I'm a hooch-monster.

So Phil was welcoming me to the club back then, feeding me tuners, from 'Guys And Dolls' to 'Sweet Charity' to Sondheim's 'Company' and giving me solid advice on how to stay off the booze, just as he had been doing for nearly a year.

He also played me these old recordings of George M Cohan, the guy originally called Keohane that everyone assumes is Jewish, who was played by James Cagney in 'Yankee Doodle Dandy' and who wrote 'Give My Regards To Broadway' – and who brought so much to the tuner game that they eventually put up a statue of him on Broadway. They only turned out the lights for one minute for Al Jolson.

Phil tells me all this and he plays me this old Cohan stuff and I'm mad for it; he seems to know I'll connect with it, he says I'm ready to do the best work of my life.

I'm buzzing. I can't understand why Cohan hasn't been claimed more aggressively by the Irish, who claim every other Irishman who went to the States, or even thought about it. I get all these ideas very fast about the forgotten contribution of the Irish to Broadway and, in my head, I can hear this new music that sounds Irish-American to me and which I really don't think has ever been done before – this classic Broadway tuner music on the surface, with all this Irish stuff going on in the lyrics, and even more crazy Irish stuff deep down in the guts of it. Rapping with Phil half the night, I'm soon seeing my mate Matt Dillon crooning on top of this mix. I'm seeing Matt as Jack Rooney, the one true star of an Irish-American showbiz family, who tries to break with the old ways before they break him. It all makes complete sense, the music is starting to sound sensational in my head, and when I eventually get home to whack down a demo, I have what seems like the makings of a meisterwork.

Nearly seven years later I feel like stopping the car to tell Phil, and Jamaica too, that I'm not up to it; to say to them, just listen to Sondheim, I can't do that thing. "You can and you must," she will say. And really, there's a limited number of useful things you can decently do with your life after you nearly cracked it but didn't. Trying to keep busy. Trying not to be bitter. Still trying.

Back then I thought this tuner would connect all the wires again, I got excited about it, I felt I was going to crack it and this time I'd take America too, because I'd be sober. This time, I believed that AA line which promised a life beyond your wildest dreams, if you stayed on the programme and did the steps. I wrote the bones of most of the songs during that honeymoon period, when I felt the wires connecting, when I was sparking again in a way that brought me back to the first time I hit a chord and heard the roar coming out of the speakers. Maybe I have stayed on the programme all this time, and stuck with the tuner, because of that one feeling, that one connection, that one memory of the roar of a cheap Gibson Les Paul copy.

Seven years later, I end up here in a car going back to Nottingham, a sentimental journey, except today I have a different feeling. Today, I just feel like a guy who can't write tuners.

By the time we reach Phil's house, near the Nottingham Forest football ground, I'm also feeling like the third man. Like I said, Phil appreciates fine women. So he appreciates Jamaica, and she appreciates him with his big, Springsteen energy, his upper class manners and his general English togetherness, which has got numerous rock'n'roll assholes around the world, and back too, in one piece.

I figure she's falling just a little bit in love with him when she sees his place, a 1930s end-of-terrace house that Phil has converted into a shrine to the musical theatre and to his first love, to rock'n'roll and the big beat.

She spends about an hour being shown around the main room with the bay window facing the street, just an ordinary-sized room but one which reeks of showbiz class and atmosphere. This is not a living room, it's a sanctuary. She stops at every framed poster of a Broadway tuner or a classic photograph from the West End, to have it explained to her by the ever-meticulous Phil. And he, in turn, is greatly taken by her Jack Rooney sketches and logos, which could go straight onto a billboard in Times Square, if only there was a show to promote.

I sink back into one of the comfortable couches, flicking through the latest edition of Variety. I don't know why I didn't anticipate this ugly twist.

Her jaw is sinking to the floor now, as Phil takes her through his awe-inspiring record collection, not just at the size of it, but the fact that he has special black shelves in-built for the CD's and for the hundreds of rare vinyl records he has squirreled away here, many treasures lurking among them.

Here is a man who looks after his stuff. Here is a man who has stuff to look after.

Here is a man who gave up the drink a year before I did, but who seems to be about a thousand years ahead of me in terms of furnishing and décor and general quality-of-life issues.

He's got a handle on food as well.

When they eventually notice that I'm still there, Phil disappears into the kitchen, which, of course, he designed himself and decorated in a sort of black-and-white checkerboard pattern. And with Jamaica still groaning with pleasure as she checks out the sleeve notes on some original and incredibly rare Kurt Weill waxing, Phil comes back with a delicious brunch, for each of us on separate trays.

We are three again, though I've got a whole couch to myself while they share the two-seater, tucking in to the brilliant food, facing the television near the window, and Sky News.

I suppose I don't know Jamaica that well, I'm just nuts about her and supposedly she's just nuts about me. But I think we're going to have some bother about this, bother that is set in the present day, not in the mists of time, not back during the Renaissance, when I feel I was doing some of my best work while Jamaica was just a common whore.

"What are you havin' mate?" Phil says to me. "Bit of Sondheim?"

"What about you?" I say to Jamaica. "I've seen all this stuff."

I try to make it seem as commonplace as possible.

"Sondheim would be sensational," she says to Phil. Sen-say-shon-al.

"'Company'? I've got 'Company' recorded at the Donmar Warehouse, directed by Sam Mendes," he says. He takes his tray back to the kitchen and goes looking for the video.

At this Jamaica gets up from the couch and starts ogling his CD collection again; I am convinced it's because she suspects, and rightly so, that I'm about to make a move and join her on the two-seater, to assuage my anxiety.

I suspect she's heading me off at the pass. I suspect that since she's met Phil, she has in some small way started to despise me. I suspect that my inadequacies have started to crystallise.

She even loves his food, as if food had no meaning for her until he started cooking it. I don't know Jamaica that well, but I know other women, and they tend to give big respect to a man like Phil who can basically look after himself and even live in some style, all on his own. I should have anticipated this, but it would have been grossly immature to put off this weekend for fear they might hit it off too well. And gross immaturity is something I must put behind me. Somehow.

But I think of that car-load of my rubbish that Jamaica took up to Wicklow for me, and I am ashamed. I am seeing it now through her eyes, how impressed she must be by Phil's set-up in comparison to mine, his taste, the way he lives. Like a woman really, except he's a large man with an air of Springsteen about him; in fact at this stage he probably knows The Boss personally and he's probably great in bed too, having roamed all over the world deciding who gets a backstage pass and who doesn't.

He's setting up the video.

"Like a beer or something? The off-licence is just across the street," he says to her.

"No, no, 'Company' will be perfect," she says.

"Not my company," I think. But I don't say it. I'm not that petty.

Well I am, I just need to control myself here.

"If you want anything later, wine or anything..." Phil says.

"Not right now, braddah," she says.

"So you've given it up again have you?" I think.

But I don't say that. Nor do I add that she seems a lot more sensitive about drinking in front of Phil than in front of me. I don't add that, because she gives me a little sign then that I might be judging her harshly. She comes over and she gives me a great big hug.

As the effects wear off, I analyse the hug as being a bit on the sisterly side for my liking. But I'm grateful for it.

She redeems herself again by moving to Phil's rocking-chair, the Kennedy chair, as he calls it. I can look at 'Company' now with less of that lacerating jealousy in my heart. I mean, I'm not madly jealous of Phil any more – I've moved on to Sondheim again.

And Sam Mendes.

There's Jamaica in the Kennedy chair looking at big numbers like 'Being Alive' and 'The Ladies Who Lunch', listening to that perfectly pitched New York pessimism of Sondheim, that sublime late-night melancholia, all that accomplishment and integrity and sheer class. And she just has to be wondering why she is wasting her time doing costumes for my tuner, which will probably never happen, when she could be making them for Sondheim, or for Sam Mendes, whose tuners happen – not to mention his plays and his Oscar-winning movies.

I've got the latest Jack Rooney demo and it never sounds better than when it's coming out of Phil's speakers, in this room bursting with the spirit of old Broadway. But I'm losing heart again.

'Company' ends. It adds somewhat to my sense of discomfort that we've been watching a tuner about a guy in his thirties, who can't bring himself to live like other men and women, who get married and live together and all that.

Phil is going out, just being a gent, leaving us to ourselves. He asks her again if she wants anything to drink.

"A drop of wine perhaps?" she says, looking to me automatically, to check if it's kosher. I shrug.

"Red wine?" he says.

"One o' dem half-bottles?" she says.

I sit listening to the windchimes on the back window, a vaguely sinister echo of Jamaica's windchimes in the gate lodge, while Jamaica has another rummage through Phil's outstanding collection of quality sounds. She turns to me and I see her in the soft light the way Phil must see her, top of the range, mate, top of the range.

"Phil... he's cool about the drinkin'? I mean, about other people drinkin' around him..." she says.

"He feels safe with us," I say.

"Is he a batty guy?" she says. "Is he a gay man?"

"Ehhh... I don't think so," I say, quite delighted really that the thought has crossed her mind.

"Terrible cliché... he likes musicals he must be a batty guy... stop it, woman," she admonishes herself.

I see the dark side now, maybe she's sussing out his sexuality so it'll cool when she claims him.

"I like musicals," I say. "Am I gay?"

"You're uptight... are you uptight?" she says.

"Tired," I say.

She hunkers down in front of me, insisting we make eye contact, that what we say is true.

"You know the time we met in your old flat, and I said I had issues with alcohol, the time when I thought I was goin' bananas?"

"Sort of," I say.

"Tell me how bananas dis is... I t'ink... right? I t'ink you need a drink, mon."

I slump back into the chair. She takes my hands and pulls me back to face her.

From the look of womanly kindness in those eyes you'd think she was doing me a big favour. But she's not. She's destroying me.

She doesn't get it, people don't get it at all, they really don't get it when they live on the other side of alcoholism. They think they get it, and some of them nearly get it, and Jamaica is one of them. But they don't.

She hasn't a clue really. She hasn't even a shred of a clue. Otherwise she couldn't possibly be doing this to me.

You don't offer a hunger-striker roast beef and Yorkshire pudding and you don't suggest that your alcoholic lover might loosen up with a drink, unless you're trying to break his spirit. And Jamaica is trying to lift me up here, she's trying to set me free. She thinks.

The problem is, by any normal standard, she's right. I do need a drink. I'll always need a drink, either in some small way or the way that I need one now, which is savagely. But I need to stay sober. Even more so, even more than I need a drink, I need to stay sober. For my own reasons, for all that I've put into this, for all the time I spent in the rooms and all the suffering that led me there and the serenity which I am starting to find. I need to stay sober, for the good of the cause. And just to stay alive.

I need a drink.

"I would love a drink," I say, as she grips me by the hand.

"You would, mon?" she says, squeezing my hand until it hurts.

"But I'll pass."

"Glass o' wine? Does wine count as alcohol?" she says, easing her grip. She knows it does.

"Wine counts," I say.

"It must seem irresponsible of me..."

"Right..." I say.

"Right, but I want to put my side of it because I want us to be..."

"Sorted," I say.

"Look, you're a good man to be doin' what you're doin', I have humungous respect for what you're givin' up here, but you've done all dis on your own. I'm in your life now and I t'ink I can make a difference."

She has hew-mung-guss respect for me.

"No doubt about that," I say.

"What's so bad about havin' two or three drinks and just stoppin' it there? The two of us, lookin' after each other?"

"That sounds super," I say. "Except I've never had two or three without wanting to have nine or ten. In fact, I'd say two or three is the worst torture. I mean, you wouldn't give a junkie just a little bit of heroin and say that's your lot, have a nice night now. Well, I want it as much as any junkie, so maybe I'll pass, this time."

"Then why not have nine or ten?" she says. "Once a week, once a month, whatever you like, mon. Have a wild night and den chill for a while. We can look after each other."

Why is she doing this to me?

"You think I haven't tried that?" I say, weakly.

"You haven't tried it with Jamaica," she says, really forcing it.

"You don't need it like me," I say.

"It is not that I need it. I just... I want it."

True, she didn't say she didn't want it when she came back from New York, just that she didn't need it in her life. So a lawyer would say she's acting according to the letter of the agreement, if not exactly the spirit. A bit early to be thinking about lawyers.

"I love what you're saying," I say, trying to find some way out of this without losing big. "But I'm either on it all the time or off it all the time. I can't control it. Otherwise, I promise you, I would."

"It's been what now? Six years?"

"... eight months, three weeks, five days, fourteen hours..."

"So maybe you can control it now... after all this time..."

"That would be lovely... me and you... bottle of wine..." I say.

"That's what I mean... that's exactly what I want," she interrupts.

"You don't want me drinking," I say quietly. "Wine. White wine, red wine, any sort of wine, or beer or whiskey or whatever, with a meal or without a meal, any time, any place, anywhere. No-one, and I mean no-one, has ever wanted me drinking."

"You want to stay uptight, mon?" she says, slumping back in frustration.

She's got me cornered now, she's making me play a card I don't want to play, but I don't think there's any other way out of this. It's time for a story, straight from the end of the last century.

"I want to tell you what I did once," I say. I grab her by the wrists. I put my face close to hers. I try to give off a sense of controlled intensity, though I can't rightly say I am in control of anything any more, starting with myself.

"This is what I did once," I repeat. And for one blinding moment I know I am about to tell her everything about that night in Camden Town, I know our relationship can stand it, I know she'll be cool about it. And then this is what I say: "The night of that barbecue... when Grace Bannon saw us and we were rubbish? That night my friend Bill and I left that house with an armful of beer and a girl about our own age who wore horrible thick glasses but who for some reason thought we were a bit special. OK?"

I say the last bit too loud.

"She was a fool," I continue, the moment of truth gone again. "And she was drunk, but so were we. Now I want to tell you what we did to her, because I've never told anyone this before, OK?"

"OK," Jamaica says, and I tighten my grip on her wrists.

"What we did, is we took her up to this place called the ferns, just a few acres full of ferns, where you could do nearly anything without being seen. And we kept drinking and she kept drinking, but not enough that she would let us do whatever we wanted to do. So we had to make her.

"We made her take off her clothes, and then we had a few more drinks there, with her naked and us wearing our clothes, and I really have no idea what was going on in her head, but it can't have been pretty. And then we fucked her. One after the other, we fucked her. Bill fucked her and then I fucked her. She didn't try to stop us, she was too far gone, but I remember this, I remember she kept her glasses on. So we decided to take them with us. And then we picked up her clothes and ran away with her clothes, laughing."

I stop. The wind has gone out of me.

"Listen, you don't want me drinking," I say quietly.

I loosen my grip in her wrists. She looks down at the floor, like she is running through what I have said a second time.

"You don't want me drinking," I repeat.

At first I think she's crying, but then I realise her shoulders are shaking with laughter.

She grabs me by the wrists exactly as I did to her.

"So... fuckin'... what?" she says, losing all trace of the Caribbean in her voice.

"So... you wouldn't mind that happening to you?" I say with a new sense of dread.

"You were kids, for Gad's sake," she says, rolling away from me and writhing on the floor in frustration. "Spotty adolescents. I don't want to come over like some Wicklow fucking lunatic here, but me and the country girls were getting drunk and getting fucked in the woods most nights of the week for fun. For fun, I tell you. And we don't get cross about it, we just know better now, and it's like, it's all right... seen?" she says, returning to the patois.

"The thing is, I did know better," I say.

I could put in another way. I could put it more graphically. I could say we raped that girl. But I don't even know if this would make any difference. And to tell the truth, I just don't have the stomach for it, to say that word and to find out what it means to her at this moment, one way or the other.

I can't argue with her any more. I see something ferocious and defiant in her eyes that I recognise in myself, a total inability to know the difference between right and wrong when there's a drink at the end of it. I'm looking at myself, twisted into a knot and I think: I tried to tell her the truth but it wasn't in me. Now I can't do anything else except give up on that, and give up on her attitude to drink, just give up before this gets any uglier. But I still can't give up on the rest of her, not when she's stretched out there on the floor like that, all mine to redeem. There's only one thing I can safely do with her at this moment, to keep us together. I smile at her resignedly. She smiles back.

"You winding me up, mon?" she says, rolling back to me.

The "mon" irritates me, it strikes that odd false note, but even now in her voice I can still hear the music of a Caribbean childhood, warm and true.

"I want to take you upstairs now," I say. "That's what I want."

"You're not too uptight?" she says, holding back for a moment.

" I'll think about it, OK?" I say. "I'll think about everything you've said."

"Will you, braddah?" she says, now sounding full of kindness.

"Just leave it with me," I say.

"For another six years, whatever?"

"Tomorrow," I say.

She kisses me on the lips.

"Tomorrow," she says, together again. Upful.

"Now... upstairs," I say.

"What about Phil comin' back with the bottle o' wine?"

"Half-bottle," I say, a stickler for precision. "You'll need it all when I'm finished with you."

I lead her by the hand upstairs to the futon, which Phil has prepared for us in the small front bedroom. Nothing but sex, and sex fast, will put me out of this misery she has laid on me. I feel we must do it now or we're history.

I put everything I've got into it. I'm really giving this woman a good time, if I say so myself. I'm doing it all for her. I hear Phil opening the front door and I take it up to another level. I hear Phil playing Sondheim below, something from 'Sunday In The Park With George'.

I make Jamaica come with the incandescent harmonies of 'Sunday' playing in the background. Then it's my turn to go over the top, and after, we take another few minutes to savour the mystery of it, face to adoring face on the futon, our bodies glowing in the orange light of the street-lamps.

I am in hell.

Nine

"Don't know why mate, I thought she was black," Phil says, handing me a mug of morning coffee in his custom-built black-and-white kitchen.

"Quarter Spanish, something like that," I say.

"I guess Jamaica... black," he says.

"That's alright," I say. "She thought you were gay."

"Joking, mate," he says, as we push through the swing doors into the living-room, the sanctuary. I detect the faintest note of disappointment in his voice.

But I love Phil, really. Lest we forget, he's the only man alive who knows the full Jesse Nestor story, as well as the bullshit story about the ferns I've been telling for so long in the rooms, I almost believe it myself. I told Phil because we have been rock'n'rollers together. We've been down to the crossroads. And of course it has occurred to me, yes it has, that Phil's knowing covers my ass for Step 5, where we admitted to God, to ourselves, "and to another human being" the exact nature of our wrongs. Though the man himself explained to me that the quest on which we have embarked in the rooms is about slightly more than covering our asses.

I start to relate the previous night's events to Phil and he stops me at the point where I'm about to tell Jamaica the truth, the whole truth.

"Don't," he says.

"Right," I say.

"Don't tell anyone that stuff," he says. And he gestures upstairs to where Jamaica is sleeping. "Not yet anyway."

"Right," I say. I'm not arguing, because I trust Phil's judgement – and anyway, what he's telling me is what I want to hear. Or at least it is until he gets to the next part.

"Never tell anyone about shit you've done that's basically illegal, mate, a serious criminal offence; you never know where they're coming from. Always talk to your sponsor first..." he says.

In my silence, Phil senses guilt.

"You've not got a sponsor yet," he says.

"I'm getting one," I say, thinking about Theo.

Phil seems satisfied by this, but then he tells me something else I don't want to hear.

"Just do it," he says. "Doing something is always better than not doing it."

"But you said not to tell Jamaica..." I say, starting to sound childish.

"I said talk to your sponsor first... and then use your discretion, obviously," he says, with the superior shrug of a grown man.

Then I tell him the Jackson Browne story, the one about Jamaica's old man naming her after the song, and he likes it but he doesn't really believe it. "Crazy people," he says.

BBC Radio 4 murmurs away in the background, 'Loose Ends' probably. When Phil speaks of these crazy people I guess he's not excluding the one who is directly above us, having the swinish sleep after staying up late on her own, listening to the original Broadway cast albums of 'West Side Story' and 'Cabaret', with a full bottle of wine and numerous cans of beer – which Phil had assumed was a weekend's supply. As an habituee of the rooms, Phil would already be thinking I've got a wee problem here.

"So what would you do, Phil?" I say."Would you join that woman for a drink and a late-night tuner session, or would you say your prayers and then shuffle off to the rooms?"

"It's Casablanca," he says. "She's Bergman and you're Bogart..."

"And there's a war going on," I add.

"She wants you to leave it all behind and go with her. And you want to go with her, don't you?"

"With all my heart," I growl.

"But..."

"But in the end I can't go with her. I've got principles; it's more important to save the world," I say.

"To save your world."

"All we need now is for the band to strike up the Marseillaise," I say.

"That's all, mate," he says.

"And Phil, mate, you're an attractive man, you don't by any chance see yourself as Victor Lazlo in this? Do you? You know, Bergman's other bloke? You won't by any chance be on that plane tomorrow and me on the tarmac?" I say, rapping with Phil, the call and the response like it was the old times, heading him off at the pass as well.

"I'm Sam," he says. "I play 'As Time Goes By'."

"Play it," I say.

It goes without saying that Phil has 'As Time Goes By' somewhere in his collection. He finds it quickly and we listen to it, like the suckers we are.

"Of all the coffee-shops in all the world she had to walk into mine," I say.

"That's enough," he says, as the music ends.

I go to make another coffee.

"That's the difference isn't it? Of all the gin-joints... Bogart could drink."

"So can you," Phil says. "Technically."

I make two more mugs of coffee.

"I'm losing it here, Phil," I say.

"You need a meeting," he says. "I'll take you."

"She should be up by the time we get back," I say. "What do I do then?"

"Maybe she needs a meeting," he says.

"She's not one of us, Phil. Not yet anyway," I say. But I don't rightly believe that any more.

"I mean Al-Anon. She meets a few wives and girlfriends of alcoholics," he says.

For some reason Al-Anon always makes me think of George Best, and all the beautiful, tragic women who might have gone there to ponder the eternal mystery of the man.

"A special section for the wives and girlfriends... you think that might clinch it for George Best?" I say.

We laugh, thinking about all that George might have brought to Al Anon, to the movement as a whole.

"Jamaica should be in there already," Phil says. "She's a natural for Al-Anon. There's a seat in there with her name on it, mate. A couch. Ninety-nine per cent of her relations are drunks and druggies, I promise you. All those Wicklow types are the same. Like, her father was hanging out with West Coast geezers in the 1970s; I suspect he took a drink, and the rest of it too. The mother knocked around with Jagger, she was a boozer. And she's knocking around with you... there's something in the blood up there..."

Cheers, mate.

I can't face a meeting. Instead we get into a long discussion of the greatness of Kander and Ebb, who wrote 'Cabaret' and 'Chicago' and 'New York, New York', and Phil tells me one of them is up in the hospital. No details, just that he's up in the hospital, probably driven to exhaustion by some tuner which won't come right for him. A sad but heroic image to take with me, as Phil works to keep my spirits up, thinking about either John Kander or Fred Ebb, who have done it again and again, but who are still committed enough to the cause to be up in the hospital for it.

"Talk about crazy, mate. Writing tuners is crazy on top of crazy, multiplied by crazy a hundred times," Phil says, hamming it up for my benefit. He plays a side of a Kander and Ebb compilation in tribute to the boys. Phil puts these compilations together himself, because no record company could make such astute selections, with notes where appropriate.

He makes copies for me to take back, to keep me focussed on my own endeavour. Just to show me how it's done, if you know how to do it. I'm not sure if it'll inspire or depress me, but I take it anyway.

In the afternoon I go for a walk with Jamaica on the banks of the Trent. She doesn't start into the drink again, which I take as a good sign; I would always need a beer for breakfast after the sort of night she's just had. I explain to her that Phil moved here because he's a fanatical Nottingham Forest fan. He moved here around the time that the young Roy Keane was playing for them, so now he can go to all the home matches, while living well away from the taverns of old Camden Town. But not too far away either, by train, if the mood were to strike.

Ultimately, it was a football decision. And I sense that Jamaica is a tad unimpressed by this, so in some totally disgraceful way I start to feel better.

She doesn't bring up our talk of last night, how we were going to get stuck into this drink stuff tomorrow. It is tomorrow now, but Jamaica is hung-over and maybe her drinker's guilt is steering her away from that topic.

So I feel it's a good time to make my stand, looking down at her, way down at her on the low moral ground. I suggest we stop walking. We sit on the grass beside the Trent.

"You're Bergman and I'm Bogart," I start. "Casablanca."

"You t'ink?" she says, her brain stirring.

"You want me to leave it all behind and go with you... and that's what I want too."

"You know, I don't see you as Bogart," she interjects.

I'm stalled.

"You see me as Bergman?" I say.

Trying to be funny.

"I always see Bogart with the bottle o' gin," she laughs.

"OK, it's not Casablanca," I say.

"No, don't give up, go with it, mon. Maybe I'm Bergman and you're the straight guy, her husband."

"Victor."

"You're Victor. That's better, mon."

"I don't think it is, no," I say.

"What I like about it is dat she ends up with Victor, she flies away wit' him on de aeroplane," she explains.

"He's no fun though, is he?"

I can't believe I just said that, without flinching.

"He is a good man. A good person like you."

"He's up in the futon studying the ceiling while you're downstairs drinking and having a wonderful time."

She breaks up laughing. She rolls on top of me, mauling me, purging all her pent-up guilt. I can't do that. I'm still not comfortable enough with my body.

As she settles on top of me, I take my chance. I speak slowly and quietly.

"Every relationship I have ever had, has been wrecked by drink," I say. "By my drinking, not by the other person's. Though once or twice by a bit of both. But mainly we're talking about me here."

I swallow hard.

"And that's fine. You can do that maybe ten, twenty, thirty, forty times and you move on and start all over again. Most of the time..."

"Hang on," she interrupts. "Hang on. You're talkin' big numbers here. Thirty, forty?"

"It just feels like that," I say. "It was probably three or four or five, but it feels like thirty or forty. And the feeling is what counts."

"Go on so," she says, with a faint note of triumph, the Jamaican accent carrying that odd echo of Cork. "Go on so, boy."

"There's a moral truth here," I say. "Don't get hung up on the numbers."

"Like, it's not how much you drink, it's what it does to you?" she says, this time more the willing pupil, even more Cork.

"Very good," I say. "So... most of the time when those women sat there dumping me, looking me straight in the eye and telling me in a sisterly way that I had a wee problem, and they couldn't go on, it just bugged me – because I couldn't just get up and go and have a proper drink. They would detain me for a while, with these formalities.

"Some of them wanted to confirm that I never loved them in the first place, and I'd oblige them. I'd agree whether it was true or not, and then they would feel fine.

"And, most of the time, I guess it doesn't matter. It's just life. Forty, fifty times even, you can walk away from it and return to your first love, the old hooch, and your true friends, the hooch-monsters. And pretty soon there'll be another little cutie along to tell your troubles to; at least that's what I find, because people tend to like me straight off, and they sometimes still like me enough at the finish, just about, to offer me words of sound advice on any future dealings with women.

"So, as sure as night follows day, another cutie steps up to the plate and you're off again, you're going to get it right this time, if anything she's drinking more than you, no way will this one be blowing you out with a sisterly look or worse still, a motherly look. But she does... she does.

"Yes, even she, who drank fifteen pints on the night you met, who has a real taste for it, even she can't hack it with you. And you know what you dream of? You dream that one day you'll meet and fall in love with a full-blown alcoholic, a whiskey-first-thing-in-the-morning type of gal, and then you'll be sorted. That's what you want, a relationship with an alcoholic. That's the dream.

"And still, not for a moment does it occur to you that if you're thinking in this way, you might need to address certain aspects of your lifestyle, and your general state of mind. You just hope your luck will change. And mine did. At last, one day, I got lucky. I met an absolute raving alcoholic and we had about three amazing, beautiful weeks of drunk love, and then you know what she did to me?"

Jamaica shakes her head on cue.

"She gave it up. She disappeared into the rooms. The bitch." I can feel a cold sweat creeping down underneath my shirt. "I'm a free man again," I say, "looking for love in a looking-glass world. And you know what happens, maybe the fifty-third time, or the fifty-fourth time? You know what happens?"

Jamaica shakes her head again.

"You start... to see... a pattern."

Jamaica bows her head so that I'm talking into her jet-black hair.

Then a voice rises from below.

"My apologies," she says.

She rolls off me. We sit looking at the smooth waters of the Trent.

"You don't understand it, but that's OK. I don't understand how you can stay up drinking half the night and not want to start again the next day. We all have our blind spots."

"But if I don't understand it..." she starts.

"You have to go through it to understand it," I say. "And you don't want to go through it, do you?"

"Obviously not," she says.

"Well, take my word, if I join you for a glass or two of wine, you'll go through it."

She stretches out on the grass. The Trent rolls by calmly, looking distinctly artificial, reminding me of a painting on an English chocolate-box. Which I like.

"De earth... de sky... I want us to bond in a pagan ceremony... in de woods... we two makin' love on the grass... a circle of women dancin' around us... naked," she says.

"Maybe just the two of us... ." I say with a twinge of apprehension, like the son of a primary teacher that I am.

"Any time," she says.

Then she cracks up laughing.

"You kno' what I was just goin' to say? I was just goin' to say... come on, I need a drink."

"There's a pub at Trent Bridge..." I say.

"It's alright... really... forget about it," she says.

"You need a drink, you need a drink," I insist.

"What about you, braddah?"

"I'll watch."

"Is it all right?" she says, cheekily squeezing my crotch.

"No problem."

"Listen... if I'm startin' to overdo it... like I said, I reckon I drink more than some of de people I know in de AA..."

"Would I tell you?" I say.

"I mean, I'm not Shane MacGowan or anyt'ing. Gad Almighty..."

We stroll back towards Trent Bridge. I'm feeling strong again, like I'm ahead on this one, after the reversal of last night. It seems to me now I chose the wrong weapon. I needed a story that couldn't be dissed as a teenage atrocity. I wanted to give her a sense of the collateral damage, when in fact I've done more damage to myself than anyone else in drink – it's just that people outside the rooms don't feel so bad about that. You have to make them fear for other people.

But I can't quite forget that defiant look in her eye, when she just charged on regardless, my soul-mate in ways I maybe don't want to address yet, or at least not today.

"I'll tell you a funny thing... I don't think Shane MacGowan is an alcoholic," I say.

"Right," she says, and she laughs.

"I'm serious. He just drinks a lot of alcohol. Which is not exactly the same thing as being an alcoholic. He drinks a lot and it's terrible for his health but the drink doesn't really change him. Not like it changes me."

"You are right," she says. "I don't understand it. Truly, braddah, I do not. Forgive me."

We enter the pub, dark and cool in the afternoon.

"It's not the amount you drink, it's what it does to you," I say, broadening my theme.

"Although, of course, the amount Shane drinks is... significant," I add, woozing at the thought.

We get a seat beside a flashing fruit machine. She has a glass of red wine, I have a Coke.

"Roy Keane now, that's another matter," I say. I always have this strange sense of Roy's presence when I'm here in Nottingham. I guess he leaves his mark everywhere, though he was just a kid when he played for Forest. Maybe it was his presence, suggesting that Cork note to me, in the voice of Jamaica.

"You're tellin' me that Roy Keane has a drink problem but Shane doesn't? Sorry..." She actually does look confused.

"We know Roy has some sort of a drink problem, right? I mean, he says himself it's got him into a lot of bad situations, OK?"

"OK, so?"

"Shane, to my mind, doesn't have a drink problem in that way. Drink is not really a problem for him. It's a problem maybe for a lot of other people, who maybe should be more concerned with their own problems, but it seems to me that Shane can live with it."

Jamaica smiles knowingly, as if I'm winding her up again.

"Just one t'ing," she says. "Call it window-dressin', but Shane can hardly walk any more, and Roy plays every week for Manchester United."

"Fuck it," I say, "you can't really make comparisons like that, because everyone's unique. I'm just trying to get it across that this stuff is exactly what they say it is in the rooms. It's cunning, baffling, powerful."

We clink glasses. I'm still feeling strong, not a million miles from invincible.

"I want what you have," she says, the way she said it that night on the phone from New York.

"Here's looking at you, kid," I growl.

Ten

I fear the approach of Christmas. We get back from Nottingham and we're dug into each other even more, the way it can be when you've come through a scare. But as the serious drinking season looms, I worry about where the alcohol will take her the next time, and whether I'll be able to hold it together.

In the rooms I say I am responsible for myself, and if she wants to go off and get drunk as any normal person might from time to time, well, that's her responsibility, not mine. But walking home on winter nights, that all starts to sound a bit theoretical and the dread rises.

Drink works its own voodoo; it was working on her that night in Nottingham when she tried to get me back on the drink and then stayed up boozing by herself, and she couldn't control it and it damn near got the better of me too, me, with all my hard-won experience.

But I still have to keep telling myself that shit happens, that in the rooms we can become obsessed with drink as the cause of every bad thing that has ever happened in this world, when in fact there are perfectly healthy people out there drinking, and drinking a lot from time to time, who are not addicted to anything because they're just not made that way. I'm still seeing Jamaica as one of them. But I'm also seeing that look in her eye that I saw that night in Phil's place when she laughed at my story; it was the defiant look of the true drinker. It takes one to know it.

And I know it's a thin line, and I know she went over it that night, but she pulled back from it pretty quickly. She was normal the next day. At least she drank normally.

In fact drink is entirely absent from our lives for the whole of November; she decides to do that Irish thing of giving it up for the month before Christmas, except most of the Irish people that I've encountered do it so that they can feel better about getting totally legless when they go back on it.

Jamaica shows no sign of wanting to do this. One night she asks how I'd feel about us sharing a few joints to celebrate our love, and I want it so badly, I am immediately seized by the euphoric recall of nights doped up listening to the finest reggae. Ah yes, I want it so badly but I can't have it, and when I tell her how I am torn, she seems to understand. No spliff, for God's sake, and no reggae either; I can't have one without the other.

Deep into December, she's still spending several nights a week with me rapping about 'Jack Rooney' and watching videos and just being man and woman, she having the odd can of beer and the odd half-bottle of wine. Though in fact the only odd thing about it is that she doesn't just move in with me altogether.

We say it's almost like a superstition now, this half-and-half arrangement. It's working, so we don't want to mess with it, partly out of habit I guess, partly because her little fashion empire operates out of the big house, she's still got work to do, for which people will gladly pay money. Even now, Eddie and the boys are shifting all her stuff towards the back of the house, converting a room off the kitchen into a new work-space, so that at least one part of the place will function, the rest for the present abandoned to chaos. Or so I hear.

As for my story of the ferns, which she heard that night in Nottingham, and what the story might mean, we just bury it.

Still I go through hours when I am pulverised by a new fear, this fear that Jamaica knows everything about Camden Town despite what Lotte says, that Lotte has been left out of the loop, basically because she's Lotte. In these hours I imagine that Jamaica knows everything about me, and what I did, and what I didn't do, and how full of shit I am when I talk the talk, about the ferns, about anything.

When I imagine these things, I have a fierce desire to be drunk, to be protected somehow, to be anaesthetised. So I put them away, these terrible thoughts, which are too big and too ugly to contemplate, and instead I get on with fearing the everyday stuff. Yes, I fear the approach of Christmas.

I get so jittery, I say to hell with superstition and start out one morning for the big house. Jittery and horny, for that matter, a bad combination. Jamaica only drove back from my place about an hour ago, but I have a serious urge to catch up with her again, to surprise her in her lair, to fuck once more like we did first thing this morning, except better this time, with the element of surprise.

But when I eventually make it up there, I can't go in. I see her through the mullioned windows, pacing up and down the room talking into the phone, drinking a glass of red wine. She seems so immersed in the talking and the wine, at eleven in the morning, I don't feel so horny any more. I just feel nostalgic, for all the wine-drinking talks I used to have on the phone, back in the day.

Then we're watching 'The Third Man' one night and from the first magical notes of the 'Harry Lime Theme' I know I've made a mistake. I deeply adore this film, but I've only ever seen it drunk. Many, many times, I watched it after coming home for the pub; as many times, its quality of Viennese nightmare seemed to suit my mood.

But, as a result, the drink and the movie are indivisible; I have no consciousness of it sober, so I have to endure the entire drama with a need for drink gnawing away at me, lashed by waves of alcoholic nostalgia, as they chase Orson through the sewers, one more time.

And then Jamaica mentions that we might go clubbing some night before Christmas. Clubbing! Maybe the darkness and the decadence of 'The Third Man' stirred her blood, but from where I'm sitting, the prospect of clubbing on one of the nights before Christmas is like being caught in the middle of some hellish stampede, nothing but shouting and crushing and destruction. But mainly shouting. All those garbled conversations, all that roaring on the disco floor.

I feel exhausted just thinking about it, but I can't just shoot the idea down either. I can't, in fairness, deny Jamaica one miserable night on the town at Christmas. We have to have some sort of a social life as a couple. It's not much to ask is it?

"I need to see some people," she says. "And they need to see you."

"Do they know I've got a disease?" I say.

"I just tell dem you don't drink and dey're enormously impressed," she says. "Enormously."

E-norm-ously.

Anyway, I was being flippant. I don't really think of it as a disease, a physical disease; I always recoil from that when I hear it in the rooms. It's definitely a disease of the spirit, but then there's a lot of that about.

"Fair enough," I ask.

"I'll look after you, braddah," she says, squeezing me with that intensity again.

I don't need to confirm that this means we'll be in the most private part of Lillie's Bordello, where it won't be so frantic, where there will be fewer madmen to disturb my spirit.

I wouldn't expect Jamaica and her country girls to be on the wrong side of the ropes.

And it works out fine. It works out so well I feel almost cheated after all the mental preparations I made, all the permutations I ran inside my head, how I would react if the night started stirring up some ghosts for me.

It feels almost ridiculous for a man like me to be coming out of Lillie's at two in the morning, a week before Christmas, in a calm state and in command of my faculties – but that's the way it happens.

Jamaica has three bottles of Heineken the whole night; she is wearing this red cocktail dress from a new collection, which will stop the traffic all across the civilised world. Her little troupe of country girls are taking it easy. I see no-one I don't want to see, or no-one who doesn't want to see me.

Jamaica walks with me to the taxi rank. Then she has a notion that she wants to go back to the country girls and go on to another club, and I have no objection to this. I guess she just wants to hear them talking about how great I am.

I let her go and I say thanks for the evening, for getting me out of the house. I am grateful, not just because I've successfully negotiated the night-club slalom, but because at some point in there, I got over my fear of Christmas.

For this year at least, I think it's going to be all right. I even share this with the taxi-driver on the way home, maybe the first time I've bared my soul to one of these guys since the days when every taxi-driver in Dublin knew the inner workings of my being.

"You're afraid you'll never get though these things when you go off the sauce," I explain. "That's what keeps a lot of us drinking, the fear of a wedding, or a funeral, or Christmas, like how the hell are we going to get though all that? But they're the easiest ones, when you think about it. You're prepared, you're on your guard, you're up for it. It's other stuff you have to worry about... stuff that creeps up on you any day of the week... like getting angry..."

"Women," the taxi-driver adds.

"That's right," I say.

"I think the point will come when men and women will have nothing to do with one another apart from procreation," he says. I sense straight away he is one of those drivers who has formed some pretty drastic views about life, and who has read a few books to support his case. Otherwise he seems too young to be using words like procreation.

"Right," I say.

"I was nearly an alcoholic," he explains. "I was this close to being an alcoholic."

He holds his finger and index finger about an eighth of an inch apart.

"Yeah?" I say.

"My wife used to shove the baby into my arms the minute I walked in the door after a day's work and say, 'I'm off, you look after it'. That itself is an act of violence."

"Right," I say. I am learning that even sober, I can never get up the moral courage to argue with a taxi-driver. I take this to be my last challenge for the night.

"So I spent a lot of time in the pub," he says.

"Sure," I say.

"You're on your own tonight," he remarks.

"My girlfriend went off with her mates," I say.

"If you don't mind me saying this, I had a look at her when you were getting into the taxi and you're a lucky man," he says.

"Yep," I say.

"Fair play to you," he says. "That's how it should be, if you ask me. The woman does her thing, and the man does his thing. And that way, no one gets hurt."

"Right," I say.

"She does her thing, you do your thing," he says approvingly.

"Right," I say.

"I mean, a hard day's work, you get home, you get the baby shoved at you, and she's out the door. They know what they're at, and still they keep pushing the buttons. They shouldn't do it."

"I guess they get angry too," I say.

"They keep pushing the buttons," he says.

"My one hardly ever gets angry, you know why?" I say.

"Why's that?"

"Because I'm great," I say. And I guess he's waiting for me to laugh, but I don't.

"Don't knock it, pal," he mutters.

I don't. I drank a lot on anger, especially on women making me angry. I would defy them by stalking off to the pub, where I would instantly be at peace. And I got through a lot of women that way.

The dynamic of this relationship is different. Jamaica doesn't make me angry like all the others; she's always trying to please me; she hates confrontation and so do I. So I don't get angry as often as I used to, I just get terrified that one day she will ask me again if I want to join her in a drink, and I'll be so pleased with myself I'll say, what the hell?

And then I'll be able to enjoy Christmas like everyone else.

As it turns out, I don't get angry again until… oh, until later that day. It's as if the taxi-driver has cursed me for being smart, and the baleful gods are shafting me for being smug, reminding me that the glass is always half-empty, always.

I was looking down on that taxi-driver, who will never have a girlfriend as beautiful as mine, wearing a dress like that; I was rubbing it in. I was coming across like someone who has it all and who knows it all. And it's when we think we know it all that we are perhaps in most danger, because we really don't know how we're going to feel from one hour to the next, which is why we try to live in the moment, one day at a time.

Jamaica doesn't make it back that night. I hear a car going up to the big house at about five in the morning and I hear it leaving again. I guess it's a taxi bringing her home. I go back to sleep.

She doesn't appear the next day, not that there's much day in the mid-winter.

And up here, in the Wicklow hills, when it gets dark, it gets really dark. It's late afternoon when I finally call her, and she says she's got a hangover and it sounds like a bad one, one of those 24-hour jobs that you tend to get after a night of dancing and shouting and beer and wine. She says she had a few glasses of wine in the River Club and it really knocked her sideways. Obviously her system isn't used to it after that dry November.

She sounds so wretched I offer to go up and medicate her. I've always felt that the best cure for a hangover is hangover sex. In fact I believed it so strongly I hardly had any other kind for years.

"No," she says. "No way."

"I'm coming up," I say.

"Just… no, mon," she says.

"You sound like you're dying. I want to have sex with you before you die," I say.

"Please..." she says, but I can't quite read it.

"Please?" I say.

"Please stop," she says.

"Hangover sex..." I start.

"Please... I look shit, I feel shit, dis house is shit..."

"I'll close my eyes. I won't look at you, or your house," I say.

"Look we have a deal..." she says, in plain English, and she cuts me off.

Actually we don't have a deal, I say, starting one of those imaginary conversations in which we always defeat our opponents with our almost effortless command of logic and wordplay and the irresistible moral superiority of our case.

We don't have a deal that I live down here and she lives up there and I never go up to the big house in any circumstances whatsoever, on pain of death, as she seems to be implying. No, we don't. What we have, is a friendly arrangement which suits the two of us, but which is not by any stretch of the imagination a solemn treaty carved in stone.

I'm winning this phantom argument of course, but I'm also getting angry.

It may not happen to me as often as it used to, but anger is still lethal for a man in my condition; it's like a thousand neon signs light up in my head, saying Drink, Drink, Drink.

I'm angry because I reckon she's pulling rank on me here in the shabbiest way; I resume my imaginary argument, assured of victory now, telling her how shabby it is, yes, shabby is the right word, the winning word. But, I continue, she probably can't help it, she just can't stop herself, she is a member of the landed gentry and I am not, and everyone has their place and mine happens to be down here, one step removed from the servants' quarters. And hers is up there, in her ancestral home. And she's probably not even conscious of it, certainly not after a skinful of drink, but when she set those boundaries she was also telling me that people like me may come and go, but people like her will only make it permanent with... people like her.

Of course she has no answer to that, she has no option but total surrender. And I'm about to call her back and say it all for real, when she calls me back, and says she'll be down to me straight away.

She arrives down in the Volvo estate, looking... well, she sounded a lot worse than she looks; her skin still looks sensational; she clearly has the strong constitution of her breed. And I'm about to engage her in class warfare – but she is so abjectly apologetic, I swallow it. A woman's apology always makes my anger disappear as fast as a pint of beer.

And Jamaica is a woman who doesn't hold onto anger, she's like me in that respect too.

So I guess it's only right to let it go, and I do, with a few lingering suspicions, which will stay with me, surfacing every now and then for just long enough to gnaw away at my innards.

"Look," she says. "Dis doesn't make sense I know, but not everyt'ing has to make sense. I just have a bad feelin' about that house, and us. I feel it's unlucky, whatever. Dis here is our place... dis here is our place and it will be our place for all time... can you go along with me on dis?"

I can. She's still wearing that cocktail dress and talking in her most downhome Jamaican. I make that dress fall to the floor. She's wearing nothing else, and I could question this. Instead, I slip my middle finger inside her punani, imagining that she did it just for me.

"Put your hands behind your back please," I say, politely, like a customs officer.

She does what I ask, with a nervous, sexy little grunt, like it's a game. She closes her eyes, she spreads her legs, she's getting into the zone.

With my other hand I check her body all over for any other damage, front and back, any of the mysterious bruises that come with a hangover. But no, she seems unharmed. If there's anything wrong with her, it's all on the inside. She is reeking of alcohol, the way I used to reek without realising it.

"Will we ever live together... the right way?" I say, my finger probing her punani, the punani-juice running sweetly.

I've asked the question before I even know where the thought has come from, but I say it in a light tone, and she seems to treat it lightly too. She just moans, grinding her hips in a horny rhythm, getting deeper and deeper into the rhythm, her eyes still closed, concentrating on what my finger is doing inside her.

"I'll spend Christmas here so," she says, "If dat's all right."

"I don't want to do anything... seasonal," I say.

She opens her eyes. She opens the top button of my jeans.

"You don't look too hung-over..." I say, guiding her down to the old rock'n'roll beanbag.

"I told you, braddah, it was just a few glasses o' wine," she says, in what is still the sexiest accent known to man.

"I mean, we can't have hangover sex, if you don't have a hangover," I say.

She drags me down with her.

"I'm dyin'," she says.

There's a picture of us on the social page of one of the Sunday papers coming out of Lillie's. We look terrific, even in the glare of the flashbulbs.

The caption says that we are seeing a lot of each other. Nothing about me writing a tuner, no chance that some unstable billionaire will see it and think, that sounds like something I could run with, 'Jack Rooney' is the one for me.

I feel I need to explain to the boys in the rooms that, though I have been pictured coming out of Lillie's, I am still relatively clean and sober. And by the way, even though my picture is in the paper and I seem to be enjoying myself, I am still poor. And miserable at least some of the time, as well. Very miserable.

"That's a common mistake people make," I say, sharing at a meeting two days before Christmas. "I still can't get arrested." There is a smattering of laughter.

"But then this is a hard time for a lot of us," I add, "It was hard when we were drinking as well. As I recall it, Christmas used to bring all the amateurs into the pubs; there'd be a big crush every evening, you just couldn't enjoy your drink any more."

Another mumble of amusement comes back at me.

"So I get lonely around this time for my old friend the hooch. But I also get a lot of pleasure when I see the madness and I know I'm not part of it.

"I haven't shared about this before but, as you saw in the paper, I'm in a relationship now. I find it hard to talk about it here, because it's like you're telling someone else's secrets as well as your own. All I can say is I'm trying to do the right things, I'm in the right place, and I haven't picked up a drink, at least not today. I haven't. I get plenty of wake-up calls and I try to heed them; like the other night I was talking to this taximan about how I don't get angry these days, and the next thing I know I'm as angry as hell. Just when I was getting a bit smug with the way I was handling Christmas, I was back again on the razor's edge. And maybe that's the best place for me, to stay alert, because the margins are pretty tight in our game."

I leave a space because I don't know where this is going, or what's coming next.

"I came down here thinking I'm missing out on a lot, that it takes courage to stand up here and say, 'I'm an alcoholic'. But coming in the door you know what I thought? I thought it also takes courage for one of us to stand up and say, 'I'm not an alcoholic'..."

The room is deeply silent.

"I'm not an alcoholic, I've changed my mind, I can go out there again, now that I'm with the right woman at long last. It would take courage of a sort to say that, and to take it to its logical conclusion over there in Regan's. So it would.

"So I keep seeing both sides of everything, I keep feeling one thing and then the opposite. And you know what's coming up in 2002? The World Cup."

They're all with me now. A shudder of World Cup dread goes round the room.

Their heads are full of dangerous visions.

"From early on I wanted what you guys have. But it's so hard to stop wanting what the other guys have as well. It's so hard to put up the white flag, to say I'm a coward, I can't beat this thing.

"But after a few years in the rooms, maybe I'm at least getting a small bit of sense. Because you know what? Personally, I'm not going to make any effort this Christmas."

The room laughs with me.

"No turkey, no ham, no tree, no effort. This is a selfish programme and that suits me fine. This girl of mine is staying with me over Christmas, but I've told her if she wants to get festive she can do it on her own. Because after a couple of days living together, I prefer it the way it was, her in her place and me in mine. I get lonely up there on my own, but I can get lonelier with another person around, who might want to crack open a beer and have a chat when I just want to... to... to crack open a beer. But I'm so glad we've made it this far; like I say, I'm trying to do the right things, and I reckon now the right thing is to enjoy these days together, and then get back to normal in the new year... with the help of God and the fellowship of Alcoholics Anonymous."

I catch Theo nodding vigorously. I'm getting gung-ho, I'm damn near announcing that I'm going to get down on my knees tonight and give thanks to my Higher Power, but I can't tell a lie that big. I leave it at that.

Theo insists on giving me a lift home afterwards. He has detected a demented note in my sharing and feels the need to offer me something.

He stops the car outside the gate lodge. He lights a cigarette. He won't come in.

"You don't believe in God," he says.

"Just got excited," I say.

"You don't have a sponsor, you never read the big book and you don't share much about what's going on for you up here with this woman... what I want to know is, how do you do it?"

"I don't know how I do it," I say.

But I'm thinking, this is my chance. The man has just opened up and virtually asked me explicitly if I want him to be my sponsor. He's a veteran, he can tell there's stuff bugging me deep down that I need to share. And I think of Phil telling me it's better to do something than not to do it. So I'm about to pop the question to Theo, but then I remember Phil also telling me to use my discretion, especially if I may have to talk about anything criminal. And another excuse springs to mind, because Theo after all used to be in the army, which makes the prospect of him taking me through the 12 steps even more intimidating for me, with my excellent 3-step programme. No, at this moment I'd prefer a guy with a few more character defects to take me through to the next stage.

"I don't know how I do it," I say again, and we both laugh.

"I'm only fooling. I love to listen to you," he says, maintaining his affable tone, giving no hint that maybe I have let him down, and let myself down too.

"All lies," I say.

"You're getting there," he says.

"A life beyond your wildest dreams?" I say, a note of the old sarcasm creeping in.

"In your confusion you're more honest than a lot of us. You sounded tonight... how did you sound?"

"A bit raw," I say.

"Torn between two lovers," he says.

He doesn't sound like he's fooling this time. Jamaica opens the door of the gate lodge. Theo salutes her and she waves back, just a couple of country people. She looks admiringly at the powder-blue Morris Minor. He looks at her intently for a few moments, like he's trying to take it all in.

"I've gotten used to Christmas," he says, giving me a firm handshake. "No TV, no nothing just... the quietness."

"I don't know what quietness is, Theo," I say.

"Call me any time," he says.

"I will," I say.

"I get lonely too," he says.

"I'll call," I say.

"For any reason," he says.

And he drives back to his quiet world.

Eleven

I'm swinging up and swinging down like this and that and this and that, and the tuner is still a long, long way off Broadway. But I've still got the rooms and I've still got Jamaica.

I get through the rest of Christmas by simply ignoring it, except for a visit to Susan and Stephen with presents, on St. Stephen's Day of course. Stephen being called Stephen came in handy almost straight away when Susan and I split; it just seemed right that I come around on Stephen's Day, a tradition which saves us a lot of potentially sad scenes of my coming and going on Christmas Day. I might also start getting nostalgic for that family life we never had in the first place.

Picking a present for Stephen is easy, always involving a much-needed boost for the Liverpool FC transfer fund. And I guess that over the years, Michael Owen made a decent enough role model for Stephen. And for me, for that matter, because Michael could have had anything but he goes for the simple things in life. Always did need guys like that out there, to show me the way.

I buy a bottle of wine for Susan, just a token of how far I've come under her guidance.

I get pangs of guilt all day as a result because I got Jamaica a bottle of wine too, only a much better one, a much older one, a much more expensive one, which delightfully she decides not to drink until the opening night of Jack Rooney.

Susan is knocking back her bottle of Jacob's Creek straight away, trying to decipher the meaning of Jamaica's present to me, a book of erotica.

"Maybe she's looking for a few fresh ideas from you in that department," she says.

"You think?" I say.

"Yes," she says.

But she approves of my handling of most aspects of the affair. She figures that taking the initiative and buying Jamaica a drink in Bray was the right move then; and it was still the right move, even when it all nearly went belly-up in Nottingham. She may have put me up to it herself, but she figures I compromised, and women like that. But I also held my ground, and women like that too. And of course I didn't succumb when I was given that heartbreaking invitation to drink, and that's why we're sitting here now having a pretty nice day.

I know it and she knows it.

"You said I had a fifty-fifty chance. How do you call it now?" I ask.

She thinks about it, like she's sizing up the Dow Jones.

"I'd say it's sixty–forty. I'd say you're sixty and she's forty."

"Right," I laugh.

"You're in there," she says, summing up her verdict in a way that's irritatingly inconclusive.

"Now," she says, "you tell me."

Ah, who the hell knows? Except that, talking to Susan, I get a new sense of what it means to be powerless over alcohol.

It's hard enough to grasp that powerlessness in yourself, let alone in other people. So maybe it's unwise for me to be grappling with Jamaica's alcohol issues as well as my own. Like I said at the last meeting, you can't beat this thing. Willpower won't do it, the best of intentions won't do it; like anyone else, Jamaica can go either way, and if she goes the wrong way, it will probably happen whether I like it or not.

I even get a moment of serenity; for a while I think I can let it all go. For today at least.

On the way out I nearly tell Susan that this all started back in the thirteenth century, but I'm not quite that serene.

"I saw the two of you in the paper," she says. "Looking good."

"Right," I say.

"Good legs," she says.

"Did you... eh... did you show Stephen?"

"Nope," she says.

I give her a little salute. We don't kiss any more.

In the new year, I decide I just can't go to the Westbury Hotel any more with my lawyer and the famous business plan to meet guys who hear the name Eugene O'Neill and think Ryanair. I figure I'll go at it a different way, back to the way I started. I remind myself I'm only trying to raise a huge amount because I couldn't raise a small amount in the first place. I reckon everyone remotely connected to show business, and most people in the western world with more than five thousand pounds to their name, have seen me coming up the garden path looking for a few quid to make a demo or just to keep the show on the road, and without exception they have been enthusiastic, but not quite enthusiastic enough to write a cheque. So, about four years ago, I start to figure it must be as easy not to get five million as not to get five grand. And you can't get a proper 17-piece orchestra with five grand.

But that doesn't really work either, or it hasn't so far, because there's one other aspect of the corporate mind that I am only now beginning to grasp and it's this: they all want to be associated with success, but obviously Jack Rooney is not a success, because it doesn't exist, as such. And I can't seem to get them to the other side of that barrier, no matter how hard I try.

So I'll go back to the start, I'll forget about trying to raise vast fortunes to put on a show, and try something small-time again, maybe an album of the songs, maybe a single that might get played on the radio and heard somehow by legendary 21-time-Tony-winning producer Harold Prince while he is in town, between projects, looking for a boxing musical. With Matt Dillon.

I'll try anything at this stage. I'm desperate and it shows. Jamaica tells me I shouldn't be talking to these people at all, they take pride in messing with the heads of artistic types, they can smell your desperation. I remind her I've had a few people doing all this stuff for me, but they couldn't take it either and eventually I had to fire them when they were away on one of their increasingly frequent trips to New York. I remind myself that it took Paul Simon seven years to get The Capeman on, and unlike me, Simon is a giant of popular music. And The Capeman has some lovely stuff in it, but it turkeyed.

In the Spring, Wes Barrett says he understands. Now I place my trust in Wes. His reputation rests on the Richie Earls album that made Earls huge, the soft soul Michael Bolton-style ballads, which to the original Richie Earls fans were a total sell-out. But who cares about them, when you're getting MTV awards, and your old chums are still stuck in The Baggot or Whelan's, checking out some happening little combo, and starting to lose the hearing in their good ear?

Wes comes up with ideas like that, sizing up a piece of talent and making them rich by putting that talent to one side, just for a while you understand, and doing something instead that sells records. I reckon that Richie's manager Dee Bellingham is the one who really makes it happen, but she's happy to take the money and let Wes take the blame from people who like music.

Which means that Wes is hot when I go to meet him in the Westbury, with Jamaica by my side.

This is big stuff, I'm thinking, you're not going to get two people as hot as Wes and Jamaica sitting down in the same room just for sport. And no one looking at this scene could guess how cold I am in comparison; after all, Jamaica wouldn't be with me just for moral and emotional support, she'd have to believe in the project. Wouldn't she?

So we shoot the breeze for a while about nearly everything apart from the tuner.

Wes, still looking like an indie type in denims, and sporting longish hair and goatee, being indiscreet about the stars. We gossip and we prevaricate.

What I want is for Wes to take one of the songs from the demo I sent him, and put it out on an indie label which he's been given as a plaything by the big bad label for which he makes all that money. A single, maybe an album to folllow, when the single gets the plays. A pet project for Wes. A tuner, now that tuners are getting cool again, now that pop is dying of greed and stupidity.

But Wes knows all that. It's the pitch I've been making for at least the last three years, since I started getting a bit anxious, a statement of intent I send to all my potential investors. Except I figure Wes has actually read it, and possibly even listened to the CD.

Wes, you see, is a fan. When the band was having its moment, Wes thought I was a god.

Wes knows me and my work. Wes is on my side. So this is what Wes says, when we eventually get to the tuner.

"What you don't want is to bring out some record that sells five copies. Then you've had a failure and that taints the whole project," he says.

Already he's implying that the record hasn't a prayer and he won't taint himself with it.

"What you need is what Queen and these guys are doing, a big West End show based on songs that everybody knows."

I stop him there.

"But Wes," I say. "The whole point of Jack Rooney is that it's a book-musical of the original type, like Chicago, which as you know is selling a lot of records. It's not a greatest hits package and a few dance routines put together for the fans, who prefer to sit down in a nice theatre these days because of the old arthritis. This is the real stuff."

But Wes is not for turning. He knows what puts bums on seats and Jack Rooney is not it. It's not for him.

And while Jamaica is away from the table, he gives me some helpful advice.

"If you don't mind me saying so, man, you sound somewhat bitter," he says.

Not bitter Wes, not bitter. I'm angry, which is different. I hate you, which is different.

I don't say this.

"I think you're wrong, Wes," I say, as coolly as I can.

Coming out of the hotel, Jamaica seems slightly taken aback that her work too has been rejected in some obscure way, probably a first for her. But she's not bitter.

And she's not angry. And she doesn't hate Wes.

"There's somet'ing in what he says," she tells me. "People don't buy records any more, not that type of record..."

"By guys like me," I add, undeniably veering towards self-pity at least, if not rank bitterness.

We're in a dangerous place here. We pass Bruxelles bar easy enough, but many of these streets off Grafton Street bring me back to days and nights in the Duke Lounge, the old Bailey, the tiny Dawson Lounge, and Neary's and Sheahan's and Grogan's and McDaid's and O'Neill's down in Suffolk Street, and the International Bar. I did a lot of drinking in these places. I am still prone to euphoric recall.

I never pass McDaid's without getting some race memory, of a time before I was born, when Behan and Kavanagh and Myles used to drink in these places, when alcoholism was regarded as little more than a form of self-expression, one of the few you could get away with.

And these guys were good, in their doomed way. They were great. And they could see no way of getting through this life sober. No way.

But I never see myself carousing with them in these flashbacks, because I fear their wrath and their ridicule. I can just about cope with Wes Barrett dissing me: being monstered by Brendan Behan, even in my drunken dreams, might just kill me off.

Ah, this is dangerous for me, and, I am drawn to the danger. I am running Wes Barrett's schtick over and over in my head. What Queen and those guys are doing. A big West End show. Songs that everybody knows. The anger is rising and the bitterness too. Wes isn't wrong about everything.

For, once I forget that the room in Molesworth Street is situated in the midst of all these drinking dens, known to the few. For once I am unaware of it, my head is full of pubs. I decide I'm not seeing enough of | Jamaica these days, what with all her successful projects, and I owe her one for sitting down with me, with Wes.

"Buy you a drink," I say.

She squeezes my hand and we take off for the International bar at a faster clip, at boozing speed as I used to call it, that extra yard of pace you get when there's a drink at the end of it.

I'm still hearing Behan and Kavanagh and Myles muttering darkly about Jamaica, condemning me for that too, saying "it's all you're good at, is riding." They didn't let women interfere with their alcoholism to any extent, it seems; the thought probably never even crossed their minds that a 12–step programme could resolve certain issues for them, or even a 3-step one.

Dangerous, dangerous stuff for me as we sit up at the marble bar of the International, where I must have drunk five thousand pints in my prime. Already my head is filling with images of ancient delirium. In this exact spot I went mad with joy as Ireland qualified for the quarter-final of Italia 90, and in this exact spot I started drinking two hours after the birth of Stephen at the convenient time of 10am, not stopping until I was comatose.

It's only the middle of the afternoon and I'm letting my mind wander into dark places. Jamaica orders a vodka and Coke, I'm having a fizzy water.

No, in my mind's eye I can't see any of those guys in the rooms, I can only hear the rasping mockery of Behan who, it must be said, was dead at 44. But then these guys would argue back that life has a higher purpose than just staying alive for as long as Bob Hope.

Staying alive is not an achievement. Writing great plays and poems is what it's all about, and once you've done that, it should be nobody's concern if you choose to drink yourself to death. Your cavalier attitude to the normal niceties of the bourgeois lifestyle is just another sign that you are a man apart, that you will be remembered when all the mineral-drinkers are just dead, as dead as doornails.

I'm already tensing up as Jamaica downs her vodka and Coke and orders a small bottle of white wine. First, I sense she's doing something that drinkers often tend to do when they're in the presence of a known alcoholic on the dry, going for wine when they really want vodka, trying to be good. And what really bugs me about it is that on the big nights, like a party or a wedding, their true nature emerges and they drink mercilessly while you try to be brave with your bottles of fizzy water, gallons of it.

Otherwise I'm tensing up because, well, because I always start getting tense in pubs when it looks like it's going to be a long one, several hours at least. One of the main reasons they invented drink is that it's unbelievably boring and uncomfortable to be sober while sitting on a high barstool, or even standing, for six or seven hours at a time talking rubbish. Drunk, it can be a joy.

But that's for Jamaica, not for me.

"Funny thing," I say, as she pours her white wine while I watch a second water fizz in the glass. "I used to think I was a very sociable bloke when I drank. Then I discovered I'm not sociable at all, I just liked drinking."

She touches my face affectionately, sympathetically.

"It doesn't get any better, mon?" she says.

"I can do it, don't get me wrong. Don't feel bad about it, I've got a lot of sobriety in the bank, you know? I passed the dry drunk stage about five years ago and by now I'm nearly a mystic. It's just such a strange thought, how drink can change everything."

"I'm taking it easy," she says, referring to the virtuous white wine.

"Go for it," I say, trying to be brave. "We need a social life."

"I guess you're right," she says.

Yes, I passed the dry drunk stage about five years ago, but I didn't do it by sitting in the International half the day, inhaling the bittersweet fumes of porter and smoke, while admiring the fine dark woodwork which gives this old bar the atmosphere of a holy place.

If you keep going to the barber you're bound to get a haircut, they say in the rooms. And maybe you don't need to keep going; maybe one time will do it, if you find yourself in a shop of this quality.

Jamaica is wearing my hat. I took it off going in to the Westbury because I didn't want Wes to think that I was still wearing the cowboy hat I wore on the sleeve of our first album. Jamaica minded it for me, as if it were hers, and now she's putting it on again, the gaucho in the saloon.

I think, when a woman put on a man's hat, she's ready for anything.

I am, after all, telling her to go for it and she takes me at my word. No more wine, just vodka and a lot of it. She's buying the drinks now, because I've run out of money. She's putting the disappointment of Wes behind her; the subject doesn't come up again. She gets more affectionate as the vodka goes down, stroking and kissing and looking into my eyes with vast sincerity, which only increases the strain for me.

And then she's talking about Mikey. I don't pick it up for a while because we're hard at it for a few hours now, and her voice is a just a Jamaican murmur to me, but there's something about the country-girl way she says the peasant name Mikey that snags my attention.

"Mikey out of Boyzone?" I say, perplexed.

"Nooooooooo," she says, throwing her arms around my neck. "Nooooooooo, Mikey who writes plays. The greatest playwright since fucking Sean O'Casey and fucking Sam Beckett and fucking William Shakespeare... Mikey you know? I'm workin' with him, isn't that the best t'ing?"

"Michael Wade?" I say. "You're working with Michael Wade?"

"Mikey," she corrects. "Lickle Mikey. We met at a reception."

"A lig?"

"OK, a lig."

"A lig for what?"

"For what?"

"Yes, what was the reception for?"

"Don't know actually. We just hit it for the free booze, mon."

So you met before you went to the lig, which is not exactly what you said the first time, I am thinking. But I don't say it. I don't want to come across like the Inquisition; she probably got burned by those guys in a previous incarnation.

But this is getting lethal for me. I don't know Michael Wade but I envy him greatly, because he's happening – but also because, from what I hear, he's the nearest thing to a gutter alcoholic we've had writing important work for the theatre since Behan and the boys were out there. A raw but magical voice straight out of the bogs of the midlands, they say, another natural-born Irish boozing genius, another guy getting away with it.

Bricks Melvin, the jazzman, drinks with Wade and he is also carrying on that line. Bricks tells me, any time I run into him, that AA and the therapy gang in general are a source of evil in this world, that the creative artist is king and that these bozos are trying to mess with the most private areas of the psyche, where the roots of genius are to be found. The roots of destruction, too, but these are the breaks. I always disagree with Bricks. I tell him I would never have written a note of my tuner if I was still out there, I'd just be talking about it in bars with all the other geniuses. But he tells me I'll come around again in time.

"Over-rated," I say to Jamaica. "Wade is just playing the game."

"I think he's humungously talented," she says, like she is personally offended. Hew-mung-guss-lee.

"He's humungously talented at this thing Irish playwrights do, sticking poor people and mad people from the country, or from the inner city, up on the Abbey stage, so that people from Dalkey can see them and feel grateful they'll never have to meet these savages in real life. That's what he's humungously talented at."

Jamaica is crestfallen. She can hardly look at me. It even seems to sober her up somewhat.

"Disappointed," she says.

Fired up by her snobby understatement, I get a rush of anger I can't control. Everything that irritates me about her on any level fills my head. I seize on her vision of us making love in the woods, because it's been bugging me in some peculiar way that suddenly pours out of me.

"Look, could I ask you to do me a favour?" I say, edging dangerously towards the high moral ground. "That stuff you said in Nottingham, about us having sex in the woods with the girls watching us... right? It's airy-fairy. It's not real. People like you just think people like me are impressed by that sort of free-spirit thing. But we're not. OK?"

Yes, the vision is fading very, very fast.

"Vodka and Coke," she orders spitefully. Then she takes her time. She composes herself, and delivers a few sharp words of plain English.

"I'm sorry Neil, you're not ready for this... I want to go clubbing tonight and for sure you don't want to go clubbing with me, so take this..."

She hands me a fifty-pound note.

"Taxi-fare," she explains.

I should, of course, throw it back at her, but I need to get out of here immediately, and so I need the money. If I was drunk, I would certainly throw the money back at her with royal contempt, but I'd still have to get the taxi-fare somehow. So it's not all bad, being sober.

But if I was drunk, I wouldn't be getting a taxi at all, we would stay in the International Bar until closing time, getting locked, and then we'd go clubbing and then we might indeed end up making love in the woods, like animals.

As if the effort of dismissing me was too great, she suddenly seems to descend into another level of drunkenness. Sensing a second attack from me, she sticks her fist in the air, and starts mouthing the deepest patois.

"Jah Rastafariiiiiii," she declares, staring straight ahead, defiantly. And as I am about to deliver some parting shot, she wards off my evil spirit with another "Rastafariiiiiiiii... Jah Rastafariiiii... Rrrrrrrrrastafariiiiii..." and I back away from her towards the door, nastily reassured by the looks of muted horror she is receiving from the other drinkers. In my last glimpse of her, she is waving her hands in the air, still chanting.

I fall to my knees outside the door of the International. A taxi passes. I jump into it, pushed by some instinct for survival born of a thousand hours in the rooms, and the distant dream of peace. The driver doesn't want to take me because he thinks I'm a nutter, on my knees like that.

I don't have the heart to argue with him.

"OK, I'm a nutter," I say wearily.

He thinks about it. Then he drives me home.

Twelve

She comes to my door the next morning with flowers. Not from the woods, from Interflora. I'm glad she feels so bad she's willing to spend money on making it right.

I figure she's still a bit drunk, in fact I can taste it off her as we kiss. But I'm grateful now for all the drink she had, making her guilty just for being alive. In drink, you always feel like the defendant. The sober people around you may be committing terrible crimes against humanity, but with a head full of last night's drink, you always feel you're in the wrong.

We connect again on the bean-bag. It's not exactly drunk love, but it's most acceptable just before noon.

I am so glad I got into that taxi, so glad.

I don't care this morning about all those guys who are out there drinking and getting away with it, Bricks and Mikey and the boys, still partying like it was 1955. I've still got a better-than-even chance with this woman who brings me flowers and then screws me senseless and they'll never have that, because they prefer pints in McDaids. So who's ahead on that deal?

"Let's go to New York City for two weeks," she says."Let's do it now, mon."

"Yeah?" I say.

"My treat," she says.

I'm too wary to say a word.

"Money in me pocket but I just can't get no love," she sings, the Dennis Brown classic.

The difficult subject.

"I'm expecting a cheque in about a week," I say. "Otherwise, I have literally no money."

"I'll give you money, mon," she says.

"No thanks," I say.

"Money in me pocket but I just can't get no love", she sings again.

"No thanks", I say.

"I mean, for the musical," she says.

That's different.

"You never use your own money," I say.

"Let us do some reasoning here," she says. "Say I form a production company... and dis company is developin' dis musical... which means you're on a wage..."

"You're still using your own money," I say.

"Is it not better than money from Babylon? It is what we call development money."

"It is what we call charity," I say.

But I'll take it. I can't refuse it. I suggest two hundred a week, the bare minimum to keep me from temptation and to assuage my guilt. And being the sophisticates we are, we crack a few jokes about me earning my corn as we have another bash at reconciliation sex, a big one that must last us until we reach the New World.

It's a perfect way for me to go, to have it landed on me like that, so I don't have time to stew on the thought of visiting New York sober for the first time. Drunk, the band and me went crazy over there, limos everywhere for a week, like we were Aerosmith, except we couldn't sell any records. Another melancholy note, which I will hear again under that old Manhattan moon.

Of course, you can't see the moon in Manhattan, something I discovered on that trip with the band.

Walking down Broadway drunk one night, I couldn't find it up there, anywhere, and this song starts in my head, the song that kicked off the tuner for me, 'Manhattan Moon'.

I've worked it up now into something of a showstopper for old Julia

Rooney, a coming-to-America song with a sort of history of popular music built in.

But Julia travelled in a heaving boat and we're going first class, because Jamaica is a guest of some fashion house which would like to pay her a few million a year to do that thing she does. Or that's what I'm hearing. But she doesn't fancy it, as she fears losing artistic control.

Still, she'll talk to them anyway, because it's fun.

And we'll go to a few Broadway tuners so I can size up the competition and diss them and find renewed hope for my own effort. And maybe even try to hook up with Matt, because it's not a boxing musical, it's a boxing musical with Matt Dillon.

So I guess it's time the same Matt was informed.

I must earn my wages, after all.

"I can do a few jobs around the house if you like," I quip as the airport taxi collects her at the front door of the grey mansion.

She keeps talking about the absolute shambles the place is in, how she's so ashamed of it, how Eddie and the workers are doing their best but it's hopeless, quite hopeless.

I just think she prefers it like this, with my territory and her territory clearly defined. Even if my territory is not exactly mine.

Anyway, we're a mile high and I don't have any bad thoughts about anything at all as I look at her sleeping in the window-seat beside me, bound for New York. I could be thinking this is the way the upper-classes do it, they'll have you around the place for as long as your face fits, they'll even pay you for your excellent company, and then they'll just move you on when you start to get tedious.

But I harbour a deep-seated hope, that in some obscure way amounts to an article of faith, that there's something deeply philanthropic about Jamaica and her kind, that they will take a lot of nonsense from creative types if they reckon they're worth it – that they understand the struggle like no-one else does except maybe the Jews. Especially if there are serious drink problems involved, as there invariably tend to be.

The fashionistas know who's hot, so they send a white limo to collect us at JFK, a white limo with a freshly-stocked bar which we do not touch.

Jamaica decides we won't be staying in the glitzy hotel they've booked, it's too Babylon; she wants a certain little place she knows near Broadway for us, for me. She gets the limo-driver to make the arrangements. He's not familiar with the hotel so she directs him to it. As the engine purrs and we make our way towards the heart of the metropolis something stirs in my gut.

This is what it's about; this is what the goddam tuner is about. It comes from that part of me which is forever mesmerised by the first sight of Manhattan, by the notion that someone from some mad place, say, Roscommon, could arrive here and have a look at this place, and have a go, and even possibly win.It's the most intoxicating thought, better than drink. It's the greatest notion, a holy thing, which is why the mullahs hate it so.

I'm wearing my hat as we check into our hotel, feeling a little bit like Jon Voight in 'Midnight Cowboy'. But I have no immediate need to hit the midnight bars; I've got a fine woman on my arm and I've even got something like a proper job, or a few bob coming in, at any rate. And anyway, I have dined with eight people one of whom was Bob Dylan, who complimented me on this very hat, and who's probably wearing one exactly like it, wherever he is.

So I'm happy here. I'm in a state of inner peace. On my scale of recovery, Step 3 is not easy, but it's looking distinctly attainable. Which reminds me, I must get a meeting tomorrow. I will be exactly seven years sober.

As we lie in our hotel bed high above this sparkling city, I'm looking forward to a Manhattan meeting like it was my first month in the rooms, when your heart soars at the thought of the new life to come, if you can make it. If, if, if...

After six years, eleven months, four weeks and a day I think I'm making it.

So I check out that meeting, and it's cool, full of Broadway actors and their ilk, all seriously well-versed in the language of recovery, talking the AA talk like old-timers, and no doubt walking the therapy walk at least twice a week. I feel like a greenhorn again among these guys, but I decide to share anyway.

"I'm Neil and I'm an alcoholic," I say. "I know other people want to get in, so I'll be brief. I'm seven years sober today, thanks to the fellowship of Alcoholics Anonymous."

I get a round of applause. It feels sensational. It's not exactly the Broadway ovation I've dreamed of, but it will do for today.

"Sometimes sobriety is a terrible thing," I continue."Sometimes you feel like you're losing your mind. But today is not one of those days for me. Today I'm in the right place. I come to this room and I hear you all sharing, and I might as well be in a little room in a village hall where I come from. I feel these rooms are our true home. That's it. Thank you."

And while Jamaica is spending most of the days talking to rich people about clothes, I'm stopping at the statue of George M Cohan every morning on my way to buy tickets for shows. "Give My Regards To Broadway," the legend says, put there by Oscar Hammerstein, who knew better than the Irish that Cohan was the main man. I have a few quiet words with Cohan's statue each day, a legacy from the drinking days perhaps, except I don't move my lips any more.

I tell Cohan I invented a new kind of Irish-American music like he did, that it will blow away all the official anthems and the mother-macree stuff, and generally address the situation whereby the most musical people on earth hold a St Patrick's Day parade on Fifth Avenue each year, at which the music is all total rubbish.

Cohan is the key, the lost leader. So he wrapped himself in Old Glory. So what? A dedicated liberal like Hammerstein thought he was worth a statue, end of story.

I muse on these matters while eating vast breakfasts in the diners of Broadway. I never had breakfast in New York until now, and I savour it wiping my plate like a savage. It helps me understand what those guys in the rooms mean when they speak in almost erotic terms about their rediscovery of food.

For me it only works in New York City, but it's a start. We sort out a regular evening meal in Joe Allen's restaurant, a place well known to me from Phil's descriptions of his numerous pilgrimages to the Great White Way.

I check out the memorabilia on the walls, posters of all these Broadway shows that flopped, images of heroic failure, which make me feel I'm in pretty good company. I think of all these fine actors who are revered on Broadway, but virtually unknown to the wider world. I tell Jamaica about the great Bob Fosse, who won the Oscar for directing 'Cabaret', the Tony for 'Pippin' and the Emmy for 'Liza With A Z', all in the same year, the triple crown never done before or since. I tell her about John Raitt, who starred in the original 'Carousel', probably my favourite tuner, John Raitt who created the role of Billy Bigelow and who is the father of Bonnie Raitt, Bonnie who is herself recovering from her rock'n'roll years. And I gush about the immortal Zero Mostel singing 'If I Were A Rich Man'.

Yes, I imagine that Bob Fosse downed a few in these parts, Bob the master choreographer, who drank and drugged and screwed incessantly, another guy who got away with it, if you discount the minor detail that it killed him. And one night after a show I see Stockard Channing in person, Stockard and a few friends brushing past our table in Joe Allen's. I think I see Marvin Hamlisch the next night, having a quick drink at the bar.

And he, the lucky so-and-so, gets to see Jamaica, exotic even in this city of amazement.

I can't raise Matt; he's off in Bulgaria or somewhere.

But tomorrow there will be another show to catch in one of these theatres I know so well from the framed posters in Phil's place: The Schubert, The Nederlander, The Gershwin. I'm getting a real boost from what I'm seeing, because most of them are refreshingly worse than 'Jack Rooney' could ever be. The way I see it, they're reaching the end of that Andrew Lloyd Webber dodgy English operetta phase and they're trying to get back to the classic American tuner – but they're not there yet. They haven't got the old confidence back yet. They lost too many friends along the way, until they were left mainly with an audience of elderly gay men and people who like Andrew Lloyd Webber.

But I have to watch the old cynicism that Theo warns me about, it'll eat me away before my time if I give it free rein. I must forget all my old prejudices about men who can turn the Crucifixion of Christ or the life of a Latin-American dictator into an all-singing, all-dancing spectacular. I'm here to change all that. I've got the smell of it now, a really distinctive smell that you get in these old theatres as you sit up front, getting the full whack of your matchless Broadway tuner orchestra.

This smell, it's a subtle perfume that lingers like the scent of a lover from way back.

And I want it again with my name on the marquee. I want it.

'Rent' alone depresses me because it works so well on the night – but then I saw a pretty vicious version of it in Dublin, the memory of which still gives me much hope.

And we meet up with the great Jason O'Brien, who comes to our hotel and who takes a couple of 'Jack Rooney' CDs away with him, vowing to run them by some of the most powerful people in the entertainment business, if not the world.

I read Jason well at this stage, as I read most alcoholics. Our differences aside, we're all the same in the end. He comes to the little hotel bar so I won't have to suffer the agonies of the late-night New York boozing scene, which we all adore. And so that he won't have to suffer me suffering. He doesn't want me on his conscience. And he's got a new Japanese girlfriend, who maybe doesn't know him well enough yet; she figures his ideal night out is a quiet evening with friends at their discreet hotel, slowly sipping a cold beer.

He met his new beautiful girlfriend working with Leonard Cohen, a choice morsel he is able to admit to me now. Running his eye over Jamaica, he reckons I'll be able to take it.

Good old Jason, he's indestructible. But he's right that I can take it now, because I actually don't resent the fact that he's getting away with it; I'm starting to feel it's too much like hard work to be going through girlfriends the way Jason is. An alcoholic like Jason, or like me for that matter, puts himself under terrible strain with his constant chasing and capturing of women, who can never ultimately compete with his ferocious love of drink. These days I get tired just thinking about it, but if I ever start missing it, and the thrill of it all, I look through my phone book and the names of all those mysterious lost sweethearts. Then a terrible weariness comes over me and I feel fine again.

So the next day I'm on the good foot, walking down Broadway like Nathan Detroit. I decide to take a look inside the prestigious Drama Bookshop opposite the Palace Theatre, to further my education.

I leaf through a copy of Moss Hart's great biography 'Act One', which I can't resist. I also pick up a copy of Sondheim's 'Assassins'. And then I see something else, something that disturbs my spirit.

It's a book entitled 'New Plays by Michael Wade'. I know I have no right, and probably no worthwhile reason, to be disturbed by this. No, I should be glad for him, a guy from nowhere making his mark. But I am disturbed. I can't help it. 'New Plays By Michael Wade'. It's got a plain black cover with distinguished-looking white lettering. And, yes, I know this is a shop for theatre anoraks, but it's still pretty big stuff for old Mikey from the midlands, to be sitting here, on these shelves, alongside Mr. Tennessee Williams and Mr Arthur Miller and Mr. David Mamet.

I know he's had a few raves from the New York critics for a couple of his plays, which – I take pleasure in the recollection – were staged in tiny venues. But it's pretty impressive all the same, to see his works between two covers in this high-class bookshop. And in the impromptu spirit of the city, I feel like standing up here right now and telling these people the truth about Michael Wade, that his famous monologues merely demonstrate his total inability to write a proper play with more than one character in it. And that the violence in his work is only startling if you're a middle-class theatre-goer in a fur coat who likes a bit of rough, but who also likes to get home to Dalkey in one piece, with a fine supper inside you.

That's Wade, and anyway the drink will get him eventually. That's what I want to say. The drink will get him eventually. But these people, in this shop, don't know that yet. They're off to their auditions thinking Wade is hot, and this I must accept. I guess I'll keep my wisdom to myself. I'll let it go.

So I'm letting it go and I'm turning it into something constructive. I decide to buy a copy of Wade's book, which is big of me. In fact I decide to buy a copy for Jamaica, which is even bigger of me.

I'm flicking through the pages landing on a line here and there, and, in fairness to old Mikey, I'm getting that feeling I always get when I look at the text of a half-decent play, a sense that it's written in some strange language known only to these characters. In this case, Mikey's bog-speak.

Then I see a line that strikes an unmistakable chord. "Six years, eight months, three weeks, five days, fourteen hours," it goes. It's spoken by a character called Tim in a new play, called 'Dry Drunk'. Christ Jesus.

My eyes race across another chunk, which seems familiar to me, about how eventually you begin to see a pattern in your broken relationships. My eye runs down the page to another speech in which Tim tells a character called Jill that he doesn't think Shane McGowan is an alcoholic.

My hands start to shake. I can't read any more. I put the book back on the shelf.

I can't buy Moss Hart or Sondheim either, I can't wait at the checkout, I just need to get out of here. Now.

I'm back on the sidewalk again, wandering like some New York basket case, drifting left and then right, looking at my feet first, then the sky and then staring straight ahead. I feel like I'm going to vomit.

Dazed, I stumble back to the hotel. Jamaica is out.

I lie back on the bed watching the planes ascending, one every few minutes, right on cue.

There's a message from Jason saying he's getting an awesome response to the Jack Rooney CD, just awesome.

Maybe I'll enjoy that tomorrow. Not now.

I've got a play to think about today. A play with me in it; I can see that even at a first glance.

I decide to let it go. Today.

If I can. Today.

I don't exactly know what I'm letting go; it could be nothing; a writer uses anything that comes his way.

But I am resolved. I'll be grown-up about it, because I am grown-up. And if I'm not, I've wasted the last seven years.

So it's like this. Jamaica's keeping nothing from me, she tells me she's working with the guy, people have lunch, they talk.

Maybe I'll wait until I see the play. Maybe I'll wait until I see it here on Broadway.

I'll assume nothing today, except that old Mikey is now writing plays with more than one character in them. He's growing.

But as the day wears on, my heart sickens. And my mind is getting sick too, as I sit in Joe Allen's that evening waiting for Jamaica to arrive. All this time I've been worried about things in my past life, about one thing in particular, that I have secreted away – and now it's possible that she is keeping something from me.

At Christmas when she came down to the gate lodge and we had hangover sex... no, it didn't feel right then, when she came down from the big house, and the whole episode is feeling increasingly wrong as I sit here in Joe Allen's waiting. Always, it's me who is waiting.

Yes, there's this nausea coming over me. Yes, my head is filling with a dumb, jealous fantasy.

I imagine her coming through the door in a few moments very, very drunk.

And drunk in a way that's new to me, giddy, giving off some anxiety which I never thought she had in her. Of course I don't imagine her falling on her face. Nothing so calamitous or inappropriate. She's still Jamaica, wearing a little black dress and wearing it well, on this warm New York evening. But when she sits down and starts talking, she looks flushed, like she's running on nervous energy instead of the usual tank-full of cool passion.

I imagine the waiter arriving, he knows us well by now, but Jamaica waves him away, like she's got something big to tell me. I've never seen her waving anyone away before, even in a fantasy, so there's something shocking about the image, the way its burned into the imagination. Then the fantasy turns to dialogue.

"First of all there's no damage done, nothing that can't be fixed," I hear her say, in plain English.

"Right," I reply.

"Straight up, I've been waxed," she appears to say.

In the vision that's consuming me, I am confused for a moment; it sounds like axed, like she's been sacked by the fashionistas. Then I get it. I take a quick look under the table at her newly-smooth legs. Because it's a vision, I stare at her legs for about three minutes.

"Wow," I say at last.

"What's done, is done," she says, like she's struggling with it.

"Can I touch?" I say.

Still imagining, I reach under the table, but she pulls back, a rare rejection.

"I should have asked you about it, I really should have," she says.

"That's OK," I say.

"Legs, under the arms... everything," she says, businesslike, none of that West Indian warmth wasted on this.

"Like... everything?" I say.

In the vision, she nods emphatically.

"You name it," she says.

"Right," I say, my fantasy self quite composed.

"I just couldn't stop them," she whispers.

"You were, like, forced to do it or something?"

At this, the object of my vision leans back in her seat, like she is pondering the meaning of it all. The waiter comes again, grinning, happy to take another rude dismissal for a good look at these smooth legs, these great legs. This time I imagine her muttering to him the name of a bottle of some French wine, and he leaves briskly. The dialogue continues.

"Well, it wasn't exactly my idea," she says. "We were doing some work downtown, trying out a few things, and we got into a little wine and then a little more wine and then one of the models produces a little coke and it all gets cranked up and the talk gets wild, and the next thing I know I've agreed to be waxed like a swimwear model..."

"Coke?" I say, just to confirm it amid the babble.

At this stage of the dream-sequence, she seems to be talking louder.

"They simply couldn't believe I was walking around with all that pubic hair... they called it the rain forest," she says, jabbering away.

"And the rain-forest has, like... disappeared?" I say, my fictional self still totally in control.

She grabs me by the wrist, melodramatically.

"Do you hate it?" she says.

"I don't know," I say.

"Oh, Gad Almighty," she says, sounding genuinely worried. "Gad Almighty." She says it the Jamaica way.

"No, obviously I don't hate it," I say. "In fact I love it."

"Anyway it's growin' again, it's flourishin'," she says, sounding a bit more like her real self through the chimerical haze.

The dreamy waiter brings the bottle of wine for her, and we order our usual steaks and salads without blinking. I'm still thinking about the rainforest, thinking hard.

"It's just... it all just sounds a bit... girly... like, something you'd hear about at a hen party... I mean... waxing... I thought it was against your religion..."

I'm blubbering now, losing control. In my troubled imagination I'm babbling.

"Uh-huh?" she says, leaning back in her seat, distancing herself from me, cold again."You mean... other women are more... well, basically, more fun?" she says.

"But I like that about you," I say. "I like your serious side."

"You like that?" she says, as if liking it is nowhere near enough.

"I love it," I say, and I know how she feels in this part of the fantasy, because everyone says they like Jack Rooney, they just don't love it. "I love that... intellectual side of you."

"An intellectual with a cunt?" she snaps.

And at this she lapses into the first moody silence of our relationship. And even though it's all happening in my mind, and nowhere else, it hurts. It almost makes me snap out of my dark imaginings, but I'm hanging on to this scene because this is most untypical of her; it really is one of the things I like most about her, how rational she is, her fairness, her beautiful mind, how she will always discuss things reasonably, rather than hit me with the silence, which I hate so much.

Then I say something that makes me proud of myself, even if it's all just happening in my head.

"I suppose what's bugging me about it... I suppose my one objection is that you've done this because Mikey asked you to do it. Sure, the models may have helped you along, but this is all about Mikey, and how he likes a shaved cunt, as he calls it. And the reason he likes a shaved cunt, is that he saw something like it in one of those cheap porno flicks that they get down in the midlands... am I right? Is this the bog-monster's way of claiming his territory?"

Yes, I am savouring this rancid scene as the real Jamaica walks into the restaurant. Reluctantly I let it go, noting straight away that she is looking in rude health, and apparently so glad to see me I am ashamed at the horrible thoughts I have been entertaining.

But I hang on to that mood of defiance long enough to say at least one of the things I need to say.

"Before we eat," I say, " I want to make a suggestion. When we get home, I want us to live together... just that."

"Soon come," she says.

"I want that," I say.

"Soon come," she says.

"When come?" I say.

"Look," she says, full of sweet reason."I have got some hard, hard work coming up and for the next couple a' months I will really not be the homely type..."

"That's all good stuff... that's natural," I say, with a hint of belligerence. "What is unnatural is that I'm basically barred from the big house."

"You are not barred!" she laughs."Don't be non-sens-i-cal!"

Oh, I like the way she says that. But I am not deflected.

"Look, I've been barred from a few places in my time and I know the feeling. What the hell have you got going on up there?" I say.

"Cock!" she declares." Jamaica loves cock, and loads of booze, and that's what I got goin' on up dere, mon."

Cock. I like the way she says that too. And booze. I like that as well.

"Alright," I say, letting it go.

"Look, I'll bring you up dere any time," she says soothingly."It's nothin' more than a superstition, the superstition is in mi blood I suppose... but I'll compromise, I see your point of view."

"I just don't want anything happening to you... when I'm not there," I say.

"Seen," she says, squeezing my hand tightly. And she signals to the waiter.

"Let's live together... the right way," I say.

She seems to get a rush, she seizes the moment.

"Let's celebrate so... can you look at me drinkin' a glass of champagne?" she says. Her eyes widen with anticipation, almost manically.

"Go for it," I say. Yes, in those wide eyes I can see a long night in front of me.

It seems she hasn't eaten all day, and with a bottle of champagne at hand she doesn't want any of Joe Allen's food, so tonight Jamaica gets drunk rapidly. She has another bottle of champagne, and then a brandy. Or two. I try to forget those visions of Mikey, as Jamaica slips away from me into her champagne world; I make my point and then rise above it in Joe Allen's, in a way that pleases me, another sign that I haven't totally wasted the last seven years in the rooms, that I am really learning how to handle a scene like this, to accept the things I cannot change.

But it's still a sad old situation as I steer her back to the hotel and she collapses onto the bed. It shouldn't be like this. We should still be talking about living together, but with the champagne-for-one it got away from us, we couldn't strike a common chord. Or that's what I'm thinking.

I'm playing it all back in my head as I watch her lying on the bed, naked after a shower which she wanted – but didn't have. At first I think she's just slumped there, refusing to communicate, so it's actually a relief when I hear a little grunt coming out of her, telling me she's having some of that swinish sleep that the Bard mentioned.

I gaze at her unwaxed body, stretched out there, this gorgeous drunk woman that I have found, and that I most certainly don't want to lose.

On two counts I am reassured. She is unwaxed, and she says she'll take me up the big house any time.

I am probably just being paranoid.

So we'll both have sick heads in the morning.

Thirteen

Jamaica turns down everything Manhattan has to offer. She decides she's launching her own designer brand instead of hiring out her talents. I guess that's an attitude you're born with, an attitude that keeps you and your people going, and thriving since way back in the 17th century, on large estates in Wicklow, regardless of the addictions and the personality disorders.

Some of which they probably invented themselves.

I just want a break, but it's not coming.

I'm back in Wicklow a few weeks when Jason calls me, raving about this bar he's found down the Bronx, where he'll be able to watch Ireland in the World Cup. Then he raves again about the awesome response he's getting to 'Jack Rooney'. He raves for about forty minutes from a bar, where it sounds busy for the early afternoon. Jason is getting there.

Maybe he'll remember this when he gets back to the rooms, and it will make him shudder just a little. But hopefully not too much. He'll have bigger issues to address than this, the day he bullshitted his old buddy about his tuner.

There's nothing in what he says, nothing solid, just the usual nonsense from people who can hear something in it, and who don't exactly want to let it go, but who won't buy it either. They like the sound of it, they really, really like the sound of the business plan. But it's just talk.

I can always give up.

I take this thought with me to my first meeting in the village since the homecoming.

It even sounds like quite a positive thought.

I can always give up.

I tell the boys I'm thinking of giving up the tuner, because where once it was an inspiration, now it probably poses a threat to my recovery. There's only so much rejection a man can take on the wagon.

The boys laugh it off. Then they introduce a darker note, telling me that Kay B has given up. In a big way.

She's out there again. Worse than ever.

Theo gives me a masterclass over coffee, suggesting that the tuner might well be my version of the Higher Power, and I should beware of letting it go. He suggests music in general may be my Higher Power, which is remarkably generous of him, given that the elder lemons are usually pretty orthodox about the Higher Power. You can tell them Van Morrison is your Higher Power and they won't diss you, but they'll smile knowingly.

Ah yes, they were young and foolish too.

It will pass, it will pass, Theo keeps saying, one of those AA statements of the bleeding obvious which are still tantalisingly hard to grasp. I guess that's what the Higher Power is about: it's about playing the long game, knowing that on any given day you will be prey to all manner of gibberish, which just arrives in your head like the morning mail. And like the mail, you feel you have to deal with it, but in fact you don't. Most of it doesn't matter, no matter what you think at the time. It doesn't matter a damn.

You just hand it over to whatever you deem to be your Higher Power, be it Jesus Christ or Jack Rooney or Jesse Nestor, and let Him deal with it. You swing up, you swing down, it's all-important stuff at the time but it doesn't count. None of it. Attacking the boys in the rooms for all their guff about a Higher Power doesn't count either. It's just an excuse. The only thing that counts is not taking up that drink. The rest will pass.

I tell Theo that with Jack Rooney I am playing the longest game in the history of showbusiness. He tells me humour can get you through it too. We both grimace at that.

In these high, sober, post-meeting spirits, I invite him up to the gate lodge that evening, to watch this supermodels show on TV, live from The Point Theatre, some charity bash at which Naomi and Jasmine and all the rest of those bootilicious babes will be giving something back. Jamaica is down there already, preparing her contribution to the show. Naomi will probably strut Jamaica's stuff, because Naomi is the best, and Jamaica is the best, and these people find each other.

Jamaica is still resisting the hard truth that these gala nights are not for me, not for us as a couple.

"I want you to come," she says.

I'm not arguing. I'm just not going, and she knows it.

"I need you to come," she persists.

She stares at me like she's genuinely worried about my attitude, the fact that I'm the only man alive who would turn down the chance to be in the same building, the same room, as Naomi, possibly when she's taking her clothes off. Jamaica still fights it, but she knows deep down I just can't do those big gigs any more. There's too much rock'n'roll in the air, and the way she works, we wouldn't see each other anyway until the nightclub afterwards, when there's even more rock'n'roll in the air, toxic quantities of it.

And, sure, it kills me that I can't go with her, it makes me feel like some sad old woman – "I would only be a burden on you, my dear" – but you have to make pretty horrible choices in this game, the payback being that when I see Jamaica tomorrow, I will want to make love with her, and when I kiss her, my mouth will not be caked with vomit. Little things like that.

Otherwise I can't enlighten Theo much when he asks me about Jamaica's work. Clothes mystify me. I recognise that Jamaica's clothes are beautiful, I just don't understand how it works, how she puts it all together. And, unlike me, she's a real artist, she just does it, rather than talking about it. There's a broadly bohemian feel to her stuff, in fact I have seen her make a pin-striped suit look bohemian, with a pin here and a pin there and a few minor alterations. But fashion and food I don't understand.

Music and drink are more my thing.

"Come up tonight Theo, and we'll try to figure it out," I say.

I can still change my mind and go to The Point, of course, and for a few mad moments I get all fired up thinking how nice it would be to meet

Bono again, and Simon Carmody, all my rock'n'roll chums who have a mutual admiration thing going with the bootilicious babes. And maybe I'd meet a few of those boyband guys hanging out backstage, who would acclaim me and maybe give me some of that money they stole from the kids. I could probably handle that now, at this stage of my life.

But instead I figure there's someone else I'm going to proposition tonight, the fit-looking sixty-year-old man sitting opposite me.

Doing something is always better than not doing it, Phil said. So tonight I think I'm going to do as he suggests. I'm going to ask Theo to be my sponsor.

There's something almost playful about it when he arrives at the gate lodge. He clearly knows what I'm going to ask him, so I decide to get it over with quick. I use the remote to turn down the sound as Jasmine bounces down the catwalk, and I say, "will you be my sponsor?" and he says "yes, sure," and then we look at the girls for a while.

We drink tea and he smokes cigarettes and we make a lot of supportive noises when Naomi does her thing, wearing Jamaica's stuff. We celebrate this great night of fashion with more tea, and to be perfectly honest, as I look at what's happening down The Point, I feel better where I am. Of course I don't pity Bono or Simon out there in the front row, but I don't really want to be with them either, not having whatever they're having, trying to explain why my tuner is taking longer to get done than U2's last three mega-selling albums and the world tours which accompanied them, combined.

No, I'm in the right place here, with Theo, my friend and confidante. And so, having reached this important milestone in my recovery, I prepare to tell Theo about my real rock bottom, that night in Camden Town. I am going through it in my mind, every detail from the flight over to London to the night in the Devonshire and then back to Jesse's. I will lay it out for Theo exactly as it happened, just the facts. But as I'm thinking it through I become strangely detached from it, like I am describing something that somebody else did. Yes, this must be how it works, you come clean and, by this very process, you leave behind the person you were, or at least the badness that was in you.

But I don't want to sound detached as I'm telling this to Theo, so I decide I'll keep it simple, like the Big Book says.

"Theo?" I say, as we watch Gavin Friday on the catwalk. "You know that story about the ferns is bullshit, that wasn't my rock bottom."

"Sure," he says, smoking, completely relaxed. He turns to me, encouraging me to continue.

"What I did... and I wasn't a kid any more when I did it... in London, in Camden Town, I was present when a woman was raped... two of us... it was rape... no excuses..."

Theo puts out his cigarette. He says nothing. He doesn't exactly look away from me, but his bright blue eyes are not making contact with me either, not in any meaningful sense. He seems to leave me in spirit. He picks up the remote and turns the sound down, leaving just the silence.

I need to stop that silence, quickly.

"Remember we were having coffee one day down in the village and I see Jamaica outside with these two other women?" I say.

If Theo remembers, he's not acknowledging it. So I keep talking into the void.

"One of them is called Grace, she knows this woman... this Camden Town woman... we were all at a party, years ago it was, the rich kids' party... the party I talked about in the rooms?"

I shape it like a question but there's not even the hint of an answer.

Theo starts to pick at his light blue V-necked sweater, blanking me out. I can't bear any more of the silence he is hitting me with, so I keep talking. I ramble. Like a sleepwalker in a maze.

"So if the Camden Town woman knows Grace and Grace is down here talking to Jamaica... I don't think Jamaica knows about it, but I am intending to tell her and maybe you could..."

"What?" he says, startling me.

"Maybe you could... advise me... if it would be wise to... you know... ?"

"Why would you tell her?" he asks, his tone suddenly reeking of contempt. He is turned towards me, but he still can't bring himself to make eye contact.

"Because... I want her to know..." I say, the fear flowing through me.

"And it wouldn't be right if she found out from someone else?" he says, still contemptuous.

"No," I mutter.

"Because what would happen then?" he says, toying with me.

"Stop it Theo, please," I say.

"Because then, she'd think badly of you and she wouldn't fuck you any more. Would that be about right?"

Theo gets up from his couch. I think he is going to do some damage.

"The fifth step Theo," I say, grabbing a lifeline. "The fifth step, admitting the nature of our wrongs. And the eighth and ninth steps, listing all the people we have harmed, being willing to make amends to them. That's what I'm on about, Theo. These are the steps and you're supposed to be doing them with me," I say, a feverish, pleading tone in my voice.

I have a feeling he's going to hit me, maybe he's going to kill me, and I might welcome death at this moment, as long as he does it quickly. Which he could, with his vigour. But then I decide he's not going to hit me, he's too controlled. He takes up my challenge about the 12 steps.

"Make amends?" he says, like it's a bizarre notion in this case.

"Right," I say.

"What's her name so? What's the girl's name?"

"The girl in Camden Town?" I say, sensing doom.

"If you're thinking of making amends, you'd need to know the girl's name, wouldn't you?"

"I don't know it, Theo. I'm sorry, I just don't remember, maybe I never knew it. I'm bad with names," I say.

"Even her first name?" he says, apparently talking to himself now, not really expecting an answer.

He could probably keep poking at me for a while yet. But I sense that he's backing off, that the rage in him is dying. And something else is coming in its place, an unfathomable look of pain or despair, that he somehow contains as he walks slowly past me and out the door with the wind chimes, leaving me broken, behind him.

I am fit for nothing. It takes me about an hour sitting in the lingering silence to collect myself enough to make a cup of tea. Then I search through my pockets to find a few scraps of paper with phone-numbers of guys in the rooms scribbled on them, stashed away for moments like this, which we hope will never come.

I am confused. Wounded. I ring up a few of the local guys, and ask what I need to ask. I start to piece together Theo's story, the part of it that I haven't heard in the rooms.

Something terrible happened to Theo. Ten years ago. Something crippling and full of dread. He had a daughter who had just turned twenty-one, a drama student at Trinity College. Theo had just started to get to know her, really, he'd missed a lot of her childhood with his drinking. He would go up to Dublin once a week, get a meeting in Molesworth Street, and have lunch with her. It was the great joy of his life.

One day she didn't arrive for lunch. She was lying dead in her flat, raped and murdered by an ex-boyfriend.

Theo was crushed. He went back on the drink with a vengeance. Eventually he got back to the rooms, but for all his toughness and his serenity, he doesn't talk about it there. Not even in that little room down in the village hall, where I guess he won't be seeing me for a while.

I don't know what to do.

Now I remember that Friday might outside the hall with Theo, when we both said that we wanted a drink. I remember that moment when some darkness seemed to descend on Theo, when he had teased the story of the ferns out of me. But the moment passed and then he was philosophical. I guess he decided I was just a kid then, but now I'm man. Or at least, that's what he took me to be. Then.

Round midnight I phone Phil, who told me in relation to getting a sponsor that doing something is always better than not doing it. He was wrong.

This is the second time I've cried over the phone to Phil. The first was when Stephen was born.

Sometimes, not doing something is better. I want to scream it.

Sometimes not doing something is better.

I'm only getting the odd meeting these days, on trips to the city, but there are more people in my life now, or so it seems. In the weeks after New York, Jamaica keeps bringing these country girls to meet me at the lodge, Susanna and Poppy and Sorcha and Lucy. Straight away she asks me if I want to spend a few days up in the big house watching them working, but somehow, once I am asked, I lose interest. So they look me over and I look them over, warming again to that midsummer night vision of nakedness in the woods.

But that's not real. They're all working with Jamaica or modelling for her and they all defer to her in some fundamental way. She's more the boss than ever. And the more she works, the less she cares about how she looks in the conventional sense. Or so it seems.

It strikes me one morning as I watch her getting dressed that Jamaica actually looks quite, what's the word, dirty these days. It's not just the traditional carefree dishevelled look either, she's wearing the same jeans since New York and a white knitted top I said I liked one night in Joe Allen's, which she still wears well, but which is not very white any more.

I tell her she's driven like Roy Keane and she teases me again about my Shane McGowan theory. I'd tell her about Theo but obviously I can't, because then I might have to tell her about Camden Town. And somehow I don't think I'll be telling anyone else about Camden Town.

She likes to work through the night. We make love down here when she gets the chance, maybe three times a week, during the day. She says the work is wasting her but she loves it. And she fears she won't be able to get it right; she is driven by fear as well as desire, the fear of how much it will hurt if she doesn't get it down exactly as she sees it in her head, the fear it will get away from her because she didn't give it everything.

And it is a beautiful thing to see, all that ambition and talent and energy combusting in the right here and now, and everyone knowing it. This is her moment.

All of us in show business who have had even minor success, know that this is the best time of all, the few weeks or months just before you make it, when you know you're going to, it just hasn't exploded yet.

I know, because it even happened to me, that lovely time when it had become clear from the advance orders and all the airplay, that the debut album was going to be a hit, and we couldn't see beyond that, we were too happy. Too busy as well, but we would have toured Afghanistan in a Hiace van at that time, knowing what we knew. I can sense that Jamaica's in that place now, or close to it, and while these all-nighters may be hard on her physically, deep down she loves being there, she knows she's making magic.

So we're not doing much more than sex, and pretty gentle sex by our standards, just to keep connected it seems, like we're keeping up the payments on our massive investment in each other.

And I figure this is the only way she stays vaguely presentable to bourgeois society because she usually has a shower afterwards. So at least she doesn't smell of sex when she leaves here, though she's in a kind of permanent sweat. Sometimes she washes her thick black hair in the shower, sometimes not. It's looking wilder all the time, but wild suits her.

And sometimes I catch her lost in some reverie, like the first time she showed me this place, and I felt she was remembering something that happened here, maybe that story about her mother and Jagger, and her father outside pruning the roses. But the moment passes. As the retired drinker and New York wild boy Pete Hamill put it, quoting Gabriel Garcia Marquez, we all have a public life, a private life, and a secret life – and unless I'm invited, I don't want to barge into her secret life.

It's working well for me in its way, this routine. We drinkers are creatures of habit. Eventually we end up not just in the same pub every night but on the same stool, drinking our usual tipple out of our favourite glass. So a steady stream of uncomplicated sex appeals to our psyches; it's kind of payback for all the nights we spent roaring at women in nightclubs, maddened by the wine.

I'm still sick about the falling out with Theo, and nearly every day I hope he'll phone me, and nearly every day I decide I'll phone him, but I can't actually pick up the receiver and do it. And as each day goes by, and he doesn't call me, it just seems harder.

I'm not missing the rooms too much, I've gone to so many meetings over the years I can probably get by for a while on the surplus.

And it suits me too that there's less of those hellish nights, those nights with Jamaica drinking and me not drinking. The last time down in Regan's, the village pub, I'm starting to go ga-ga after about five hours on the water when she asks me again what am I having, and I bark at her, "Oh, take a wild fucking guess."

Less of that is bound to improve my mood. What's more, I'm looking forward to my second World Cup sober, another landmark. And on the day the Irish team leaves for Japan, I feel genuinely elated. So, in some bizarre way, my life enters a period of relative serenity after the trauma with Theo. And in this mood and with no particular purpose of which I'm aware in mind, I get it up again to raise the topic of Mr Michael Wade.

Jamaica's just out of the shower, and getting dressed, so it's a casual scene. Just shooting the breeze.

"Mikey", I say. "The one and only... I have got to tell you this, it's probably no big deal, but I happened across a play of his, a new play... you know the one?"

She smiles in recognition. Not in guilt, I note, just in recognition.

"Go on," she says.

"In New York, actually, I'm browsing through a book of his new plays and I see parts of it that are familiar to me," I say. "This guy talking to this woman about drink?"

"Gad, it's probably all about you. You and me. Is it all about you and me?" she says.

"I didn't read it all", I say. "Just the good bits."

"You got to watch what you say around lickle Mikey," she says, checking herself in the mirrored door. "We're workin' on this other play and I guess I'm reasoning about you and me, and issues around alcohol. He loves anything to do with alcohol, he is to-tally obsessed with it. Obsessed with drinkin' it too, Gad Almighty. Anyway he tells me it's de first of a trilogy..."

"So you'd just be talking about me being off the drink," I cut in.

"The fellowship of Alcoholics Anonymous," she says. Ah yes, how sweet the sound, Al-co-hol-ics An-on-ee-muss.

"And old Mikey would be squirelling it all away?"

"You're like him, you're a writer. You know these t'ings," she says, flattering me.

"So I could go to see this play then, whenever, and I wouldn't be unhappy?"

"You know how it works," she says, all mellow Jamaica. "There's bits of you in it, bits of me in it, bits of other people, bits of Mikey himself. I never read plays. Mikey asked me to read it but I said no, go away, I never read plays. They make no sense to me at all, mon, unless they're up on a stage."

"So it's not actually you and me?" I say.

"I suppose he just robbed a few of de good bits, like you say," she says chirpily. "Anyway he's a savage in rehearsals, he keeps changin' his plays, like Mister Bob Dylan changes his songs. It'll probably all get chopped out anyhow," she adds, blowing me a kiss as she returns to her lair.

Fair enough, I feel I'll be able to read this play now. I want to read it. The thing has embedded itself in the bottom of my brain and it won't go away. I have to read it. But I have to be prepared for something which might disturb my spirit. I always have to be prepared for that.

I make a day of it, a bus into Dublin, a lunchtime meeting in Molesworth Street, a ramble around the record shops blowing my 'Jack Rooney' wages, if that's the word, on a new clutch of CDs, and a read of Mikey's play as I sip a mug of white coffee in Bewley's. Jamaica doesn't actually hand me my wages in cash, I have a hole-in-the-wall card to preserve whatever is left of my financial dignity.

Flush with my latest withdrawal of two-hundred big ones from the bank in Westmoreland Street, I buy the book of plays in Waterstone's. The other two in the collection have already been produced to massive acclaim, and now 'Dry Drunk' is much anticipated, it says on the back. It may also be the first of a trilogy, it says. But they don't need to tell me that.

Jamaica is right. You have to be highly trained to be able to read a play on the page and know whether it's any good or not. In fact I'll no idea whether or not the script of the 'Jack Rooney' show is any good, not until I workshop it at least, which I can't afford to do.

All I know is that the songs have something. The songs have heart. Ultimately the songs are the story.

In fact I'm saying something to that effect in the early pages of 'Dry Drunk'. I'm a songwriter called Tim, who has this idea about writing a musical, an idea so patently insane it attracts the eccentric Jill, who soon learns that the mad musician is also going mad from lack of drink.

I still can't tell if the play is any good or not, my nerves are jangling too much.

I'm kind-of expecting the drink bits, which come next, based on the snatches I've seen in New York, so I fly through that, noting in one scary line that Tim is banging on about drink while he's lying with Jill on the bank of a river.

I need all my hard-won serenity for what comes next, the arrival of Jamie, an alcoholic writer who starts an alcoholic affair with Jill. They make this arrangement, that Jamie is her drunk lover, and Tim is her sober one.

A neat idea.

I don't read any more. This is a play, it's not real. I didn't spend seven years keeping it real, keeping it in the day, without developing a sure instinct for stuff I shouldn't be letting into my head. And I don't want Michael Wade in my head, or anywhere in my vicinity. But he is.

I get out of Bewley's fast. I know now what I must do, and by tomorrow morning, it will be done. If I want to find out what's happening in my life, I won't find it in this book of plays.

But I'll find it.

Fourteen

She won't be at the gate lodge. She'll be working through the night.

I know what I must do.

She said the work is wasting her, but she loves it.

I should probably get a taxi, for comfort, but I blow my wages on CDs. A different kind of comfort. So I get the bus back home, a journey shortened by the evening paper screaming the news about Roy Keane and the catastrophe of Saipan. The hero walks out in the middle of the biggest play of his life. It looks like we'll all be finding out where we stand in the days to come.

Night falls and I don't sleep at all. I have the small television working on the floor; Sky News is following up the Keane story, running the same piece all night until the next demented instalment arrives, from a different time zone, another world.

Roy is helping me out here, filling my head with something other than the task I have given myself for the morning, the prospect of which night otherwise be too horrible to contemplate.

Roy's fracas with Mick McCarthy is no surprise to me, of course. I feel I have a special knowledge of how Roy must be suffering. When a man has what Jamaica calls issues with alcohol, and he's trying to tackle them, the last thing he needs is a month away with a bunch of boys, who keep him awake at night drinking beer and singing.

So it's like I'm keeping vigil up here for Roy. He's complaining about the state of the gear and the pitch; I'm just thinking about him in that room in Saipan, trying to get through it.

It's tearing me up but I feel it couldn't be otherwise.

All year I've been wondering how Roy could endure it without going berserk. And now, I can't help but admire what he's doing, coming home like this, getting out before a deeper madness gets into him.

I only wish he could say that; it would be an inspiration to us all. Instead we'll have to listen to this garbage about footballs not arriving on time, about failing to prepare and preparing to fail, jargon really, but not the jargon Roy needs right now.

But I can relate to that too. Us boys in the rooms can always find a reason.

So we'll all have to get through it somehow without mentioning the one thing that needs to be mentioned, the old hooch, and the lack of it, and what it can do to you.

And now Sky is saying the people are split down the middle on this, and it's true, but not in the way Sky thinks. Superficially we will be at each other's throats; deep down the split is within ourselves, the split between the rational and the irrational.

I know all about this. I am a rational man who, for the best years of my life, chose to be drunk. And I think there might still be another drink in me, though I know that same drink will probably kill me about twenty-five years before my time, almost certainly in a very bad way, if I have it.

But I can still see myself savouring that first drink, and many more drinks, sitting up at the bar of the International reading the Irish Times, asking the barman in an urbane fashion to switch to the RTE News for the sport and the weather. Just like that.

Maybe the trauma of Saipan is pushing me a few millimetres closer, but tonight it seems to come almost as a blessing, someone else's problem to think about, some sadness that lodges itself inside me but doesn't directly concern me.

Jamaica will be remembering that thing I said over in Nottingham, that Roy Keane has a drink problem in a way that Shane McGowan doesn't. Hell, Mikey put it in the play. Soon the whole world will know it.

And Roy is running away like we'd all love to do sometime, but he even runs away in a confrontational way. He's running away from football but he's facing up to something else, running away but getting closer to what he needs for the rest of his life.

Yes, even the World Cup will pass.

I'm thinking of writing him a note as I sit here sleepless, to help pass these empty hours before the morning, when I must go up to that big house and deal with whatever I find there.

I suspect Roy knows who I am. I've always had this weird feeling he saw us on Top Of The Pops and thought we were rubbish and felt better about himself as a result, and went on from there.

I could write him a note telling him that if he's still available for the next World Cup, and if he keeps doing the right things, by then he might be able to endure a couple of hours at the barbecue with the boys, and join in their laughter. And then to bed, smiling in the knowledge that he will wake up with a light heart, while they will wake up feeling like diseased rats.

I think he needs to hear that kind of thing right now, not the hellish media babble.

I wonder does he want to invest in a tuner?

Ah, I'll leave him alone; I don't suppose he'll be dealing with his mail for a while anyway.

I'd have written that note if I was still drinking, when staying up all night was just part of the routine. I'd scrawl a few pages that not even I could understand in the sharp light of day. But not any more. The biro stays in the jar.

You hold back a lot more when you go into the rooms, you stop making a disgrace of yourself, you stop sitting in night-clubs telling people you love them. But you feel safe in some odd way when you stay up all night drinking, safer than I feel tonight.

You can tell anybody anything and it doesn't really occur to you that you might be very close to death. You just have another drink. You wouldn't be there at all without the drink, it would be ludicrous.

So tonight is the first night I can recall staying up like this without a drink since the first night I heard 'Blonde On Blonde'. Which changed my life. And in the morning, I think my life will change again.

I've got the Blonde On Blonde CD here, it's one I'd never part with. I turn down Sky and put Dylan on. I don't have cigarettes any more, but I've still got Bob. I'm 17 again, things are about to happen for me. My heart is full of anger, but I know there's something on the other side of it, if I keep believing. I'm 17 again and this man knows exactly how I feel. I'm 17 again and Dylan is telling me to hang on in there, I'm not wrong.

And now I'm grown-up. I can't deny I'm grown-up, I wouldn't want to deny it any more.

I'm still hearing what these great songs are telling me, but I know now I have to face down the demons myself. In my own words. In my own time.

And I fear it, because I have all this time to think it over, so much time to look at the situation from all sides, first a moment of doubt, then an hour of suspicion, now this long, long night of deepening dread. So much time.

Which is another big advantage of sobriety, but also its curse.

Out with the hooch-monsters, there might be bombs going off all around you and you just keep staggering through the wreckage with a glass in your hand.

Now, with all this time, you can prepare yourself for anything. And they'll still get you.

It's eight in the morning, by the Sky clock. I hear Eddie coming through the front gate on his Suzuki. I change into a flowery shirt to give my spirits a lift. I'm feeling stiff after my sleepless night. I select a dark brown bomber jacket and the hat that Dylan likes. I take a copy of the latest 'Jack Rooney' CD, as I always do when visiting. Call me superstitious.

I walk up the lane, a long stretch of what feels like about a thousand yards, until I turn the corner and see the old grey mansion. I walk another thousand yards and I'm passing the flowerbeds. The nerves are starting to jangle but then I tell myself to calm down, I know what I'm going to find here, I'm not a fool, it's no mystery to me any more. But it still has to be done.

I catch sight of Eddie off to the right, coming out of a shed. I hold up the 'Jack Rooney' demo, which seems to mean something to him, though in truth I don't think Eddie cares about the goings-on between people like Jamaica and me, he just works.

He directs me around the back. I salute him. I walk around the building like it's my second home, though of course I've never set foot in the place before. This is her territory, which she says is a total shambles, and she speaks the truth about that.

God, the state of it.

I push open a door at the back. I am in a huge kitchen with terracotta floor-tiles. But apart from being a kitchen with a large dining table that hasn't been cleared for what looks like a long time, and an old black range, it is also a work place, strewn with yards of fabrics and dressmaking equipment and materials and designs.

It is also a bar, littered with empty bottles and half-empty bottles of booze, like the aftermath of the last night of a Motörhead farewell tour. Except there's been no party up here that I know of, not that I know everything, of course. For whatever reason, serious drinking is taking place here.

And it is also a bedroom. There's a mattress on the floor. Two people are asleep under a huge white duvet. Jamaica and Michael Wade. I knew what to expect, but still it tears me up.

I knew it could not be otherwise. Once that line in the play about the drunk lover and the sober lover kicked in, a lot of things about Jamaica started to make sense. I know a few things about drunk love. In fact I know more than a few things about drunk love. Now I know just a little bit more.

It's still hard to look at them there, knowing that your sober love could never be enough. That it never had a chance. That it's over.

And there's a smell of ganja in the room. The stuff she only smokes on special occasions? She must have found this occasion special enough.

I get an urge to kick Wade to death as he lies there, a few day's growth making his jaundiced face look a bit like Val Kilmer in some western, rough but cute, a bog-monster with fine cheekbones. Another gaucho.

With one blow of a bottle to the head, he would die in his sleep, which he will probably do anyway after some colossal bender, which will shoot him straight away to the highest rank of dead drunk Irish geniuses. I'd be doing him a favour really.

And there's Jamaica. Wonderful Jamaica, with her mouth open and the occasional snort coming out of her, not sleeping any more, just sleeping it off, the swinish sleep.

Obviously she didn't want me coming up here and that worked easy enough. But it must have been hard for her to keep everything going. I know, because I've done it all my life.

When I was out there, would I have done this to someone like me? Yes. Would I have thought I'd get away with it? Probably. I was seeing three women once, and while I was with each of them I swore I loved them truly and I think I truly did, in my fashion, in my way.

She has issues with alcohol, it's nearly the first thing she tells me, and that adds up too.

Most of us know we're not quite right, we have our suspicions, it's the next part we can't get our heads around, the need for change. We think we just need a change of speed. So Jamaica would be drinking a little with me, and drinking a lot sometimes, but any alcoholic worthy of the name can behave themselves if they have to, a few quiet drinks with the normal people and then the serious drinking can begin when the normal people have all gone to their beds, leaving the night to the night-people.

And while they can't keep it up forever, they can keep it up for a very long time.

I hate her at this moment, but I also know where's she's coming from, and where she's going to. There's always been that connection between us, from way back.

So I know she'll go with the drunk guy. Drunks don't want to get found out, but most of all they don't want to stop drinking. She'll even resent me for being such a pain in the ass and wrecking it all in my meddlesome way.

I need to get out of here now, with one thought for consolation. She doesn't love him.

She can't love him. She loves the booze in those bottles, and what it does to her, that's what she loves.

I know all this, I know how it works. But it's still tearing me up.

I drop a 'Jack Rooney' CD on the duvet.

My calling card.

Fifteen

Back at the gate lodge, I get the first sign that I'm starting to lose it.

I have this fierce urge to ring up Susan, to tell her we should give it another try.

I want to tell her I'm better now, you see, and we can live as a family, just the three of us. I can almost hear it in my head, a Nat King Cole voice over lush strings. "I'm better now, you see/We can live as a family/Just the three of us... "

It's 9 o'clock on Sky, still early, which is all that's stopping me making the call.

Until I think this is exactly the sort of thing a drunk guy would do, and I'm not one of those guys any more. I'm playing the long game. I don't make the call. Yet.

But I'm losing it. By any standards I'm losing it. I can take myself off to a meeting at lunchtime and the boys will tell me that this too will pass, but I don't think it will.

I think I'm stuck with this one.

I'm wasted now after that sleepless night. In the rooms, they say you have to watch it when you get tired. But then you have to watch everything, don't you? You have to be eternally vigilant, and still you can miss those little things, like the fact that Jamaica is screwing someone else. For how long?

I stick on this video of an all-star Sondheim tribute at Carnegie Hall. Something in his songs always comforts me, some plaintive note he strikes.

Maybe that night she rang from New York, putting me in bad form, maybe then the madness was starting. I'll ask old Jason O'Brien about it some day; Jase always has the inside track.

And I wonder if it bothered her that Mikey was writing the story of our lives?

Probably not, because a lot of the mad things we drinkers do tend to appear pretty reasonable to us at the time. On top of which, she has that bohemian chutzpah that says she can do just about anything and get away with it. It's other people who have the problem, we're fine, we're keeping it together.

So I guess she can handle it. It might even turn out to be an important work by Mikey, the most distinctive voice of his generation. And with the addict's love of secrecy, what better way to keep a secret than to open it up for everyone to see? Most writers use material from their own lives, but they tart it up, they play with it; they make it up, if it comes to it. Only the hardcore will do what Mikey is doing, and in some twisted way I can't help but admire him for it, for his ruthlessness, his total indifference.

I don't think I could do that, just put it all out there, raw.

Which is maybe why Mikey is happening and I'm not, and why he's walking down the lane at this moment with my woman.

They're coming to see me. Jamaica's face is partly hidden behind her very long purple scarf, but Mikey is striding out with no apparent inhibitions. I guess Mikey just wants to get this sorted; it's boring him.

I can see them now, waking up still banjoed, seeing the Jack Rooney CD and knowing they have a situation on their hands. First they're guilt-ridden, then quickly they see the funny side. And with the fever of the drink still working, making them giddy, they call it this way. Maybe a swig of wine to take the edge off it, then a strange feeling of relief, a sense that it will be simpler from now on, just the two of them and a room full of drink. But first there's a chore to do, so they might as well get it over with. I am that chore, and they are coming now to do me.

They're coming. Now. I open the door to them. I want to say that this is the quickest response I've ever had to a Jack Rooney CD, but I let it pass. I reckon it's up to them to make with the awkward jokes. Mikey goes and sits in the corner, chewing gum, his knees sticking out through the large holes in his denims, his expression one of glassy-eyed amusement. I notice his teeth are very white, an oddly wholesome thing in a man who is otherwise trying to look like one of The Ramones.

Jamaica slopes past me, most of her face now invisible behind the big purple scarf. But she raises her eyebrows knowingly, an eloquent gesture. It says sorry, but let's not make a federal case out of it. It says sorry, but not too sorry. It says sorry, but you know yourself...

I know, I am reading the signals. We are all going to be sophisticated about this. We are not going to have a slanging match like we're on 'Brookside'. We are going to get through this like the enlightened individuals we are, three alcoholics, two of them rampant, the third feeling a bit left out.

I have a bottle of wine under the kitchen sink, the one that I gave Jamaica for Christmas, and that she said she wouldn't drink until the opening night of 'Jack Rooney'.

"I've got some wine here," I say.

"Cheers," Mikey says, all earthy.

I take the bottle out. I open it in front of them. I give them each a wine glass and I pour the red wine expertly, with that little flourish, that twist, at the end, like a waiter.

"The best in the house," I say, admiring the label.

"Neil is writing a musical, as we know," Jamaica says, taking a sip, then looking towards the Sondheim video, and some prodigious adolescent doing 'Broadway Baby'. The bottle of wine seems to mean nothing to her, there isn't the slightest flicker of recognition, it's just wine, wine, wine, spo-de-oh-de...

"Very smart, writing a musical, very, very smart," Jamaica adds.

She sounds weary, like she's talking to herself. I think it'll be plain English for today.

Mikey is engrossed in the video.

"Broadway," Mikey says to no-one in particular. "The new Marina Carr play will go to Broadway."

I'm not exactly looking at Mikey in a kindly light at this moment, but even the way he says the word "play" is irritating me, his flat midlands accent flattened out even further for effect. These guys are always pretending to be more unschooled than they are, just fellas off the bog writin' oul' plaaaays. The Dalkey matrons must have their bit of rough.

"Good," I say.

Jamaica lowers the scarf. She drinks her wine. In the morning light, she looks better than a wine-for-breakfast woman has a right to look.

"It sounds like a musical, a real show," she says, apparently still referring to 'Jack Rooney'.

"Listen to Sondheim, I can't do that thing," I say, my modest contribution to the theatre talk.

"You can and you must. And you must let me do the costumes," she says, still sounding sincere, the way they do at wrap-parties when they swear they'll work with each other again.

"Have a drink," I say.

I fill her glass again. The smell of the wine is killing me.

"You must listen to Neil's musical," she says to Mikey. "It's a boxing musical, you might bring something to it." Still she calls it mew-zee-cal – not mus-i-cle – a final mark of respect.

And Mikey just laughs, puts his hand up like a cop stopping the traffic and starts to sing in this Broadway rhythm, "a little bit gay, a little bit ho-mo-sexual, a little bit gay..."

I think he is dissing me. I laugh like I'm too big to take offence. I put another splash of red in their glasses.

"Marina Carr is the best, she ought to be on Broadway," I say. I hope this is a taunt, because Carr is from the same part of the world as Mikey, making Mikey not even the number one playwright in the Irish midlands.

"She's a woman," Mikey says, with what I take to be a note of sarcasm.

"She's gettin' there," Jamaica says,

"Like me and my musical," I add, dissing myself, with what I hope is a touch of class.

We all laugh, just because we can.

"A boxing musical," he says, sounding genuinely baffled.

"A boxing musical with Matt Dillon," I add.

"Mikey's a total savage in the rehearsal room," she says to me, like I need to know. "If you can get it past him, it will run for ever..."

I hunker down beside her, confiding in her.

"I don't want to work with Mikey," I say quietly. "And Mikey doesn't want to work with me. I think you're full of shit."

I take the bottle into the kitchen. The smell is killing me. I think we've reached the end of our theatre talk.

Jamaica leans back in the couch. She stares into her wine. It seems she's not going to strike back at my insult, she'll just absorb it, along with the morning wine. She raises her eyebrows again in that way. Mikey gets up out of the corner. He turns off the sound on the Sondheim video, like he knows all that now, and he can move on. He brushes past me into the kitchen. He takes what's left of the wine with him into the toilet.

I guess they've arranged for Mikey to leave us a few moments together, like the condemned man with the next of kin. But I don't suppose Jamaica wants to discuss anything in depth with me.

She gets up from the couch like she is carrying a great weight. She comes to me, and she wraps the long scarf around me. With the wrapping, I get the impression I'm about to be posted abroad for Christmas.

Then she wraps both of us in it. She tries to kiss me but I pull away. She giggles, trying to lighten it up, but I'm not playing.

"What must you be t'inking?" she says, oozing humility.

I'm thinking she's reeking of drink.

"You must tell me about it some time," I say.

Her expression turns serious, like she is absorbing a very wise statement.

"We have known each other a long time," she says.

This is not exactly true. I have known her since last year. She has known me a long time, since the thirteenth century she says. She saw me first. You could even say she waited for me. Waited all that time until the day we connected, and then took it as far as she could, until the old hooch started to take her somewhere else.

So maybe I'll let her down easy this time. For that dash of freckles on that gorgeous skin, I won't be too unkind. In exchange for the day in this room when we listened to 'Jamaica Say You Will', maybe I'll go quietly. And it goes without saying that Phil was right. I don't believe that Jackson Browne story of hers any more. But I still like it... I still want it to be true.

"I've got a meeting, and then I'll leave," I say. On the silent Sondheim video, Liza Minnelli is dancing on a grand piano. Liza has a meeting too.

"It's not that I want you out of dis place, it's more I want him in it," she says.

"He'll do good work here... with his plaaaaaaays," I say, unable to resist the midlands drawl.

The audience is starting to rise to Sondheim. She still needs to talk; maybe it's just the drink, but she can't stop.

"Our t'ing, it's becoming something else now. We become more alike, we move away from each other," she says, sounding almost excited at this new phase in our relationship.

"That's OK," I say. I just want her to stop now.

"You will hate this, but it feels to me... organic," she says.

"I hate that," I confirm.

Mikey comes out of the toilet, without the bottle of wine.

"Are you getting all this down, Mikey?" I say.

"Michael," he says with a smile. "It's Michael Wade. Listen, one thing I can't figure out. How come a well-known fella like you can't get his musical on? Do all these rock'n'roll business types not remember you?"

He sounds genuinely curious.

"No," I say, keeping it simple.

They're making their move for the exit, the hard work done.

"Neil..." Jamaica starts, but I get in ahead of her. I just want her to go away now.

"I might take up painting," I say. "All these old rock'n'roll guys are taking up painting."

"We're the rock'n'roll stars now," he says. "Fellas writin' plays."

Jamaica is gently steering him to the door.

"Well, monologues," I say.

And he laughs. I guess he can afford to.

I look at them walking up the lane. I see Jamaica's hand on his shoulder. I wonder how much drinking they've got left in them. Another five years maybe for her, and as for Michael Wade, if the critics keep writing him love-letters he might never give it up.

Another five years maybe, of sick heads and a sick relationship, if they're lucky. But at this moment they must be feeling pretty wonderful; the day must be full of promise, and the night too.

I think I might take that, you know, if it was offered to me right now.

I think I might take it, in exchange for another five years of being good. Half-cut in the middle of the morning, a room full of drink and a woman to drink it with, I want my old life back again.

I feel mean now, about that monologue jibe. The guy's just more talented than me.

He has the gift; I just have the rooms.

And he's growing. The drink will take him to stranger places still, it might even give him that extra ten per cent, it might make him the next Tennessee Williams – and if it poisons him like a dog after that, so what?

I go to the toilet. I check the bottle of wine. It's empty.

I throw it with full force against the mirrored door. I shield my eyes and then I get out of there fast, slamming the door behind me, leaving behind a room, full of broken glass.

Sixteen

I walk quickly towards the village. There's a meeting on at eleven and I can make it, but I don't think I'm going to. I keep walking anyway, like an automoton.

If Theo comes along now and gives me a lift I'll get to that meeting and then maybe I'll be fine. But I don't think that's going to happen, and anyway I don't want to feel fine anymore. I want to feel drunk.

I want to go into a pub and order a pint of Guinness and read the paper. I want to take my pint out to the beer garden in the afternoon. I want to watch the World Cup and drink. I want to watch the World Cup on the island, and drink.

The island.

Where did it come from, this notion, this great notion of going to the island for the World Cup? It first came to me when I spent a week on the island eight years ago, watching the World Cup Final between Brazil and Italy in Pasadena, a pint and a chaser in front of me: there I was, thinking I'd love to do this right some time, take in the whole tournament, maybe the next time Ireland qualify.

Take in the whole tournament, three perfect weeks of it, on the island.

But where in my head did it come from? The addict's need for escape, they'd say, to put some physical distance between you and reality, to feel nothing but the addict's love of drink and sport and escape, they'd say.

They never miss a chance to condemn these pleasures. I've spent seven years condemning them myself, seven years sitting in the rooms with men lamenting all the fun they used to have, or that they thought they were having at the time until they realised they weren't having fun at all and it was so much better fun to be sitting in a bare room on a Friday night with a bunch of alcoholics talking about their Higher Power than it was drinking and chasing women in bars.

Well, I don't believe it any more.

I think it works for some, but in the end it doesn't work for me. And I don't know if going back on the drink will work for me either, but the way it is, I'm stronger now, drunk or sober. And drunk is better. The way I'm feeling now it is. Drunk. Better.

Now I have this ecstatic vision of hitting the open road to the west, all the way to the other side of the country, and sauntering into that harbour bar for a few leisurely pints before getting the boat.

I take off down a side road away from the village. I'm not going to get that meeting now, I know it in my blood – and now I'm making sure of it. Everything inside me seems to be pumping, like I'm running as fast as I can. But I'm just walking. And thinking.

I'm thinking, I am going to drink again, and that's OK.

I stop walking. I look at my watch. I am nine minutes late for the meeting. And I am going to drink again, and that's OK, after 7 years, 122 days, 11 hours and 9 minutes.

I am mad with joy at this moment. I stand there on the side of the road, delirious with the thought of what is to come. I start walking again, back to the gate lodge. I must do this now before the fever dies down and the boys in the rooms reach out to take me back. I must return to the gate lodge and find a number for Gray's Hotel on the island and make a booking. For three weeks. All the way through to the final whistle and beyond.

I hear a car coming, I am terrified it might be Theo and he will stop for me and take me to a meeting in a spirit of reconciliation, and all will be lost. But it's not Theo. I half-expect the driver to stop, to get out and help me like I've been in an accident, but he just keeps driving. It feels like he's ignoring my trauma, that's been brought on by this appalling thought that's kicking away inside me. But I'm forgetting again that it's not an appalling thought; if you look at it with any sense of reason or detachment it's a perfectly normal thought, to want to have a few pints and watch a few football matches; in fact it's an extremely pleasant way

THE ROOMS

to spend the day, if not the rest of your days.

It's just that in this moment of revelation I feel I am the only man in the world who has ever had this thought. I'm like Roy over there in Saipan, thinking, I can't just go home from the World Cup, can I? Can I?

Actually I can and I will.

So we're thinking the unthinkable, me and Roy. In our different ways. Roy and me.

I am going to drink again, and that's OK.

I am not going to let it pass, I am going to let it happen.

I am going to make it happen.

I start to run. I get back to the gate lodge and crunch my way thought the broken glass to get to the mobile. I call directory enquiries looking for the number of Gray's Hotel. I dial the number without writing it down, just in case I change my mind while I'm looking for a pen.

I book a room in the hotel for three weeks. I ask the woman if there's a television in the room and she says there is. There's also a big screen in the bar. I have dreamed of such a thing. A big screen.

I tell her my name and she recognises me. She used to be a fan of the band. I take this as a good omen.

Money, I need money. Drink costs money, a shocking amount these days, so I'm led to believe. But then I never knew these pleasures to be cheap.

I've got enough cash to do me a couple of nights. Maybe I'll get Susan to bung me a few hundred from her latest win on the Dow Jones: I'll be feeling guilty about taking money from her, but I think I'll get over it once I get into my island routine, the drink, the football, the fellowship. Or, better still, maybe I'll just ask Jamaica for my wages; yes, that's the one, that's another sweet revelation coming through to me, clear as a bell.

I will get to the island and then I will call Jamaica and ask her for my wages. To be delivered in person, by her and by her alone. And by the way, could she bring a bottle of that red wine she's been throwing into Mikey, because you can't get a decent vintage over here?

I'm booked in, I'm breaking out, I'm ready to rock. I'm getting lucky too; I see Eddie has left his Suzuki just up the lane. I fancy I'll borrow that, if for no other reason than that it'll save me a lot of bus-fare I could be spending on drink. And it's there, right now, no queueing, no stopping to pick up old women on the way.

Ah Eddie, we never did have that talk about motorbikes. I close the door of the gate lodge quietly. I get to the Suzuki and start it up. I put on Eddie's helmet. The miracle is it fits. But I knew it would all work for me today. I'm back in the fast lane again.

I ride out of the estate. Sorry Eddie, I have to work too. And I've got seven years of a backlog.

I gain speed as I ride though the village, suddenly sick with dread again, that the boys in the rooms will hear me passing and know somehow that it's me and run out in front of the Suzuki like maniacs, or call the emergency services or the cops.

I dread this, even though I'm wearing Eddie's helmet. I give the old village hall, built in 1928, just one glance, for old time's sake. I love those guys, but I can't do that any more.

From the vantage point of the bike, that place doesn't look serene to me, it just looks dead. I can hardly believe I spent so much time in there when I could have been out here. I pass the speed limit sign, a black circle and a line cutting through it. I'm on the road.

I am going to drink again, and that's OK.

I ride from town to town mostly by the back roads, no particular route in mind, taking each signpost as it comes, hardly a coherent thought in my head, just the primitive pull of the west, just the adrenaline ripping through me. There's a feeling of frustration setting in. The Suzuki has an efficient whine, but what I needed for this trip was the growl of a Harley. I am stiff. I am sore. I am almost falling asleep at the boredom of it, as the minutes stretch into hours and my arse starts to feel an unfamiliar ache from the badly designed seat.

I stop for a couple of minutes in Athlone to get a can of Coke from a machine, and to fill up the tank with petrol. Then I ride on into county Galway with its stone walls, passing through the little towns of Connaught, thinking now of nothing, nothing but my destination.

When I get there, I park the Suzuki near the pier. Near the harbour bar.

If I go in here and have this drink, I will die. Maybe not today, but soon, and it will be a very ugly scene.

That's what they tell me anyway, in the rooms.

But I'm going in anyway, a guy going into a bar like any other guy going into a bar. I'm going into this harbour bar to have my first drink in more that seven years and once I've got that inside me, I'll be ready for the journey across to the island, where the real drinking can commence. And since the boat leaves in two hours, I will actually have time for more than one drink here, on the mainland, for a few drinks in fact, provided I can keep the first one down, which is by no means certain. After so long without it, maybe the first one will just kill me stone dead.

But I've come a long way. And today, I'm not really afraid of dying.

I can see the boat that will take me over to the island, the same ferry that took me across eight years ago, when I still had a few months drinking in me. From the bar, I can smell the beer; it has never really left me, the waft of a bottle of beer on a summer's evening, 15 years old and Bob Seger's 'Night Moves' playing on the cassette machine, a bunch of boys in the sand-dunes watching the girls swimming in the sea. Twenty years later, I am still visited by these blasts of euphoric recall, as if the first tang of adulthood had been tasted a matter of months ago.

It may take me another twenty years to stop this time, but today is not about stopping. It's about starting again in this harbour bar.

For a moment I am frozen. I am frozen in that moment I saw her...

And even now as I walk into this pub I can still turn around and ride home. I mean physically I can do it, of course, but my spirit is hogtied. I have made a call and I'm not wrong about it. The voice inside my head keeps insisting. I'm on my own now. But I'm not wrong. I guess Roy Keane feels like this on his way back from Saipan, like he's standing up for something, like sometimes if the world doesn't see it your way, then the world has got to change. Not you.

It's a lonesome place to be but that's OK, as we say in the rooms. That's

OK, we keep saying that's OK, like, I'm longing for a drink today but that's OK, like, I shot a man in Reno just to watch him die, but that's OK, like, everything is OK – everything except a drop of the old hooch.

So, all things considered, I wish Roy had made his stand some other time, because it's like Roy's living in my head right now, as I pick my spot at the bar with the old fire rising inside of me. Roy is living in all our heads, dividing us within ourselves.

We wake up hating him for putting us through this, and we go to bed seeing him as a Shakespearean hero, knowing that a lesser man could have handled this better. Yes, that's the tragic part. And they say there's still a slim chance he'll turn around and go back to Japan and play for us, and we'll win the World Cup. But I don't think he'll do that. I think he should just do what I'm about to do now. He should have a drink or two and hunker down and watch the World Cup, even though they say he shouldn't be drinking at all.

They'll say that about me too, about a lot of people who probably don't have too much wrong with them, apart from a few bad habits. I was saying this about Roy when he was showing all the signs of what to my expert eye looked like that ol' dry drunk syndrome, a guy bursting for booze with no help from the rooms, nothing but willpower which only goes so far, and which leaves you open to the odd slip, especially if you're a top man like Roy, who's used to the best.

But of course in the rooms we all agree it would be even worse than missing the World Cup and living with a lifetime of regrets if he just broke out and had a beer. In the rooms we claim Roy as one of our own and we won't be persuaded otherwise. We just know deep down.

Well, I don't know any of that any more. I don't know how it ever got into me either, all that shit, as I inhale the atmosphere of this lounge bar, the beer, the smoke, the whiff of last night's beer. It all went away, it evaporated this morning, for a lot of reasons which are clear, and some which I can't rightly explain, except I heard about this kind of thing in the rooms, how a guy who was solid AA for 21 years runs into this American lady he used to know, and they start talking on the street and the talk turns to books, which the guy finds interesting, and she suggests a drink and he goes with her and has a drink and he's off, just like that. Drinking again after 21 years, after all the things he said.

After 21 years, a slip, as we call it in the rooms, a slip being a pretty fine description of this guy falling off the wagon hard, knowing the craziness is going to be a lot worse this time, because now he knows too much, he knows just about everything, except how to stop it happening to him when the old fire sweeps him away. Maybe going back on the drink is like going off it in the first place. When your time comes, you'll know it. My time has come, I feel; I could sense this weight lifting from me this morning with just one thought that came into my head: I am going to drink again, and that's OK.

I have fought the bottle and now I need a new challenge. I need a new start, here in this harbour bar. To fight the battle in a different way.

What will I have? Will I have a pint or will I have a short? My earlier visions swim back into focus. I think I will have a pint. But what will I have a pint of? Sweet Jesus, show me the way.

By the time I get a bit of service in this place I may have changed my mind again. I have this side of the bar all to myself, so I can still run out the door and pretend this never happened, but then again I can't. It's like the proprietor knows I'm wrestling with a few issues here, and he's giving me space before I make that commitment. I could rap a coin on the counter, and demand his attention, be done with it, but at this stage I'm savouring the elaborate build-up, musing on these matters, knowing in all likelihood that there's a drink at the end of it.

Yes, they'll say it's bad craziness and I have heard it's always worse when you go back on it after being off it for any length of time, always worse, always, always, always.

I know all that and every other AA routine, but let's forget about me for a minute and put it another way: what if it's all wrong, what if the world is just going through this phase, a bit of an attitude problem, and all these people who think they're alcoholics can be fixed a lot easier than they think?

Attitudes change, the bar is raised and lowered all the time. Twenty years ago you needed to have three bottles of whiskey for breakfast before you could be rated an alcoholic, now you hear some American dude plugging away on the radio telling you that even thinking about whisky is enough to qualify you.

I get a new surge of determination when this thought hits me. I want to spite that American. I want that barman to come to me immediately. My heart is pounding again like it was pounding at the side of the road this morning. I am joyous at the possibilities that have just opened up for me, 7 years, 122 days, 16 hours and 15 minutes by the pub clock, since my last drink.

Yes, what if there's nothing wrong with us except we lost the thread for a while? I mean such thoughts have occurred to me before, but I put it down to this thing called alcoholism, just the old devil working in me. Now I'm not so sure. The question isn't going away this time. And it's raising all these other old questions that have troubled me over these dry years, like, how can I say in the rooms that I'm handing it all over to a Higher Power when I don't believe that Higher Power exists?

I've got no beef with God, or what my rock'n'roll chums call The Mainman, I just have this eerie feeling His work is wasted on me. In truth I've been feeling this for some time; in fact I've always felt the absence of the Mainman in my life, and maybe I just came clean about it for the first time in years, this morning at the side of the road.

For a long time I couldn't completely put down this Higher Power jazz because, in the rooms, you're too anxious to stay sober. In the rooms such a bad thought, such a dangerous vision, can terrify you like the thought of giving up drink did when you were out there every night. You hold firm and then it just drifts away.

It's not drifting away any more. In fact as I stand here in this bar, looking for a drink like anyone else, I can't quite understand how I could have stayed in the rooms for so long; I actually feel embarrassed that I've spent seven years listening to people mouthing about a Higher Power, like we used to mumble the prayers at Mass when we knew no better. I think of all the hassle I gave Jamaica over the drink and now I figure she's got good reason to be finished with me. It seems to me, as this revelation dawns, that there isn't much wrong with her, but there's most certainly something wrong with me, that I swallow every line I hear in the rooms and feed it back to her like it's gold, like that line I gave her when she wanted me to have two or three drinks with her, and I said two or three is the worst of all, it just makes you want to have nine or ten. And now I guess Jamaica was right to wonder what exactly is so wrong about a relatively healthy rock'n'roller having nine or ten anyway? Or eleven or twelve if it comes to that? What if the only thing wrong with him, is that he's not big enough to drink and take the consequences? Yes, that's why Jamaica is blowing me out. And that's OK. That's OK. That's OK.

What kind of a fool was I?

I want to call her right now, from the pay-phone in the pub, and tell her I can drink again and it's cool and to get her ass over here straight away. I'm thinking now that maybe she just had a couple of drunken one-night stands with Mikey, maybe once at Christmas and again last night. I want her to leave Mikey up there now, with his first rejection.

So she kept me away from the big house because she was superstitious?

Very superstitious.

I want to call her right now.

No, I'll do it when I get to the island. I'm a bit down on myself right now, giving myself a hard time, another bad habit I picked up in the rooms. I want this day all to myself, and I want the night too, for as long as it lasts. I want to prove I can drink and not wake up feeling crucified with guilt and fear and sickness. I want to prove I can drink this first drink because I haven't exactly done it yet, I'm crossing the line in principle, but I haven't actually put that drink inside me, I haven't officially had a slip.

I can still turn back, me and Roy can still have the World Cup we once intended, clean and sober. But he's on his way back to Manchester and I've already landed on this barstool, so it's getting down to the wire.

I settle myself on the bar-stool and it feels like I'm home from the war. It feels right, in this harbour bar, to say 'I'll have a pint, please'. I am already half-drunk on the smell of beer from the lounge, where maybe half-a-dozen drinkers, mostly on pints of Guinness, are watching Sky News. These men with their brokendown fishermen's faces never bothered themselves with thoughts of addiction, let alone received thirty days of residential treatment for it. They're just men, drinking and smoking and watching the news. They're just men.

And that's all I am, after seven years of sobriety and rooms. And that'll do me for now, as I give the signal to the barman and say the words I've been preparing all the way over on the bike, in what I hope is a nonchalant tone, while my stomach turns over inside me.

"Have you Macardles ale?"

The barman thinks about it. He's about twenty years older than me. His cardigan is about twenty years older again. He's thinking about it. Jesus is he going to refuse me?

Of course he's not, it's just when you've been preaching about drink for seven years, you're like a teenager again, convinced that everyone is looking at you aghast, when you walk into a pub.

"Macardles," he says. "They don't make it any more."

"Smithwicks then," I say.

He pulls the pint and places it in front of me without a word. It's like he knows I shouldn't be doing this. It's like he's seen right through me.

I hand him a ten euro note.

"Keane is out walking the dog," he says.

"Jesus," I say.

"Back in Manchester, walking the dog."

I raise the pint of Smithwicks.

"There's still time," I say, although I know it isn't true.

The smell of the beer hits me, starting a flood of remembrance and a promise of sweet release. I'm ordering a beer instead of a whiskey because I doubt if my alcohol-free system could stand the first belt of the whiskey, and the beer has sentimental value, it brings me back to the first one I ever had.

I put the pint back down on the counter, to admire it, the full pint standing there, a lovely dark red pint with the white head still intact and the waft of it imploring me to just pick it up again and drink it. Ah, that first taste is going to be astonishing, beautiful. I'm fifteen again, with my life in front of me. Except this time I have the advantage of knowing how it all turned out.

I sit here dicing with the drink, elbows down on the bar counter, a nice bit of old-fashioned white formica that seems almost traditional to me next to the overall rustic ambiance about which I have my doubts. I find it a bit cold, a bit fake.

But this bare old-style section, with the white formica counter, feels like it's for elite drinkers, or drinkers with special needs, call us what you will. At this smooth white bar counter, I can immerse myself in my old ways, I can rekindle the desire, surrender to the black seduction of the booze. I am back at the altar where I worshipped for so long.

We're in semi-darkness here, day or night. I had forgotten how wonderful it feels, just to sit in a darkened pub in the middle of the afternoon, with a drink in front of me. Any good pub you enter, anywhere in Ireland, gives you this feeling straight away, this feeling of peace that you get when you walk into a chapel during the day. I'm here again in the half-light, the artificial glow of the pumps with the logos a bit spruced up since last I gazed upon them, Heineken, Smithwicks, Budweiser, Beamish, Kilkenny, a new one on me. I can reach out and touch them like I'm performing some holy ritual; I can see myself doing it in an oblong mirror behind the bar, which seems to have been put there specially for me. I can see myself without flinching, facing my true nature. And next to this, on the wall behind the bar, they've pasted a load of banknotes from around the world. They've got tickets to Premiership football matches, and the Champions League quarter-final between Man United and Porto which, I recall, United won 4-0. Yes, I have been stone cold sober for much of this glorious era of theirs, the Keane era.

And then the optics, Powers whiskey, Cork Dry Gin, Smirnoff vodka, Hennessy brandy, the basic hard stuff for the hard guys here in the bar, probably there's a long line of them when you turn the corner into the lounge, bottles of tequila and Bacardi and a hundred varieties of alcopops, which have undoubtedly become more common in the west of Ireland since I was last here, freely drinking. Or maybe just free.

Yes, freedom is a thing on which I have mused much these past seven years. In the rooms, it seemed plain to me that a sober man has the freedom to drink or not to drink, he just exercises the option not to drink. But a drunk man, while seeming to be more free, actually has no option except to drink, in any conceivable situation in which he might find himself. With this pint in front of me, making me weak, I feel that I may be shutting down a lot of options for a long time, like going to the theatre or the cinema or meeting people for coffee or buying CDs. But all that aside, the one option I'm leaving myself is still looking pretty irresistible at this precise moment.

There's an old television to my left, switched off permanently, it seems, all the action now on the big screen inside in the lounge, the one with Sky News that I can just about hear from this spot, watching the men watching it as they drink and smoke.

Their smoke is reaching me in here and drawing me in there to a cigarette machine. Or maybe out here in the west they still sell you smokes behind the bar. Anyway, I think I'm going to have a cigarette to go along with this drink. I think I'm going to have my first cigarette in three years. I think so.

The two always went together for me, and when I stopped drinking, I kept smoking for a few years, but it was never the same. I needed them badly when I first went into the rooms, just to keep at least one addiction going full blast, to comfort myself when the cravings got terrible. And it's a fact that a lot of guys in the rooms smoke, the AA has no position on that, it's strictly the booze that's verboten; a simple position, which is probably why the rooms have been going for so long.

But I figured it would be easier to give up the smokes if you were off the drink, just because you had the experience of giving something up, of losing something wonderful in your life. And I did it without much bother, to tell the truth, it was like the smoking side of me had lost the will to live when it was deprived of alcohol, its constant companion.

I remember now the first smoke I had, when I was seventeen, at a party drinking a bottle of Harp, and someone offered me a Rothman's and I just smoked it and it nearly blew my head off. I think I want that to happen to me again, now that I'm losing my faith. And to those who still have the faith, I'm saying here now, it's one view of the world, that's all, and there are other views of the world, like the one I'm coming round to in this cosy bar after seven years in the rooms doing all the right things, at the end of which I'm homeless and broke and Roy Keane won't play for us in the World Cup and none of these things in itself has me here with this beer in front of me feeling the stirring of some forgotten ecstasy. Because I've got bigger problems that I can hardly name and one that I can, one called Jamaica.

I reckon it's worth having this drink and a few more, just to see if it sets off the old spark with her. We've had the two of us sober, and me sober with her drunk, but we never tried the two of us drunk. We can still put that right.

We're made of the same stuff, me and Jamaica. Though with the smell of this beer drugging me, I'm starting to doubt any opinion formed and any agreement reached during my sober years.

Again this bad, bad thought comes to me that Jamaica has known about Camden Town all along, that she's been looking at me for months in that horrible light, that she's been drinking on it. But I'll hold that bad, bad thought until I'm a bit more relaxed.

What other strangeness is about to enter my head on this day? What about this?

On the opening night of 'Jack Rooney' I'll be able to drink. I'll be able to stand in the foyer nursing a whiskey sour. The weirdest things worry you when you're sober, you are assailed by the strangest fears, like how will you be able to stay off the booze when it's all razzle dazzle on your Broadway opening night?

Now this fear is going, in fact it's gone. And I'm really, really curious to know how my songs will sound after a few drinks. I only know them sober. I only hear them with my head full of AA. I strongly suspect that the show won't happen for me because I've been thinking too cautiously, and living too cautiously. I need an extra ten per cent from somewhere.

I need a smoke.

I'll be able to drink on the opening night, but I'll have to go outside the theatre to smoke.

You might think I'm losing my nerve here, but I think I'll get a packet of cigarettes now, and have my first smoke in three years, and then the drink. The overture and then the opening number.

I realise this pint is going flat waiting for me to come through, but I've waited a long time too, 7 years, 122 days, 16 hours and 18 minutes by the pub clock. I need everything to be right.

I get off my stool and push through the adjoining door and into the lounge. Again I feel like everyone is looking at me, like I'm underage and shouldn't be here, but that's the acute sensitivity of a man fresh from the rooms. They're all following the breaking news about Roy as I go to the bar and say to the guy with the cardigan, "change for the machine, please."

He's still looking at Roy walking the dog on Sky.

"Cigarettes behind the bar," he says.

I take out a tenner.

"Thanks," I say.

He seems irritated.

"What cigarettes?" he says.

I'm so out of practice, the basic bar room etiquette has become so alien to me, I don't know what brand I want.

"Ahhhh, Marlboro," I mumble, about 95 per cent of my bar room dignity gone in that childish hesitation.

He slides the packet to me and I pick it up cleanly, thank God. He takes the tenner and he gives me the change, still mostly looking at Roy. The change consists of a few small coins, but I'm careful not to seem surprised, like I have just arrived from the last century, when you could have a full night's drinking and smoking and a four-course meal with wine for ten pee. I also need to tell this man that I need a new head on the Smithwicks, it's gone a little flat. But I feel like too much of a chump.

"Thanks," I say.

"Thanks," he says, in a manner that sounds almost friendly to me, picking up every vibration. And then he returns to the far more important scene of Roy walking the dog, who is called Triggs.

Everyone knows that now; everyone in this pub knows the name of Roy Keane's dog. They don't know me at all, as far as I can tell, though there was a point in our respective careers when Roy was with Forest, when I was slightly better known than him. Maybe for a few weeks, maybe just for that night on Top Of The Pops.

One more time I tell myself , maybe Roy saw us that night on Top Of The Pops, as he skulled a morose pint of lager in some pub near Trent Bridge, and thought, there's a crowd of Irish lads doing well for themselves, fuck them. Maybe the sight of us entering the charts at number 18 and poncing around like that, put the iron in his soul. These fantasies have a way of worming back into your mind like an old riff. Start me up. I'm going back to my spot. My quarters. I've got a fresh packet of Marlboro now and a not-so-fresh pint of Smithwicks.

This gives me a chance to get out of here sober. You could call it a sign, a personal intervention from the god of drink to one of his old disciples, a message in the garbled code of the booze, which goes something like this: I ordered a drink but I didn't partake; I had bad thoughts but I didn't do anything; and now the drink is starting to go flat, it sets me thinking that maybe this is not the day for it; the least I owe myself, after seven years off it, is a fresh drink; but that means asking for another with nothing gone out of the first one, and I don't want to be putting anyone to any trouble, or drawing attention to myself – but I don't want this bad pint either.

Not that it's bad exactly, it's probably perfectly drinkable, but if it's your first one in more than seven years, you want it more than just drinkable.

So I'm tap-dancing like this and thinking that the force is not with me, because I just can't bring myself to knock this drink back.

I still intend to drink it, I'm just having trouble picking up the glass. I think I could sit here with my hands on my knees all day just looking at it, and for someone who's coming from the rooms, that's what you might call a challenge. But it's still not a crime, of course, and as far as I'm concerned it's not a slip either, just to be looking at a drink and desiring it, frozen in this state of alcoholic suspense.

And now as I sit in this harbour bar and it's getting towards the time to leave for the island, I have another thought. A better thought.

I won't go to the island tonight. I don't feel like it now, and I certainly won't feel like it when I've had this drink. I will need some time to reflect on this momentous occasion, which I won't really be able to do on a heaving old boat with a load of sober people. I'll be having this drink here, and I'll stay for the duration. In this bar, it somehow doesn't feel right to be leaving.

I'm shattered now. My head is still too full of the rooms, even on this day when I have finally faced up to the truth, and gone with it. I'll loiter here, and I'll figure out later where to stay for the night; I'm wiped out as I sit staring at the formaica and remembering all the gibberish we tell ourselves just to stay sober. And for what?

I think I should be lecturing in universities and appearing on talkshows telling people the things I know now, just like all those twelve-stepping guys, who seem to be on a permanent tour like Dylan, except unlike him, they've got it all wrong.

But I'm wired now, this trip to the island would be wasted on me, this harbour bar is where it must happen.

I think I am here for the night. I am going to have a drink here and miss the boat, and that's OK. To miss the boat is OK.

But first I am going to have a smoke. Just to get me in the mood, to get some of that old corruption into my blood.

I don't want Marlboro, I want Rothman's. I signal to the barman and I ask him for a packet of Rothman's instead and a box of matches. I unwrap the packet in a fever.

I light the cigarette and I inhale. It nearly blows my head off, exactly like that Rothman's did when I was 17. For a moment I think I'm going to pass out, but I hold it together. It will be easier from now on.

And anyway I'm not 17 any more, I'm a man. Which is another fine thought to take with me to the island tomorrow. I'm a man and I'm going to enjoy that drink properly.

I'm not going to slug it back here like some demented adolescent and then run like a lunatic to catch the boat. I'm a man and I can sit here all night, drinking at my leisure. I'm a man just like these other men, and this is what we do on a Saturday night.

I take another lungful of Rothman's. It feels so bad for me I am almost ecstatic, I luxuriate in it. I am going to smoke forty cigarettes a day again, sixty when I'm out drinking.

The barman asks me if I'm getting the boat, because it's leaving now, and I say "no, I'm getting it tomorrow."

But I am going to drink again, and that's OK.

I am going to the island for the World Cup tomorrow and I am going to drink and drink and drink.

I'll have a good run at it tomorrow, I'll start early and I'll finish late, or whenever they finish drinking on the island, if they ever do.

"Tomorrow," I repeat to the barman.

He comes back a few moments later and puts a fresh pint in front of me. He explains that a couple of lads in the lounge recognise me from way back. They want to show their appreciation.

I feel humbled by this. I saw no-one in there who looked like a fan of the band; in my shallow way, they just looked like country people to me. I take this gesture as the final signal from the baleful gods that somehow it was meant to be, that I am doing the right thing here, yes, that I am in the right place.

"Tell them thanks," I say to the barman.

"Sure," he says, with a small smile.

"Tell them I'll be here for a while," I say.

"Alright so," he says.

I watch him wiping the counter in front of me, removing the flat pint and the cigarette wrapping. I lift the cold glass of fresh beer. I wait until he ambles back into the lounge. I take the drink.

Seventeen

It doesn't quite pack the same wallop as it did when I was 15, but it's better now, in a way. I feel in charge of the situation. I have the knowledge, and knowledge is power, as they say out here in the world. In the rooms we just admitted that we were powerless over alcohol, that the accumulated knowledge of a hundred million alcoholics was as nothing if you went out there again, if you had a slip.

Well, here I am slipping through my first pint in over seven years and it's taking me exactly where I want to go. I'm taking it very slowly. I respect this stuff now, I don't care if it takes me an hour to get through this first one, I'm in charge here.

I'm doing this for me, but I'm doing it too for all the suffering alcoholics everywhere, to prove that there is hope, that a man can take a drink without the drink taking the man. I feared it would make me drunk straight away, but the experience is too solemn for that; there is reverence in each sip and in the feeling of freedom that is coursing slowly through me.

I don't think I could get drunk tonight even if I tried. I think I will stay on the pints, maybe no more than three or four, stretched over the evening, a gentle re-entry to this planet I thought I would never see again.

Spontaneity, that's the thing you miss most. Just that sense of chucking it all, of changing your plans, of talking to strangers. Talking rubbish, we say in the rooms, as we bang on about a Higher Power that we happen to know isn't there.

But I don't want to be dissing the guys in the rooms, I never wanted that; I'd just like a few of them to be here with me tonight, having a slip and not minding it.

Not minding it at all.

I might never see some of those guys again. I might never see Theo again. It's an amazing thing that. The world of drink exists entirely apart from the world of not-drinking, and between these separate spheres there is mutual incomprehension and terror.

I'd be afraid to meet those guys now because I can't go back there, and they would be afraid to meet me, because I'm going to make this work and they'd not be able to handle that. So if I do go back to the village in the hills or to Café-En-Seine, they'll avoid me, they'll avoid the bars, they'll stick to their jargon, they'll say if you keep going to the barber you're bound to get a haircut, to which I would say, maybe you need a haircut. Maybe that's exactly what you need, buddy.

I take the final one-third of the pint into the lounge with me.

I get a signal of recognition from a couple of men sitting in the centre of the lounge, heavily-built men in Ireland jerseys who look about fifty to me, who look like they have had hard lives. My fans.

I join them. They introduce themselves as Martin and Barry, but I forget their names almost immediately. I remind myself that I always forget names, drunk or sober, so this is no indication at all that the drink might be getting to me. It's just me. It's just life.

I thank them for the drink and order three more pints from the bar, two Guinness for them, another Smithwicks for me, another quiet drink. We all seem too big for the low stools we are sitting on, and the low table, but I don't want to sound like a prat by asking them to move to a more comfortable spot, and anyway I'm already feeling more comfortable with my body.

They still seem too broad, I seem too tall, but I imagine they've endured worse over the years since I was a star. Though I never really was a star.

I start my second drink, thinking that this is what happens to people; they work at rotten jobs and they have hard lives while people like me are writing tuners and banging women called Jamaica. These guys probably think that Eugene O'Neill used to work for Ryanair, and why not?

I am really moved now, I get quite a lump in the throat, when it emerges, halfway down the second pint, that they followed the band a lot. They can tell me about gigs I can't rightly recall myself; there was one in the Leisureland in Galway when they were students, a week before we appeared on Top Of The Pops, that was a real humdinger. I still can't recall it.

They must be about the same age as me, they just seem older, but then I've been having early nights for seven years, while they've been out enjoying themselves. And I can't see how they were ever students; they look like labourers, and it turns out that's what they are, or were. They're builders now, probably millionaires, the type who have so much money they're beyond caring about what they look like, wearing Ireland jerseys and drinking all day. They went working on the buildings in London one summer, the pair of them together, and never went back to university. They saw me over in London too, in the Hammersmith Palais. I tell them I remember that because Elvis Costello came backstage to meet us that night.

I am basking in their respect as I let the second pint do what it's supposed to do.

And the respect is mutual, I can tell I've hit up with a couple of free men who are already starting to talk about continuing the night in Galway, and about whores.

And as I'm reaching the end of my second pint, feeling right, feeling strong, feeling about as happy as I've ever felt in my life, we start to argue about Roy Keane. A very civil discussion, as it happens; these guys know their stuff, they are bright men.

They think Keane is the guilty party. I don't make a big deal about it because I'll probably be thinking that too, when I hit my next mood-swing on the subject.

I guess before the end of the night I'll also be telling them that this is no ordinary drinking night for me, but at the moment I'm just immersing myself in this feeling of normality, in the idea that nothing bad is going to happen, indeed nothing much will happen at all, except we'll probably go to Galway in Martin's car, or Barry's car, and have a few more and maybe get a hotel room and get us a few whores.

Which is exactly what we decide to do. And it's not until we are leaving through the front bar in which I had my first drink, that I remember the Suzuki. I see I have left Eddie's helmet on the ground beside the barstool. I pick it up and confess to my new buddies that I have a motorbike with me. Will I follow behind them on the road to Galway? No, I'm not used to motorbikes, I might crash and wrongly attribute it to the booze.

But I savour this moment in my new drinking life, this first scene of forgetfulness. As we leave the harbour bar, I can feel a lovely wave of amnesia washing over me. I feel unencumbered again, like the last twenty years didn't happen at all, and I can seize the future, starting tonight.

Then I can seize Jamaica, starting tomorrow. Oh, what a time we will have. She'll be crazy about Galway. Oh, how we will laugh at how she left Mikey up in Wicklow in a pool of his own vomit, to be with a man who can hold his drink.

Vomit is stirring somewhere deep down inside me as the car speeds towards Galway, a big comfortable car, a Rover, I think. I'm not good on cars.

But I just roll down the window a little, and I'm fine. And the lads are giving me strength too, with their insistence that I'll be quite a trophy for them, that with a famous face like me, they might even pick up a couple of women for free.

The banter encourages me to ask them if they know anyone who wants to buy a motorbike. Maybe I'm not sounding too subtle about it, because straight away Barry offers me a grand for the Suzuki. Four hundred in cash now, the rest tomorrow.

It is a beautiful summer night and I feel sanctified, I am emerging at last from the rooms, from a bleak world in which men lose all their spontaneity, all their power to make wonderful gestures like

this: four hundred now, the rest tomorrow. And I get another gush of well-being about the World Cup starting in a few day's time, the whole country wandering around in a blissful haze of alcohol, the pubs open all night for the matches starting at seven o'clock in the morning.

The sun is going down as we speed past the stone walls on the road to Galway. Even as a child there was always some part of me that wanted to escape to Galway, to take the night train across the country and let myself go. And I respond with this primitive joy to the sunset, I think back nostalgically to festivals we played in the west, the free bar in the marquee, the beer in plastic cups. I tap Barry on the shoulder.

"You don't by any chance want to invest in a musical?" I say. And I tell them all about 'Jack Rooney' for the rest of the journey, and as we are walking through Galway, and as we push our way into a pub with an Irish name on the front I am still talking the talk.

This is the real stuff now, the frenzy. We're throwing pints into us, then squeezing through the crush at the bar, ordering two at a go. Then we're ordering large whiskies just to save time and hassle. I mix mine well with water, working my way through nearly half-a-pint of the diluted Powers, though I can still get a blast of the old firewater underneath it all.

I push my way through to the toilet. It's so strange again to be standing at a urinal with drunk guys on either side of me, guys who look about fifteen years younger then me, who maybe need a break from it like I did, before coming back to it, except in control this time, like I am doing.

By the time we get to the night-club, with the two lads jokingly using my fame to ensure entry, we have a full night's drink in us and we're ready for wine. I have Barry's four hundred in my pocket now, but the boys won't let me buy anything; they say they couldn't have got in without me, and now all I have to do is sit there being attractive to women.

'Oh What A Night' by Frankie Valli and the Four Seasons, causes a rush to the dancefloor. The song pierces my heart. I am young again and I will never grow old.

I am overwhelmed with a feeling of love and happiness, probably on some higher plane of ecstasy known only to mystics, but still aware in the pit of my being that I can't totally let myself go, that this is a shock to my system, that I'm like a Beirut hostage coming out of years of sensory deprivation into some riot of drink and sex and music, from the Hezbollah to Frankie Valli and the Four Seasons with nothing in between.

In fact I think I'm handling it pretty well. Apart from banging on a bit too much about the tuner, I reckon this is me at my drinking best. I remember now why I loved it in the first place, after dwelling on the downside for far too long.

It occurs to me that I haven't eaten all day, and that it never seemed to cross the lads' minds either, which is how it should be on a night like this. It doesn't bother me, it might only make me puke with all the excitement and I would probably blame the drink again for some perverse reason, rather than the food.

I can see the lads dancing, pointing me out to women, using me shamelessly. I marvel at their sense of freedom, I am convinced now that they're millionaires who have dedicated themselves to guilt-free enjoyment of the masculine pleasures, and if they have a few ex-wives and families about the place, they can probably look after all that too without getting too morose about it. They just have that look about them, that lightness that you miss so much in the company of self-flagellating alcoholics.

But I won't join them on the dancefloor. I prefer to just sit drinking glass after glass of red wine, listening to the music, connecting with the madness, loving it all.

And no, I'm not going to end up being butt-fucked by the lads, like Ned Beatty in 'Deliverance'. I'm not going to be sent crashing through this window onto the pavement below, breaking my legs and my skull and causing massive internal injuries which will force me to drink through a straw for the next seven years. I'm not going to get off with some sixty-year old woman who looks seventy-five in the morning light. I'm going to do nothing except sit here drinking and having a wonderful time tonight. I'm not going to argue about Roy Keane, I'm not going to argue about anything.

I know too much.

Eighteen

I wake up in a plain brown room in a small hotel in a side street in Galway. The details are written on a receipt that I can see on the dressing table of this monastic place. I think it's in Dominick Street, but I don't care really.

The man who got us in here after the night club is lying beside me, his naked back turned to me. I can't remember his name at first and then it comes back to me, it's Barry. Barry!

And Martin is the big heap lying on the floor with a brown bedspread over him, sleeping it off. Or maybe it's the other way 'round, I was never any good with names.

I turn away from Martin's bare back as I recollect that we're all in this brown room because it's the only room available and because the late-night receptionist did us a favour, letting us in at all. I have a brutal hangover in the form of a pounding head and an appalling thirst. I roll out of the bed and run into the bathroom to fill myself with water straight from the tap. Now I'm giddy, mad with the hunger. Just like old times. I wish I had something for the headache, something to numb the power drill that's driving the sweat out through my forehead with the ferocity of its assault.

I pull on my clothes. I see myself in the mirror. I look glassy-eyed and unshaven, but there's nothing ugly to show for the escapade, no cuts or bruises. I need to think for a minute and then I need to have an enormous breakfast or I will become delirious with the hunger.

I think, I did it. I went drinking last night and I survived. No, I thrived. I feel like a poisoned pup right now, but this too will pass. And looking at the boys stretched here comatose, I guess it's not a pretty scene – but we did no harm and we can pay the bill and once we're elbows down again at the bar of The Quays, we won't really care about this difficult start to the day. We'll just feel like students, except we have money to buy drink.

So, I'm not surprised at how rough I feel coming down for breakfast; it's not exactly a mystery to people like me that you might feel a bit woozy after a night's drinking and clubbing following seven years in the rooms. No, I had that one sussed without consulting the manual.

And the physical sensation of my first hangover in living memory suggests that there has been too little variety in my life, that you need to wake up feeling rough sometimes in order to appreciate the upside. Otherwise it's like they say; you'll wake up knowing that this is as good as you're going to feel all day. So you need a variety of experiences. Hell, you just need experiences.

I am first into the dining room. It's only now I check the time, it's only now I figure it's Sunday. Sunday morning coming down.

It's eight-thirty, I could have had another hour in bed before breakfast, even if it was with a large naked man who is probably still pumped full of raw, untreated lust from last night.

It's only eight-thirty; my body-clock is still set to sober time. I flash the girl a big gaucho grin and ask for the scrambled eggs. "And a leetle glass of champagne?" I say, in a Mexican style that hangs on the morning air with a slightly embarrassing note.

She says she'll check it out, and I say that's good enough for me.

I light a cigarette, the first of the day to celebrate the achievement of waking up alive.

The girl is back quickly with a miniature bottle of champagne and a glass of orange juice. I am hugely impressed. This country seems to have finally gotten it together on the old catering front, since last I was in the hangover-curing game.

I mix the champagne and the orange juice. The first gulp takes the edge off the sick head.

Then I knock it all back, and I'm ready to eat breakfast. Again I'm being conservative, ordering scrambled eggs, for me the most digestible way of cooking them. I've balked up at the sight of a few runny ones in my time;

just the look of them seems to trigger a sudden heave.

I chance another little bottle of champagne, and I silently toast Jamaica, with whom I hope to have many sparkling drinks before our time is through. I know she'd be in bed with Mikey at this moment, but she's not usually horny first thing, unless of course it's with me. And anyway I don't care.

I want to call her right now. I ring from the phone-box in the hotel and Jamaica answers straight away. She lets out a big sigh of relief when she hears my voice. Then she tells me that Jason O'Brien is dead. He fell from the 21st floor of an apartment block over there in New York, during a party. Poor Jason. They've had trouble tracking down everyone he knows, she just got the call late last night, but anyway he's been brought to Dundrum church, in Dublin this evening, funeral tomorrow.

Jamaica sounds very together, like she's organising the whole thing. She says she hopes to see me at the removal and she needs to meet me afterwards out at her place. Our coterie, the rock'n'roll troubadors, are heading for the village, for Jamaica's place. To trawl through the memories together. To do the man justice.

Poor Jason. She'd love to talk more now, but she's got to round up all the troops, she's got another fifty lunatics to contact. The way she's running this show, you'd think there's a lot of goodness in her, and you'd probably be right.

I slump in the phone-box, remembering that riff of ours about all the drinking we'd done, me and Jason, how the days on the bottle become months and then years, until one day you add it all up and you discover you've spent more than half your life in the old battle-cruiser, or generally under the influence.

I know that riff so well, it reminds me of Jason most fondly; we gave a blast of it to all our mates who came into the pub until we knew it backways, and still we kept at it. It came back to me the first time Jamaica mentioned Jason's name on the phone from New York, and it comes back to me now word-perfect, like a well-remembered lament, like the reprise of a big number in a tuner...

We were uncorking a few at the mixing desk of our old studio at about five in the morning, reminiscing, when I put it to Jason that Jimmy Carter was President of the United States when the two of us started to drink seriously, and so this riff started. We had been drinking from the time of the Carter administration, through to the end of Bill Clinton's first term. Three Republican administrations had come and gone, and we were still out there. When we started, James Callaghan was still leader of the Labour Party in Britain, and Tony Blair played in a rock'n'roll band. We drank steadily through the entire Thatcher era and deep into the time of John Major. We were drinking at the time of the Falklands War, the Iran-Iraq War, Reagan's dirty war in Nicaragua and El Salvador, the first Gulf War, the war in the former Yugoslavia, and a sizeable chunk of the war in Northern Ireland.

Jason did the sound for us at beer-maddened benefit gigs for the release of Nelson Mandela, when the prospect of Mandela ever getting out seemed remote. Indeed, for about the last ten years of Mandela's imprisonment on Robben Island, our drinking became progressively alcoholic.

We saw the Ayatollah Khomeini coming and going in a haze of booze, we were in a pub when we heard of the death of Pope John Paul 1, in fact we still believe the man was murdered in his bed. And we were drunk for much of the Pontificate of his successor Pope John Paul 2.

Comrade Leonid Brezhnev was still king-of-the-world around the time we were moving from Macardle's ale to something a bit stronger. We carried on, oblivious, still broadly sympathetic to the Soviet Union until eventually we witnessed the collapse of Communism and the fall of the Berlin Wall. Which we celebrated in the only way we knew how.

We drank through five World Cups, in Argentina, Spain, Mexico, Italy, and the USA. We drank through the entire career of Diego Maradona, from his emergence as a teenage prodigy and on through the glory years in Italy with Napoli and on again to immortality against England in Mexico, until they got him in the end, banishing him from the Argentina squad on drugs charges. And, at the end of it, we figured we were holding it together better than he was.

Five World Cups and five Olympic Games. In fact when we started,

Athletics was still purportedly an amateur sport and the world record for the 100 metres was still over 10 seconds, but we watched them whittle it down over the years, raising our glasses to each new landmark in human achievement.

Meanwhile, immersed in alcohol, we went through a seemingly endless world recession and enjoyed the boom that followed. We saw Japan rising to become an economic superpower, and then falling back to where it started, and we took it all in our boozy stride. When we joined the drinking ranks there was virtually no such thing as a video recorder. By the time the old hooch was catching up on us, we were roaring uncontrollably down the information superhighway.

We got through punk rock, new wave, powerpop, the New Romantic movement, Live Aid, World Music, raggle-taggle, grunge, Britpop, hip-hop, house, and hard house. We saw Ireland winning the Eurovision Song Contest seven times. And we never stopped drinking, we just gave it a rest from time to time, to get us up for it again.

We were going on three-day benders before MTV was invented. By our best estimate, we had not been properly sober for approximately 750 episodes of Top of the Pops, apart from the one on which I actually appeared. We saw U2's early gigs on Saturday afternoons at the Dandelion Market, drunk.

In fact Elvis Presley was still alive, just about, when alcohol was starting to play a significant part in our lives. And so was John Lennon.

We riffed like this, Jason and I, until the dawn was breaking outside the old studio and the early houses on the quays were opening. It was maybe the last great night we had together.

Poor Jason, I whisper.

But what I'm really thinking is, poor me.

I had my heart set on another day's drinking here in Galway, but now I must tear myself away from it for a day of grief.

Poor Jason. It's hitting me now, I loved that guy. And he saw me as his shining light.

Which goes to show you never can tell.

No doubt if I was still on the wagon, I'd already be judging this as yet another example of how the hooch will always get you in the end somehow. But I'm off the wagon and this morning it feels as if I'm staying off it. So I won't judge my old buddy, who so nearly got away with it, I'll just take myself off to the train station.

The lads seem heartbroken to lose me so early in the day. I tell them there's no need to get out of bed, I just have to go. They offer me outpourings of sympathy and compassion. And as we high-five for the last time, Martin tells me to give him a shout about that musical, he's seriously interested in investing in it. And I believe him. Even if his name is Barry, which it may well be.

"It was a long day's journey into night," I say, trying a long shot.

"Eugene O'Neill," Barry mutters, filling me with joy. I leave that brown room certain that my tuner is going to happen, and that we'll all be able to get blind drunk at the opening night. Then I feel sick that Jason won't be at it; Jason was always sweeping into the lobby in my vision of the opening night, with his beautiful new girlfriend.

I get a seat in the smoking carriage. Happily no one sits beside me. I like a little space on a train, especially when I'm up and down the aisle availing of the bar facilities. I start drinking as soon as the bar opens, about half-an-hour outside Galway, and once I'm off there's no stopping me.

Drinking on trains was always a speciality of mine. Some folks love drinking on planes, but I always loved drinking on trains, gin and tonics for some reason, two miniatures and one mixer at a time, and loads of ice. Repeat according to taste.

I'm having the first one while we're still about twenty miles away from Athlone, and it hits me like a jab of fine poison, a thousand volts of the mother's ruin juddering through me; I'm definitely back in business, already blasting through that first hangover and drilling for the next one. I'm getting annoyed that I haven't a Walkman with me. I always used to love Bob Seger on the Walkman singing 'Roll Me Away', looking at rural Ireland out there though gin-filled eyes.

I'm smoking constantly, like one of those laboratory dogs you used to see in the Sunday People.

Would Jason still be alive if he had stayed in the rooms? I can't avoid this question. As a born-again drinker I aim to be as honest as I can. Two days ago I would have thought it was a silly question. Now I see that Jason could have met his Maker in a thousand ways, drunk or sober, and it's only guys like me in the rooms who would call it otherwise. Like, how the fuck do I know, how does anyone know?

The Reaper isn't running a temperance crusade, he doesn't smell your breath before he takes you on board the River Styx express. Maybe the drink kept Jason alive all this time, maybe he nipped into Mulligan's on 7th Avenue for fourteen or fifteen drinks one night and, as a result, missed getting beaten and raped and decapitated by a bunch of bastards who had been waiting for him and his beautiful new girlfriend. Who knows these things?

As the train pulls out of Athlone, I know I want another couple of gins. I know I'll be nicely oiled by the time I get to Dublin, then I'll get a taxi at the station and maybe have another one or two in Mulligan's to renew old acquaintances, then a taxi out to the church in Dundrum, for the grim business of mourning my man Jason.

It's not the worst way to go, falling off a balcony like that. It might be the ultimate buzz as you fall, and then splat, you're history. I know this because when I was fourteen I spent the summer looking at my aunt dying, puking up green cancer into a bucket, because she insisted on looking at Wimbledon on the telly. I would pull the curtains and we'd watch the tennis and I'd empty her bucket of cancer into the toilet and it would begin again.

And it happened like that, because that was the only place I could watch the tennis. Hers was the only house with BBC. It seemed to make sense at the time. I need hardly add that she never touched alcohol. So maybe if she did, she'd have gone like Jason twenty years before she got cancer, and gone a lot happier.

I am radiantly happy with gin as the train pulls into Dublin. If I get another five years out of my dodgy liver, then I'll settle for that if it means I can drink on trains again. So many times I arrived drunk at this old station. Now, at last, I think I know what I'm doing. Maybe I just know my own nature better, maybe that's what the rooms have given to me, the inner knowledge that I am basically a man who must drink in order to be even remotely happy for any part of the day.

I head straight for the taxi at boozing speed, that extra yard of pace again. Am I repeating myself? Never mind. In a few minutes I'm in the old bar of Mulligan's with a pint of Guinness on the counter. Guinness always went well on top of gin for me, for some reason. Some fathomless reason.

I sip the Guinness. It is exquisite, almost unbearably bitter. Almost, but not quite. I get this deeply strange suspicion that I am going to start crying. I guess the shock of Jason's death is hitting me now, in that second wave, and my body is still adjusting to the new regime. No doubt all sorts of interesting stuff will be oozing from me until I get straightened out.

It's early afternoon and I'll need to be getting out of here soon to make the service. But I get the feeling, all of a sudden, that I'm not going to make it. No, I don't think I can make it now, I really don't.

And I don't think it would be right anyway to arrive out there with a cargo on board. And ultimately I'm sure Jason would want me to remember him this way, the few pints here in Mulligan's, like I'm just waiting for him to drop in at any moment and say it's alright.

I recall this mutual friend of ours who died young in a drinking accident, and I said to Jason it could have been any one of us, it happens a hundred times, and ninety-nine times you walk away from it. Nine-hundred-and-ninety nine-times, Jason said, and that was Jason, always raising the bar, always for him the benefit of the doubt.

I think I will phone Jamaica now, and then I think not. She'll still be rounding up the troops. I'll catch her later back at her place, like we arranged. She'll be cool about it, she's not a great one for the Christian rituals. Or not that I recall.

And once I've got my bearings again, after this mad couple of days, we'll see if the new me is more to her taste. I figure I can teach her things now, I've forgotten more about drink than Mikey will ever know. And she needs that and she knows she needs it.

She says she needs to see me. Need is good. And no matter how much

Guinness is sloshing inside of me tonight, I'll be better able for her then than I was yesterday morning, up at the gate lodge, pouring them red wine while they gutted me. And right now I can't figure out who should be more embarrassed about that, her or me? Me or her?

Me probably, for taking it. Me probably, for letting it get to that, for being too disgracefully sober to realise that Mikey, with his white teeth, was chewing her up.

It won't happen again. I'm back in town and I'm hot on the trail of drunk love. I think this could be the drunkest love of all, me and this woman with whom I have an ancient connection, certainly in this life, probably since the thirteenth century.

That's what I'll say to Mikey, I'll say 'Mikey, your trouble is, she met me in the thirteenth century. She only met you at a lig. Don't fight it'.

I drink another pint of Mulligan's finest. I run that little speech around in my head for about half-an-hour, jabbing at his chest in my mind's eye, saying 'Mikey, your trouble is, she met me in the thirteenth century, she only met you at a lig'.

That's what I'll say.

Nineteen

I'll be prepared.

As Roy put it, fail to prepare, prepare to fail.

I'll get out of Mulligan's now in the middle of the afternoon and get a taxi out to the village in Wicklow so I'll be set up in Regan's by the time the chief mourners arrive out.

A few more under my belt, and I'll be prepared for anything. Oh, how I have longed to sit in Regan's drinking pints, instead of being across the road with the boys in the rooms, not drinking pints.

Theo wanted it too, but he never made it across that road. He said we'd do it tomorrow.

As the taxi drops me at the door of the pub and I walk up to the bar of Regan's for the first time, I order a pint of Guinness and think to myself, this is tomorrow Theo, wish you were here.

I feel very close to Jason at this moment. I'm sure he'll be having a whale of a rock'n'roll send-off, some lovely Leonard Cohen stuff raising the rafters no doubt; maybe Leonard himself will do the honours. In which case I've got even heavier competition for Jamaica, if they're not out there in the woods already.

I never found my Zen master, my Higher Power or whatever it is that gives Leonard his voice, the stillness of his being, the songs that come out of self-knowledge and the knowledge of the world's most beautiful women. But Leonard, like me, has thought deeply about staying up all night drinking. He said that the first rebellious act that a man can perform is the refusal to sleep – to turn night into day, to revel, drink and womanise till the dawn, to triumph over time and death and the regenerative process with your mind and your will.

I did all that too. And then I found the rooms, where's there's a different form of rebellion going down, a counter rebellion. And now I'm rebelling again.

Turning night into day, revelling, drinking, womanising, like it was in the beginning.

The taxi-ride out here has freshened me up somewhat, I feel focussed again, not maudlin like I was getting in Mulligan's. Drink gives you that, it automatically cuts away all the stuff you don't need in your life, like funerals, like dinners, like someone else's motorbike.

But in all decency I think a minute's silence is appropriate to mourn someone else today, not just Jase, but that guy I left behind in the rooms, that other version of me...

It wasn't all bad, what happened when he was around. In fact much of it was good and true, and I probably wouldn't change it because it made me what I am today, whatever that is.

But some of it wasn't good and it wasn't true.

In vino veritas, as they said in ancient Rome, because even back then it seems that men couldn't bear thinking about all the things they'd done, without the vino to make them remember, and to make them forget again. Ah yes, to forget.

So I gave it a good shot in the rooms, but maybe not my best shot, because I was always holding something back. Stuff I would hardly admit to myself at dead of night, let alone to a room full of resting drunks. Let alone to Jamaica.

But I had certain standards during all that time, I had become better at the small things of life, and already I can feel that slipping away. For example, I don't think I'll bother cancelling that three weeks in Gray's Hotel; I doubt if those island folk are sitting up all night waiting for me to walk in. And the phone in Regan's seems to be permanently occupied.

Regan's is also lightening my load. It's unusually bright for a pub, but they've done it right, country-style, all pale blue and white wood which makes you feel soothed, not exposed. I'm focussed too, in my determination not to get involved in any discussions about Roy Keane with the crowd which is growing around me as I establish myself at the bar, lifting pints back to people who thank me from the bottom of their hearts.

I don't want this to get messy. Keane is doing people's heads in and a lot of them shouldn't be drinking on top of that, like they shouldn't drink on top of antibiotics. But they'll do it anyway.

They just won't do it with me, that's all. I don't need to be yammering away, I know it can get terribly tedious in pubs too, I'm feeling a bit of that as the afternoon drags on, but I've already factored it in. I'm still on solid ground here, that hotel breakfast is standing to me. I'm still wearing the same clothes I was wearing when I rode down that street outside, desperate to be free, but so what? I'll think about clothes some other time too, there's nothing like the drink for making you see all that stuff for what it is, stuff that is not important, stuff that you do not need, like clothes, like cinema, like theatre and books, if it comes to that.

Jamaica can make a new set of clothes for me every day if she likes. I don't care about clothes, I want to be like Shane McGowan, living and working in the same suit from one season to the next without even thinking of a new look. And I have great news for old Jamaica on the 'Jack Rooney' costumes front, now that I've finally met a couple of decent men who are prepared to give me serious money, thanks entirely to my getting drunk with them, as distinct from showing them my business plan over coffee in the Westbury Hotel.

Seven years I wasted over coffee and biscuits in piano-tinkling hotels, seven years, while all the time there were drunk people out here, in the bars and saloons, who would give me the shirt off their backs.

These are the guys.

And I'm back among them now. I'm out here again, except this time I've got the edge. I've got seven years on them, I have lived many lives.

I nearly lose this one too, with the shock of hearing my name called out by the barman.

There's a telephone call for me. I'm sure it must be Theo. I fear I am going to be abducted and taken back to the rooms.

I brace myself too for a blast from Jamaica; as I pick up the phone in the booth I get a surge of fear that she has nothing to say to me except that I left the gate lodge in an awful state, that I should go back and pick up all the broken glass myself and by the way Eddie is looking for his motorbike. But I am brave. I put the receiver to my ear anyway.

It's Jamaica.

"I'd like to see you, braddah," she says, sounding warm, mellow Jamaica, like she is curled up in a beanbag.

"I'm here in Regan's," I shout above the noise.

"I am outside this place," she says, still calm.

"Well, come in then. I'm here. I'm here at the bar," I shout, over the hubbub and the clinking glasses and the blaring TV.

There is a pause.

"Comin' in," she says.

I see her coming through the crowd, dressed in black. I see merry guys with pints in their hands doing a double-take. The moment he sees her at his shoulder, the guy beside me offers Jamaica his stool. He seems apologetic for sitting on it in the first place.

"Couldn't make the church," I say. "No excuses, I'm just on the razzle." She looks me over in a spirit of understanding and compassion. I never imagined she would be judgemental, it didn't occur to me for a moment that Jamaica couldn't rise to this occasion, the sight of the most sober man in Wicklow sitting up at the bar of Regan's skulling pints.

"It's alright," she says. "There is no need to be defensive."

I get my first spasm of real drunken anger. Women telling me not to be defensive is probably the thing that makes me madder than anything else in this life. When I am explaining something in a perfectly reasonable way, and a woman tells me to stop being so defensive, I am consumed with helpless wrath, I feel like I'm being hog-tied and baited. And that's just what I feel when I'm sober.

Heroically, I merely shrug. I still sense that she comes in peace. She settles herself properly, like a musician in the moments before the recital begins. There is some new sense of calm about her. She looks me straight in the eye and I flinch under her gaze. She seems centred, she seems to be coming from some place in the middle of the earth. The space around her grows even at this raucous bar.

"What are you having?" I say.

"Just water," she says.

"After the church? " I say. "Are you serious?"

"After a meetin'..." she says. I feel like I'm going to be sick. I flinch again from her gaze.

"You're not..." I start, but she signals me to stop. She wants to go on with her side of it.

In the back of my brain I want to tell her there's no need to be defensive, but I'm not fit for repartee. Not right now.

"It sunk in finally at the church," she says, holding my hands, a bit too sisterly.

"It was a beautiful service and still it was so tragic. Poor Jason, such talent, such a good bloke, a soul braddah, and now he's gone. It is wrong, Neil, it is all wrong. I can do nothin' about Jason but I can do somethin' about Jamaica... so I've just been to mi first meetin' across the road."

"Oh Jesus," I say. I feel really weak now, really wasted.

"I felt I was in the right place," she says, the standard AA line.

I am appalled. But I have it figured now. She's got a kind of three-day virus that people get sometimes, when they suddenly see the light and they get themselves to a room and instantly they find the meaning of life. They're amateurs, worse than the amateurs who crush into the pubs at Christmas and destroy it for everyone else. They're worse because they talk more rubbish.

"See, I had my rock bottom yesterday," she says. "It was wrong for Mikey and me to blow you out like that, drinkin' first t'ing in the mornin', mon. It was just wrong. My apologies."

"Right," I grunt.

"If it is any consolation, Mikey and me did nothin' but drinkin'..." she says.

"Enough," I snort, but somehow I know she won't desist.

"You need to know the truth about me and Mikey," she says. Christ, she's on Step 5 already, admitting to God, to ourselves, and to another human being the nature of our wrongs. Unfortunately, I am that other human being.

"Mikey was no threat to you, it was the drink that was your enemy. It was the drink took me away from you," she says.

I snort. She's one of them all right, one of those amateurs, and of all these fly-by-nights I've encountered over the years she's probably the worst. Because she's got all the rubbish I taught her as well, all of my serene wisdom, along with her own daft notions and her own special brand of supernatural gibberish. See, I always kind-of believed that line of hers, that she kept me away from the big house out of superstition, because she saw the gate lodge as our special place. We boozers are like that, superstitious, always fearing that the delicate balance of our lives will be destroyed by some dark force beyond our ken, when really it's the dark force we are throwing into ourselves in shot glasses that will do for us.

So if I heard her right, and she's claiming now that nothing fishy was going on with Mikey, or nothing much anyway, that it was just the drink, I kind-of believe that too. An alcoholic who says it was just the drink? Yes, I'm inclined to believe that, but I'm even more inclined to carry on drinking here, in peace, now that I've started.

She's still deep into Step 5.

"Mikey just likes to drink,"she says. "He drinks with me, he drinks with Susanna and Poppy and Sorcha and Lucy. Occasionally we make it back to the big house. Mostly I leave him roamin' though the city."

I raise my hand to make an interjection.

"Just one thing... I never slept with my drinking buddies," I say.

"You never crashed in the same bed?" she says, undeterred by my sarcasm.

Actually I did, come to think of it. But I don't acknowledge this, I just grunt at her.

"The truth is, towards the end I just preferred bein' with Mikey than bein' with you. I was gettin' so uptight. I wanted to be drinkin' and smokin'... Mikey and me became soul-mates, it's true... you were too good for me, braddah."

I butt in.

"So I was too good for you, and now you're too good for me," I jeer. But she is resolute.

"I was goin' to blow you out anyway," she says. "You had become a total pain in the arse."

This knocks me back a bit.

"To take just one t'ing, I understand now that you couldn't come with me to the fashion show at The Point... but you were indifferent to my work at the best of times. I went with Mikey that night. Mikey was not indifferent, he gave me support."

I shrug.

"I got it wrong sometimes," I say urbanely.

"And maybe you are wrong too, if you think you are headin' for an all-time rock bottom," she continues in a kindlier tone. "They say it's always worse if you go back on the drink after bein' in the rooms. You have your all-time rock bottom the second time around and it's worse, it's the all-time worst... but so far this is just a slip, that's all it is, a slip. So listen to me, braddah, if you put down that drink, maybe you don't need to have that rock bottom."

I take a long slug of Guinness.

"I think I'm having it now," I say.

Twenty

Ah yes, she was over there in the room with that light in her eye, saying I'm Jamaica and I'm an alcoholic, feeling ecstatic as she declared herself free from the old hooch and then looked around the room, the room where she will be spending her Friday nights from now on, as the boys told her she's in the right place. But while she was getting it off her chest, the boys were probably suffering. The boys are probably out there now walking crooked with lust and mad for porter, mercifully unaware that she's in Regan's, sitting on the bar with a fallen comrade, starting an outreach programme.

They know, like I know, that she'll be sharing like a woman possessed for a few weeks, making them horny when they just want to offer it all up to their God. And then one day in Al-co-hol-ics An-on-ee-muss, they'll notice that she's not there any more. They won't be too taken aback, they'll hope to see her back again in a few years if her Higher Power spares her, a bit more subdued, maybe less excitable. Ready at last for the long game.

She smiles at me, there's still badness in her.

"Come with me," she says. "Come on."

I think of something that Susan said. She said Jamaica has risen above it and she's done something, she's taken a risk, she's even done something about Jack Rooney.

Sometimes you get lucky in your life and someone rises above it and does something when they might just as easily let you fuck off and die.

I wish now with all my heart that she would take the easy option.

"What about Mikey?" I say.

"Mikey's still out dere," she says, implying that in his advanced state of alcoholism she can't be with him any more.

I consider this with as much nonchalance as I can. I'm feeling quite ill now.

"I've a pint coming," I say.

"OK so," she says.

I light a cigarette. Another challenge.

"Braddah, you've just had a slip, dat's all," she says. A slip. She's got the jargon already.

But she hasn't quite thought it all the way through, she hasn't questioned her new regime in the light of the fact that one of its top guys is enjoying a feed of Guinness at the bar of Regan's, and loving it.

"Listen, I think I've got a couple of investors for the tuner. Couple of guys I met in a bar..." I say.

"Go on," she says.

"Martin and Barry, or maybe it's the other way round," I say. "Anyway they're mad for it. I really think we've got a result here. They know who Eugene O'Neill is."

"I love dis," she says. "I really, really love it when you're positive. Upful. I love it when you're upful. I love it."

We are speechless for a few moments, wondering if this is the breakthrough for Jack Rooney.

"How's Theo?" I say.

"He sends you his best," she says.

"We're friends again so?"

"When were you and Theo not friends?" she says.

"He's, eh, he's not coming over to get me or anything?" I say.

"He said you would know what to do," she says.

We had our moments, me and Theo. Maybe he blames himself for my going to the bad like this, maybe he figures I had it coming. Still, I suppose I'm a little flattered that he reckons I can steer this thing home.

The pint is nearly ready. I pay the man a fiver and I tell him to keep the change. My pockets are crammed with change, just like old times.

Yes, of course I know what to do. I'm going to do it now.

I'm going to do it her way for a change.

The pint comes. I hold it up, admiring its perfection.

Then I put it back down again.

It actually seems a shame to disturb such perfection. I don't want it now, I think I can live without it tonight.

"You know what I'm going to do?" I say. "I'm going to have this pint, but I'm not going to have it now. I'm going to have it tomorrow."

She keeps it casual.

"Tomorrow," she says.

"I'm going to have it tomorrow," I say.

I am planning my exit like drunks everywhere, careful not to look drunk. I will leave the pint there untouched. I will slide off the stool and stand up. My feet are numb. I will probably be walking like some frostbitten Antarctic explorer. I suddenly feel as if I've been drinking every day since the thirteenth century, but Jamaica will steady me, she's had some experience in the field.

Then she says something that steadies me where I sit.

"If you can really leave it 'til tomorrow..." she says.

I get a rush, a blast of recognition.

"Uh-huh," I say.

"I mean if you are really able to do it," she says.

I hear a new note in her voice now. I hear all that composure breaking up.

"Yeah, I could walk away now," I say, getting her drift.

I want to give her a big smile, a big alcoholic smile, but then I realise that the game is on now, we must be sincere about this. I know what's just happened to her, I am onto it straight away. I know that feeling, I know it well, I know how all those good intentions can be vapourised if you make just one wrong move. And the way it's looking at this moment, for Jamaica, coming in here with the joint jumping and me sitting up at the bar, was one wrong move. Maybe that three-day virus I mentioned, was just a three-hour virus in her case. I sense it now. That light has gone from her eye. The serenity she found at the meeting has just worn off, the pub atmosphere has taken her from the path of righteousness.

And then there's the sight of me sitting there drinking, something she wanted for so long, something she can't resist even after all the sober promises she made to herself, and to the boys in the rooms. That's the way it happens for people like us; we are weak, and we are especially weak at the sudden prospect of a full drinking relationship with one of our own kind.

"Yes, I think I can handle it now," I say. "I've learned so much in the rooms..."

I can feel a surge of joy passing between us. The booze is bringing us together again. Maybe after admitting the nature of her wrongs to God, to herself and to another human being, after getting to Step 5 so quickly, the truth indeed has set her free.

"You really and truly were goin' to leave it until tomorrow," she says.

"You see, that was always my problem. I could never leave it until tomorrow, I had to drink it all tonight," I say, warming to the theme.

"So if you could just leave dis drink..."she says.

"I can take it or leave it..." I say.

"Could it mean... could it mean maybe you've turned the corner?"

I give her the smile of a gaucho.

"I've turned the corner, baby, and I've just run into you."

She strokes my face, not too sisterly this time.

"At de church for Jason... I so wanted what you had, the peace you found in the rooms... now I am askin' myself was it a knee-jerk kinda t'ing to be havin' big ideas at such an emotional time? And maybe dis is a bad way to come to de rooms?"

"There's no good way," I say.

So she wants what I have when I'm in the rooms, and if I'm hearing her correctly, she wants what I have when I'm out of the rooms. So what is she having?

"You're going to laugh at dis, braddah," she says, shaking her head defensively. "You are really going to fall about de place laughin'."

"I don't think so," I say.

"Vodka and Coke," she says, with a note of guilt, but still a credit to her race.

I order the drinks. I am handling the excitement pretty well myself. We have tried her drunk and me sober, we have tried the two of us sober, we have more or less tried everything except the two of us drunk, which is where the two of us truly want to be, when the night has come, and the land is dark.

I pay for the drinks with a tenner. I am running out of money, but then I remember the big room up at her place, the room full of booze and smoke where I found her with Mikey.

So we won't be stuck.

It feels beautiful now, to be drinking together. We don't talk much, but we are feeling the same deep happiness inside. Maybe we always knew we were getting to this place, maybe this was our journey.

Now I can see myself later tonight, lying beside her on the bed in the big room full of booze and smoke.

She is sipping the vodka'n'Coke, still a bit tentative, like something is still holding her back, like she hasn't fully released herself yet from all those promises.

Then Camden Town floats into my head again. Fortified, I grapple with that bad thought, the worst of all thoughts, the thought that Jamaica knows all about Camden Town, and what really happened in Jesse Nestor's place. In fact she probably knew all about it all the time, from the day I saw her with Grace Bannon, out there in the street. Yes, what if she knew about it that night in Nottingham, when I made my big confession? Awww mama, awww mama... and she probably knew about it over Christmas, when we were having that hangover sex and, yes, when I was giving her a hard time in the International Bar, she knew... and if she knew about it then, she must have known about it in New York... yes I think she knew, she knew, all that time she knew...

But hell, maybe like me she thought it was all just rock'n'roll, maybe like me she was in a place where you just bury everything that pains you... but before she buried it, she must have hated me. Even if it was just for one day. And then no doubt she had a few stiff drinks and discovered that she loved me more. And maybe when she thought about it next, she had a few more stiff drinks, this time when no-one was looking, the way you do. And so, here we are again.

I am thinking, I knew that Grace was trouble, she's the type who keeps in touch with everyone she ever knew, or at least everyone vaguely decent. This is what is going through my frazzled mind. She's the type who wants to remember in a world of people who just want to forget and move on.

But what about Lotte? Why didn't she tell me the truth when I pumped her in the café? Maybe Lotte just wasn't told the truth, because she was too flaky, too liable to go off on one, at the time.

I'm poking around in the filthy embers here, and I'm also pretty drunk. But something tells me there is one more river to cross.

I can't bury this any more, I don't even have the energy to bury it, in vino veritas.

Somehow I knew this time would come, I guess I'm just glad it has come while I'm sitting with Jamaica, fresh drinks in front of us.

"Camden Town..." I say.

Jamaica concentrates on her vodka'n'Coke,

"Fuck it, I did whatever she says I did," I say.

Jamaica carries on as if I'm just rambling away to myself.

"And I probably did worse," I say.

Jamaica considers this. She says nothing for what seems like a long time, maybe a full minute, in pub time an eternity. It's something I can never do, I always have to fill the silence. Then she turns to me as if she's thought of something new.

"Funerals... the t'ing about people dyin', is it makes you want to live," she says, rattling the ice in her vodka.

I nod in solemn agreement. We have had good times as well as bad. Her voice is still full of that Caribbean childhood. And as for me, when I close my eyes it is a summer night and I am fifteen years old, yes, I can hear it now, Bob Seger's 'Night Moves' playing on the cassette machine, a bunch of boys in the sand-dunes watching the girls swimming in the sea.

Ain't it funny how the night moves.

THE STORY OF O by Olaf Tyaransen
Described as Ireland's *Catcher In The Rye*, this tale of teenage sex, drugs, rock'n'roll – and of course music – is hysterically funny and poignantly moving in equal measure. **Price: €12.99**

"It's like The Secret Diary Of Adrian Mole, only with cannabis-induced hazes." – *Sunday Times*.

"Very funny and searingly honest" – *Irish Times*

SEX LINES by Olaf Tyaransen
Delving into the wonderful world of sex, Olaf attempts to find a Russian bride, is asked to be an extra on a porn movie shoot, attends a fetish spanking club and much more. **Price: €12.99**

"Hysterically funny" – *Sunday Independent*

PALACE OF WISDOM by Olaf Tyaransen
The "enfant terrible" of Irish journalism is back, with a remarkable book that explores the dark and dangerous currents in which artists, celebrities, musicians, writers and politicos alike – including the author himself – are wont to swim. And sometimes drown... **Price: €13.99**

"Olaf Tyaransen is the genuine article" – Robert Sabbag, author of *Snowblind*

U2: THREE CHORDS AND THE TRUTH
The International Bestseller Edited by Niall Stokes
Critical, entertaining, comprehensive and revealing, *U2: Three Chords And The Truth* never misses a beat as it brings you, in words and pictures, a complete portrait of U2 in the process of becoming a legend. **Price: €11.49**

THEY ARE OF IRELAND by Declan Lynch
They Are Of Ireland is a hilarious who's who of famous Irish characters – and chancers – from the worlds of politics, sport, religion, the Arts, entertainment and the media. Written by Declan Lynch, one of Ireland's wittiest writers, this is a book of comic writing that actually makes you laugh out loud. **Price: €9.99**